FINAL WITNESS

A gang of London warehouse thieves kill a policeman during a raid. The murder is seen by three people, none of whom is anxious to come forward as a witness. David Wight, a young journalist on *Topical Truths*, becomes involved in the case, which is being handled by his godfather, Detective Superintendent Morgan of Scotland Yard. David eventually gets his 'exclusive' story, but not before there have been several attempts on his life and other murders have been committed.

Books by J. F. Straker
in the Linford Mystery Library:

A CHOICE OF VICTIMS
SWALLOW THEM UP
DEATH ON A SUNDAY MORNING
A LETTER FOR OBI
COUNTERSNATCH
ARTHUR'S NIGHT
A PITY IT WASN'T GEORGE
THE GOAT
DEATH OF A GOOD WOMAN
MISCARRIAGE OF MURDER
SIN AND JOHNNY INCH
TIGHT CIRCLE
A MAN WHO CANNOT KILL
ANOTHER MAN'S POISON
THE SHAPE OF MURDER
A COIL OF ROPE
MURDER FOR MISS EMILY
GOODBYE, AUNT CHARLOTTE

J. F. STRAKER

FINAL WITNESS

Complete and Unabridged

LINFORD
Leicester

First published in Great Britain in 1963

First Linford Edition
published 2005

British Library CIP Data

Straker. J. F. (John Foster)
Final witness.—Large print ed.—
Linford mystery library
1. Detective and mystery stories
2. Large type books
I. Title
823.9'14 [F]

ISBN 1–84395–789–2

Published by
F. A. Thorpe (Publishing)
Anstey, Leicestershire

Set by Words & Graphics Ltd.
Anstey, Leicestershire
Printed and bound in Great Britain by
T. J. International Ltd., Padstow, Cornwall

This book is printed on acid-free paper

1

Only the wind disturbed the nocturnal silence. It blew fiercely off the river, funnelled down the narrow street in a flurry of dust, picking up scraps of paper and other refuse and juggling with them playfully before flinging them away. A sudden gust clouded the mouth of the alley where the woman stood, and she shielded her face from it and pressed her body against the high, unyielding wall of the warehouse, pulling her thin coat more closely about her and hugging herself tightly to deny access to the probing wind. She had known it cold in May before, but not as cold as this.

As the gust subsided she drew away from the wall and looked across the street to the tall, arched doorway where the couple had taken shelter. She could not distinguish them clearly, but she knew they were still there; there was the occasional movement in the shadows, the faint, unintelligible murmur of voices brought to her by the wind. She stamped her feet and blew on her numb fingers, swearing softly to herself, at herself. For what was she waiting? In the twenty minutes she had stood there she had learned nothing. It was a senseless, futile vigil.

Yet she continued to keep it. She was even able to obtain from it a strange satisfaction — the ecstatic, esoteric satisfaction of the martyr.

A low rumbling to her right caused her to peer out cautiously. Light shone on to the street from beyond the warehouse, bringing the cobbles into high relief, but too faint to illumine fully the hoardings opposite. As the rumbling ceased there came the throb of an engine, and the dark shape of a large van emerged from the warehouse yard and turned right; it stopped, and the rumbling recommenced. Silhouetted against the glow of the sidelights she could see two men tugging at the heavy sliding doors, while another stood motionless and watchful near by. If they spoke she did not hear them. The wind carried the sound of their voices away.

The woman shrank back quickly, forgetful of her vigil in the sudden panic that assailed her. She knew what the warehouse contained, and it was not difficult to guess why the men were there. As she thought of the night watchman and realized what the thieves must have done to him, anger and frustration were added to her fear. Yet she was powerless to intervene, to raise the alarm. If she ventured into the street they were bound to see her; there was no escape that way. And behind her, at the far end of the alley, there was only the river.

So far the noises had been in undertones, muffled by the wind and dictated by the need for secrecy and silence. Now they sharpened. As the heavy doors clanged together there came the sound of iron-shod feet hitting the cobbles in rhythmic urgency; away to the woman's left the dancing beam from a torch hurried towards her, swinging from side to side of the narrow street. Momentarily it flashed across the couple in the archway, and as she craned forward the woman caught a glimpse of a man's face, scared and startled. Then, as the beam neared the mouth of the alley, she retreated into the protective darkness and waited for the roar of an opening throttle to announce the thieves' departure.

It did not come. There was only the excited babel of men's voices, the patter of men's feet on the cobbles, and above them the sharp whine of the starter motor — in frantic bursts at first, and then in laboured continuity.

'Hold it, copper!' snapped a man's voice.

She had not realized that the running feet had slowed and stopped. Cautiously she peered round the corner of the warehouse. The beam from the torch was still, directed downward at a pair of highly polished black shoes that winked back at it. Silhouetted against the light was the dark shape of the policeman, his helmet seeming to tower above the buildings beyond. The starter motor whined on, its note lower, more sepulchral.

The beam lifted. As it moved slowly up the tight-fitting jeans, hesitating only slightly at the gun gleaming in the man's right hand, a piece of newspaper came sailing down the street, dipping and soaring. It reached the mouth of the alley and was sucked in, wrapping itself round the woman's face.

A voice called shrilly, 'Don't do it, Bandy! For Chris' sake don't do it!'

The woman snatched the paper away. Her spectacles came away with it, but she did not stoop to retrieve them. The torch was now steady on the man's face. To her it was little more than a blur of white, like the blanked-out faces of prisoners in a newspaper photograph. Yet because the torch pinpointed it in the darkness she watched it.

The policeman stood his ground. In a brisk, authoritative voice he said, 'Better hand over that gun, lad. It might go off.'

The van's engine erupted into noisy life, drowning all other sound. But suddenly there were no faces, no voices, no human shapes; only a thin pencil of light along the cobbles, through which the polished shoes of the gunman moved briefly into obscurity, and behind the light the huddled figure of the fallen policeman. There came the brisk revving of the engine, and the van moved off with a hurried, untidy changing of gears, head-lights dancing as the wheels bounced on the cobbles. As the noise died and the lights vanished round a corner the woman saw the couple leave the shelter of their archway, heard the sound of their footsteps. But she did not follow. The purpose of her self-appointed vigil was forgotten, submerged in the tragic urgency of this new situation. She came out from the alley and ran to kneel beside the dead policeman.

2

The Centipede Club is in Streatham. It is a respectable club in a respectable district, although it gets its share of drunks. There was one there that Tuesday evening; an irascible, burly six-footer, with bloodshot eyes and a bulging stomach, who had discarded his jacket at an early stage and whose flapping shirt was wet with sweat. Between double whiskies he cavorted round the room with maniacal fury, pressing his partner, a tired-looking little brunette, against his damp bosom and glaring angrily at any couple who dared to impede him. As the evening advanced these became fewer. The women, if not the men, saw to it that his progress went unhindered.

'Who's the drunk, Jimmy?' asked David Wight.

The barman scowled. 'Name of Chapman. Country member. Don't come in often, thank goodness! Haven't seen him for months.'

'He's making up for it now. How long before he passes out?'

'He don't pass out. Never has yet, anyways. Just keeps going till he gets the urge to quit.' Expertly Jimmy snapped the top off a bottle of light ale and buried the neck in a glass. 'I hope he gets it soon. Could be trouble else.'

David leant against the bar and watched the dancers jiving and twisting round the room. Like the drunk, he did not come to the club often. It was a cosy room, discreetly lit, with a good floor and a modern radiogram. An enormous and elongated black centipede formed a mural round three of the yellow walls; according to Jimmy, who claimed to have counted them, the creature had exactly one hundred legs, one for each of the hundred members to which the club was limited. David wondered who had imposed that limitation. To him it seemed unnecessary. He had never seen more than a score of people present at one time, and in general they were the same people.

That evening there were thirteen; six couples and himself. The women had an average share of good looks, but the men were an unattractive lot. Apart from the drunk, whose fat face was now almost incandescent, three of the men were young and noisily exuberant, one was a West Indian, and the sixth a bearded, thickset man who solemnly jigged his partner up and down in a dark corner of the room, a meerschaum pipe stuck between his teeth, a monocle dangling from a ribbon round his neck. Occasionally he would cease jigging, remove the pipe, and smother the girl's face with kisses. Then back would go the pipe, and the jigging recommenced.

It was the West Indian who interested David the most. In the middle thirties, he was lithe and sparely built, with a slim waist accentuated by a jacket of exaggerated cut. To David he suggested a mixture of several races. He had the high, severe cheekbones and taut skin of the Hindu, yet the full lips and thick woolly hair denoted negroid blood; his alert, inquisitive eyes had an oriental slant. His

9

shoulders were narrow and sloping, his fingers long and supple; the pointed shoes probably added several inches to feet that were small. A thin chevron of a moustache decorated his upper lip, and diagonally across the high, domed forehead ran a jagged scar, thick and long and ugly, over which the dark skin had failed to knit. His partner was a woman David knew only as Nora; a tall, brittle blonde, with a good figure and a tight, impassive face. They danced well together, the woman a trifle stiffly, following the man's intricate, rather exaggerated pattern of steps with the minimum of motion. And as they danced the man talked incessantly, his mouth close to his partner's ear. David wondered at the theme of his monologue. It did not appear to be of absorbing interest to the woman.

'Who's the darky?' he asked. 'Never seen one here before.'

The barman shrugged. 'Couldn't say. Nora brought him.'

'Don't we have a colour bar?'

'Not yet we don't. There could be one brewing.'

David knew what he meant. Chapman had stopped dancing. He stood at the far end of the bar, whisky in one hand and his free arm encircling his partner's waist, bloodshot eyes glowering at the dancers. But it was at Nora and the West Indian that most of his resentment was directed. Each time the couple passed him he commented loudly and disparagingly on the man's colour and parentage and on the probable morals of his partner. That they ignored him only increased his resentment and sharpened the insults.

When the dance ended they joined the other couples at the bar. David grinned at Nora, and she gave him a stiff little smile. There was a rumbling in Chapman's throat. He removed an arm from his partner's waist and banged a large fist on the counter, making the glasses rattle.

'We don't want bloody niggers here,' he growled. 'They stink. Tell him to get the hell out of it, Jimmy.'

The chatter died. Unheeding, Jimmy went on pouring the drinks. Chapman's partner clutched at his sweat-soaked shirt.

'Stop it, Wilfred!' she said plaintively. She had a squeaky little voice. 'Don't make a scene, dear.'

The big man shook her off. He leaned across the counter and grabbed Jimmy's arm, jerking him violently forward. Whisky splashed on the polished oak.

'Hear what I said? Tell that nigger to beat it.'

The barman put down the glass. He looked more annoyed than frightened. 'You tell him,' he said. 'I only work here.' Almost delicately he unpicked the hand from his sleeve, lifting it finger by finger. 'Me, I prefer niggers to drunks. They're less expensive.'

The allusion was lost on Chapman. Nora was between him and his quarry, and he pushed her away and stuck his crimson face close to the dark face of the West Indian. The latter stood his ground; but there were little flecks of white foam at the corners of his mouth, and he licked his full lips nervously.

'You going, nigger?' Chapman brandished an enormous fist, on the little finger of which was a heavy gold signet-ring. 'Or do I throw you out?'

The young couples at the bar drifted away, the men led willingly enough by their anxious partners. David braced himself; he was disinclined for trouble, but he had no intention of running from it. With relief he saw the bearded man release his clutch on the girl, screw his monocle into his eye, and advance on the bar. The meerschaum was still between his teeth, but he looked a man who would stand no nonsense.

Nora's face was pale under the make-up, her eyes troubled. She said quietly, 'You'd better go, George. I was afraid something like this would happen. That's why I didn't want you to come. But you insisted, and . . . ' She shrugged. 'I'm sorry.'

The West Indian nodded, his eyes fixed warily on the drunk. Perhaps he feared a sudden attack. But he looked neither surprised nor resentful of the insults; no doubt he was used to them. He finished his drink, flashed his white and gold teeth in a smile at Nora, and, passing his tormentor in a wide arc, walked briskly to the door, his body swaying from the hips.

In silence they watched him go. At the door he turned. In a high-pitched, clipped voice he said, staring back at Chapman, 'I'm going, man. But I ain't going because you tell me. I just don't like drunks. Like you said, they stink.'

With a roar Chapman released his hold on the bar and charged drunkenly. As he passed the bearded man the latter put out his foot and gave him a sharp tap on the ankle, and with a crash that shook the room Chapman tripped over himself and fell headlong. David waited expectantly for the ensuing uproar, but it did not materialize; it was clear that Chapman did not know how he had come to fall. For a few moments he stayed prostrate. Then he sat up, glared dazedly at the watchful faces above him, and rose awkwardly to his feet. Swaying unsteadily, he tottered across to a chair and sat down, the chair legs scraping the floor in protest.

David said to the bearded man, 'Neat, chum. Very neat indeed.'

The other removed the pipe from his

mouth. In a transatlantic drawl he said, 'Know what I like about you British? No segregation. The coloured man is your friend and brother. It makes us Southerners feel real mean.'

He stuck the pipe back and returned to his partner.

Someone put a record on the radiogram. David asked Nora to dance. He had two styles of dancing, neither of which was of text-book quality; Susan Long had classified them as 'the quick and the dead.' Susan herself was usually treated to the 'quick.' The 'dead' was reserved for David's more elderly or unfamiliar partners; it consisted of a series of lateral shuffles and forward or backward glides, the feet never leaving the floor, the trunk erect and rigid. Nora followed it easily enough, her body as stiff and unyielding as his. Under his hand her waist felt as though it were encased in steel.

'The shouting and the tumult dies,' David said. 'But it was unpleasant while it lasted. Particularly for you. I thought your friend behaved damned well.'

'He's used to it. And it doesn't help to lose one's temper. Not when the other man is so much bigger.'

Cynical philosophy, he thought, and wondered what her relationship with her coloured friend had been — or still was. She was probably the elder by several years; he doubted if she would see forty again. The eyes betrayed her age; the eyes and the neck, where no artistry could hide the telltale lines. Nor was she beautiful. The careful make-up and the slim, tightly corseted figure, the platinum blonde hair piled high on her head (too high, thought David, for such a tall woman) provided a veneer of glamour, but they did not give her beauty. The black velvet dress, high necked and short skirted, hugged her figure. He thought her legs too thin, but her ankles were good.

She was a patient listener, but David found himself unable to emulate her former partner's ceaseless flow of words. There was nothing about Nora to inspire him. Half-way through the dance he ran out of conversation, and they finished it in silence.

At the bar Jimmy said, 'Now we can all have a nice, peaceful evening.' He looked apologetically at Nora. 'I'm sorry your friend had to leave. There wasn't nothing I could do about it, was there?'

She gave him a fleeting smile and shook her head. David noticed with surprise that Chapman had gone. But his partner had not. She came up to the bar and added her apologies to Jimmy's.

'Drunken brute!' she exclaimed, as angrily as her plaintive little voice would permit. 'Spoiling everyone's evening like that. And then he just walks out on me. Didn't even offer to pay for my taxi.' She grimaced. 'Oh, well! But I'll have something to say to Mr Wilfred Chapman if ever I see him again. Which I probably won't.'

She accepted eagerly the drink which David offered. Nora said, 'You're not a member here, are you?'

No, she said, she was not a member. Jimmy began to enumerate the advantages of joining; he received a percentage of the takings and a bonus for enrolling new members. David asked Nora to dance.

'I'd rather sit for a while,' she said. 'I'm tired.' She nodded at the brunette. 'Why not ask her?'

'I'll sit too,' he said firmly. He felt in no way drawn to Nora, but at least her voice did not irritate him. It was cool and impersonal, and pleasantly low. And she did not chatter.

In an effort to be sociable he told her about his job. When she learned that he was a journalist she evinced her first show of interest.

'What paper?'

'Not a paper — *Topical Truths*. It's a weekly magazine.'

'I know. Elsie takes it. She and I share a flat. But I'm afraid I've never read it.' To soften the blow she added, 'I'm not much of a reader.'

He laughed. 'You don't have to apologize. It's not much of a magazine. Just a scandal sheet. 'The truth behind the news.' But not the front-page news; not the big stuff. We're not interested in politics or economics or world affairs.

Sex, crime, gossip — it's dirt we go for. We wallow in it. So do our readers.'

He did not sound bitter. 'Do you like it?' she asked. 'The work, I mean?'

'It's a job. And a beginning. One doesn't have to like it.'

Her hard blue eyes surveyed him. He was an untidy creature; hair thick and unruly, tie adrift, his suit obviously bought off the wrong peg and unpressed since. The scarecrow type, she thought; needs mothering. He had a long, lean body which looked unco-ordinated, and had felt unco-ordinated on the dance-floor. His face too was lean, with a sharp, pointed nose and a strong chin; the wide mouth seemed to split it in two when he smiled, to show sharp, uneven teeth which gave him a faintly wolfish look. His hands were hard, and she liked that. It was a pity about the mangled nails and the brown, tobacco-stained fingers. Yet somehow the nails went with the tie and the suit and the general air of untidiness. He had not yet learned self-discipline, she thought, never quite matured.

Her thoughts drifted away, and she

sighed. David said, 'As bad as that, am I?'

'Eh?'

'Been looking me over, haven't you? I presume the sigh indicated you didn't like what you saw.' He shook his head in mock regret. 'And I thought I was making an impression!'

She gave one of her rare, fleeting smiles. He suspected they were controlled by the heavy make-up; it might crack if she gave way to them unrestrainedly.

'It was a private sigh. Not for publication.'

They danced again. David tried to make her talk about herself; not from curiosity, but because he had exhausted his own career as a conversational peg. But Nora was unresponsive, and he soon desisted. He learned that her name was Nora Winstone, that she worked as a manicurist near Victoria, and that she shared a Kennington flat with a girl called Elsie; but these were bald facts, and she enlarged on none of them. He was not particularly anxious that she should. They had been thrown together by an unfortunate mischance. It was unlikely that they would be thrown together again.

They had one more dance, and then Nora said she was leaving. It was nearly midnight, and Jimmy was preparing to close the bar. The bearded man was still there; still jigging, and with the meerschaum still between his teeth. Two of the young couples had left, and so had Chapman's girl-friend. She had borrowed her taxi fare from the bar.

'Said she'd post it.' Jimmy shook his head. 'Me, I just kissed it good-bye.'

He said it so cheerfully that David guessed it had not come from his own pocket. 'Did you sign her on as a member?' he asked.

'Sign? That dame don't sign nothing that'll cost her money. She likes it coming her way. All the time.'

David laughed. 'I'll see you home,' he told Nora. 'The heap's outside.'

She did not ask if she would be taking him out of his way; it was clear that the offer was expected. As he waited for her at the foot of the wide steps he wondered what else would be expected of him. Just what sort of a woman was she? He was sufficiently conventional to mistrust white women who chose the companionship of coloured men.

The Centipede occupied the ground floor and basement of an old house that was scheduled to be demolished when its lease expired. The houses on either side of it had already gone; their empty sites provided convenient parking-space for the club's members. As he helped Nora to stumble across the uneven, rubble-strewn ground David regretted he had no torch. She did not complain, but she was undoubtedly suffering. So, he suspected, were her shoes and stockings.

'Well, here we are,' he said, trying to keep the pride out of his voice. 'There's the heap.'

She looked at it aghast. 'What is it?'

'Alvis Twelve-Fifty.' The polished aluminium body gleamed in the moonlight, and he stroked it tenderly. The Alvis had been his for only a few months. 'Nineteen twenty-five model. One of the earliest. Real vintage motor-car.'

'I thought it was only wines that had vintages.' She ran a hand along the side, seeking the door-handle. 'How does one get in? There's no door.'

Clearly she was not impressed. That's what it means to grow old, he thought sadly. No feeling for adventure. She'd prefer one of those plush, modern hot-boxes.

'Hop over the side,' he told her. 'Here, let me give you a hand. We'll leave the hood down, eh? It's a warm night.'

She was too occupied in climbing into the car to answer. Gratefully he took her silence for consent.

'Hang on to your hair,' he warned, letting in the clutch. 'It could be breezy.'

With a crisp roar the Alvis bumped out on to the unlit street and accelerated nobly towards Streatham Hill, its head-lamps splitting the darkness, the noise of the exhaust bouncing back at them off the tall, closely packed buildings. Nora clutched with both hands at her flimsy scarf and huddled down behind the low wind-screen. But speed was more implicit than real. Once into top gear David's foot was light on the throttle. He held the steering-wheel with one hand, leaning away from his passenger, his overlong hair blown across his face and whipping into his eyes. He delighted in the feeling of power that the one-and-a-half-litre engine gave him, but he did not necessarily want to squander that power. It was enough to know it was there, to feel it under his foot. Occasionally he jabbed lightly at the throttle, exulting in the ready response, or leaned still farther to the right to watch the big wheels bouncing smoothly under the narrow, sloping wings. And for much of the time he sang — a wordless, tuneless song that was swept away by the breeze.

They went down Brixton Hill and along the Brixton Road to the Oval. Here David slowed, looking to the woman for guidance. She directed him across the traffic lights into Harleyford Road, and round the Oval into Vauxhall Street. It was a part of London foreign to David, and he was appalled by what he saw. Open expanses of waste land, grim, empty houses with the windows boarded up, houses partially demolished or in an advanced stage of decay; all, he supposed, the result of war-time bomb damage that none had yet seen fit to repair or replace. Some of the buildings were occupied, and he wondered how people could live in such surroundings. Among the rubble and the decay were rows of little villas, scarred and blackened, where light still showed in a few of the windows; dreary little shops with cracked panes that seemed withdrawn into themselves in an agony of despair and shame; and the occasional larger building, cut off from its fellows and standing, alone and forlorn, in a desolate waste of rubble and tumbled earth and weed.

The street in which Nora lived was less grim than the others, but it too shared the general air of depression and decay. David stopped the Alvis where she directed, and sat for a moment in silence looking up at the tall, blackened building. It stood back from the road, with steps leading to what appeared to be a large porch. Years ago, no doubt, it had been a family residence of some grandeur. Now it was no longer grand, and housed not one family but several. It had grown old and decrepit and gaunt and tremendously pathetic.

A light showed in a top window. Nora had told him she lived on the top floor. He said, 'Looks like your friend has waited up for you.'

'She's a late bird herself.'

A car was parked a short way up the street, its lights towards them. Otherwise the street was deserted. David climbed out of the Alvis and went round to help Nora. As she stood up her handbag slipped from her lap to the floor, scattering its contents, and she swore. David was shocked. It was an oath he had not previously heard on the lips of a woman.

'Let's get you out first,' he said. 'I'll salvage your valuables later.'

She stood on the pavement while he rummaged on the floor and under the seat. Lipstick, powder-compact, spectacles, sundry coins, paper tissues, comb, pencil — gradually he collected them and put them in the bag, sweeping the floor with his hand to ensure that he had missed nothing.

'I think that's the lot,' he said, handing her the bag. 'Care to check?'

'There was nothing of value,' she said. 'It doesn't matter.'

There was cloud over the moon, the night had grown suddenly chill. They stood side by side on the bleak pavement, looking up at the house. David wondered what his next move should be. What did the woman expect?

Nora shivered. She said, 'Well, I'm going in. Thanks for the lift.' And, when he said nothing, 'Aren't you going to kiss me good-night?'

'The thought had crossed my mind.' Keep it on a facetious level, he decided. He wanted nothing from her, but he had to play along. 'How will you have it? Long or short, hot or cold, wet or dry? They come all shapes and sizes with me.'

'As it comes. I'm not fussy.'

It was short, cold, and dry. Her lips were soft and sticky, their pressure automatic. He suspected that she got no more pleasure than himself from the embrace. Certainly there was no effort to detain him when he desisted.

'Thanks for a pleasant evening,'he said cheerfully. 'We must do it again some time.'

He knew they never would.

She waited by the steps until the engine crackled into life, and gave him a listless wave of the hand as he shouted good-night and let in the clutch. As he passed the stationary car ahead he saw that it was a black Zodiac saloon, its gleaming paintwork and crisp, modern lines looking out of place in that grey, sad neighbourhood.

He wondered a little about Nora as he made his way back to the Harleyford Road, but by the time he reached Vauxhall Bridge he had forgotten her. Delighting in the empty streets and the crackle of the Alvis's exhaust, he sang lustily all the way back to Fulham.

* * *

It was not until the next evening, when he was cleaning the interior of the car, that he found the diary. There was no reason why he should have missed it the previous night (it was on the carpeted floor, near where the passenger's feet would be); but he had missed it, and it was up to him to return it. It had Nora's name inside the cover, and as he flipped idly through the pages he saw that she had kept no day-to-day record. It was filled mainly with addresses and telephone numbers and what he supposed were appointments; although now and again she seemed to have made a brief record of events, and there were occasional comments. The writing was squarely childish. He did not scan it closely enough to judge its literacy or spelling.

Since he did not know her address he could not post it to her. But he had no doubt he could find the house again; he would return it after supper. He hoped she would be out. Then he could leave it with her friend or push it through the letter-box, and avoid the possibility of further entanglement. Women like Nora, he thought, with all the impudence of youth, must be short on escorts. He had no wish to fill the gap.

In the fading May sunlight the neighbourhood looked even more depressing than it had the night before. Now he could see it as a composite whole, and he did not like what he saw. There might be something here for *Topical Truths*; a scathing exposé of the shocking conditions under which these people were forced to live. In contrast to the muck and scandal in which he normally dealt, Snowball was occasionally moved to project himself as a crusader, a second-rate Beaverbrook.

The adjective was David's, not his editor's.

Two cars stood outside the house. David pulled up behind them, and as he cocked a leg over the side he saw they were police cars. A uniformed constable stood near the foot of the steps, and when David approached he moved to bar his progress.

'Which of the flats are you visiting, sir?' he asked.

'Top floor. Miss Winstone's. Why? Anything wrong?'

'I don't know, sir. But I have

instructions that no one is to go up until the superintendent gives the word. He's up there now.'

Police constables and police cars did not seem out of place in that neighbourhood, but a police superintendent was another matter. David's journalistic instincts were aroused. This was big stuff, surely.

'The divisional superintendent?' he asked.

'No, sir. Detective Superintendent Morgan. Scotland Yard.'

David whistled. He knew Morgan, had known him for years. Morgan was his godfather, had been his father's closest friend. But it was not the coincidence of the superintendent's presence there that evening that surprised him. The divisional detective inspector would normally take charge of the investigation of any crime committed within his division. That Morgan should have been called in indicated something big, something that stretched beyond the bounds of M Division.

'Is the D.D.I. with him?' he asked.

The constable did not answer. There was the sound of footsteps on the uncarpeted stairs within the house, and he sprang smartly to attention and saluted as three men came out from the dark porch and descended the worn, unscrubbed steps. One of them, a big, broad man wearing a bowler hat and carrying a neatly rolled umbrella, frowned when he saw David. Then the frown changed to a grin, and he stretched out a hand in greeting.

'Why, David!' he exclaimed. 'What the heck are you doing here? Don't tell me that rascally editor of yours has started to think up trouble before it actually happens?'

David winced. Morgan's grip was muscular.

'Snowball didn't send me. I'm not here on business, sir. Just wanted a word with Nora Winstone.'

Morgan's well-trimmed eyebrows lifted.

'You know her? I wouldn't have said she was exactly your cup of tea.'

David flushed, pushing the hair out of his eyes. The superintendent always managed to make him feel like a small boy, and he resented it.

'We're not intimates, if that's what you're inferring. We just happen to be members of the same club in Streatham. The Centipede.' Because of his resentment his tone lacked the grudging respect he usually accorded his godfather. 'We were both there last night. I drove her home.'

'You what?'

'I drove her home.' The astonishment in the superintendent's voice and look dispelled David's resentment. Curiosity replaced it. 'Anything wrong in that?'

'Not wrong, no. But definitely odd.' Morgan caught David's arm and started to propel him towards the cars. 'I think you had better come back to the station with us, my lad. You see, Nora Winstone didn't return home last night.'

'But she did! I dropped her right here.'

'You did, eh? Well, she never reached her flat. What's more, she hasn't been seen since.' Morgan shook his head. 'We're working on the assumption that the woman has been kidnapped.'

3

Detective Superintendent Rees Morgan flicked imaginary specks of dust from the seat of the swivel chair and lowered his bulk into it, carefully hitching up his well-creased trousers. When he sat his paunch became more pronounced. He was aware of this, and it worried him; he was a man who prided himself on his appearance. But he had to sit sometimes.

'Take a pew, David.'

David did as he was bid. He had followed the police cars to divisional headquarters in the Borough High Street (his godfather had politely declined the offer of a lift in the Alvis. 'I don't really go with that sort of car,' he had explained), and had waited with some impatience while Morgan and the D.D.I. had conferred with the divisional superintendent in another office. Morgan had said that Nora was missing, that she had not returned to her flat the previous night.

But he had certainly taken her there. She had been standing by the steps as he drove away, and she had only to walk up those steps and climb the stairs to her flat. Why had she not done so?

The superintendent scraped his chair closer to the wide, flat-topped desk, cloaking his paunch, and surveyed his godson with curiosity and some apprehension. He had been fond of David the boy, but as the boy grew into a man the affinity between them had gradually waned. Perhaps the fault was his; perhaps he had not tried hard enough to appreciate the difficulties that can beset a youth orphaned while still in his teens, had shelved his responsibilities too readily and too soon. Occasionally, stricken by conscience, he had attempted to remedy the fault; invited him out to dinner, dropped in at his flat for a casual chat. But the attempts had seemed doomed to failure. Inevitably the two men grated on each other. David appeared to interpret interest as interference, advice as criticism, and resented both, so that his godfather's efforts to be heartily avuncular too often ended in anger. And perhaps, thought the superintendent, with unusual humility, the lad's resentment was not entirely unjustified. For he *was* critical of his godson. He thought him irresponsible and slovenly and bumptious, and mistrusted both his judgments and his intentions.

It was those judgments and intentions that troubled him now. Hitherto their infrequent meetings had been of a social nature. What unhappy quirk of fate had decreed that David should be involved in what might well prove to be the trickiest case of his career?

He drew a paper-bag from the pocket of his smartly cut jacket, and proffered it to David.

'Have an acid-drop? No? Well, smoke if you want to. There'll be a cup of tea along shortly, I hope.' He popped an acid-drop into his mouth, placed the bag within easy reach, and leaned back. 'Now, let's have it, shall we? The whole story, from the moment you walked into the Centipede and saw Nora Winstone until you dropped her outside that ghastly flat.

Being a journalist, you probably think you can distinguish between what's important and what isn't. Well, maybe you can. But I want the 'isn't' as well.' He saw David frown, and gave what was intended as a knowing wink. 'The police are discretion personified. Anyway, this isn't going to be an official statement. It's off the record. O.K.?'

David was more than ready to oblige. He was bursting with curiosity, but he knew that he would get nothing out of Morgan until Morgan had got what he wanted out of him. Perhaps not even then; not unless it suited the superintendent's purpose. But if Morgan were prepared to talk at all he should be prepared to talk to his godson. David's appraisement of that affinity had hitherto been low; he had thought it more of a handicap than an asset. Now its status rose appreciably.

Morgan knew how to listen. He prompted, but he did not interrupt unnecessarily. Every now and again he would pop another acid-drop into his mouth (he was a non-smoker), sucking on it continuously, but never crunching it until only the last thin sliver remained. Several teeth had recently been extracted from his lower jaw, and with each particularly virile suck a little hollow would appear in his left cheek. It fascinated David.

Tea arrived before he had finished; in two thick white mugs, tepid and sickly sweet and heavy with milk. David eyed it with disfavour and sipped reluctantly. Morgan, however, appeared to find it both palatable and refreshing.

'Great stuff, tea.' He put the mug down half empty. 'Better than all your beer.' He had a soft, musical voice which was much in demand at police concerts. 'Mind if I put a few questions?'

'Help yourself.'

'Right. Well, now — these people who were at the club last night. You say you knew none of them except the Winstone woman?'

'I'd seen one or two of the younger set there before, but I don't know them. Never even spoken to them.'

'I daresay we can get their names from

the barman. Does the club keep a visitor's book? Do they have to sign in?'

David did not know. He had never taken a guest. Although he did not say so now, he preferred to seek his company and partners among the members. It came cheaper.

'And Nora? She's a Mrs, by the way, not a Miss. Or so her cell mate says.'

'Cell mate?'

'Sorry. A slip of the tongue. But their flat has a cell-like atmosphere, poor things. Very primitive and spartan.' The superintendent was a man who liked his comforts, and he shuddered at the memory. 'What about Nora?'

'I've already told you. I've seen her at the club a few times, and once or twice I've danced with her. Until last night I knew nothing about her except her Christian name. I don't know much more now. Less than you, I imagine.'

Morgan took another large draught of tea, his grey eyes fixed thoughtfully on his godson. The crumpled suit, the heavy check shirt with its soft collar, the loosely knotted tie, offended him aesthetically.

And when did the boy last have his hair cut?

'H'm!' He put down the mug. 'How long an interval was there between the departure of the darkie and Chapman?'

'I don't know. I didn't see Chapman leave. Perhaps ten minutes. Could be less.'

'And the Winstone woman told you nothing about her coloured friend?'

'No. I didn't ask, and she didn't tell me.'

Morgan belched silently behind his hand; the tea and the acid-drops were beginning to tell on his stomach. Surreptitiously he undid the top buttons of his trousers and allowed the zip to slide a little, reflecting sadly that a year ago such a concession to obesity would never have been necessary.

'All right. Go on from where you left the club together.'

There wasn't much more to tell. Just the journey back to the flat, and bidding Nora good-night, and leaving her there at the foot of the steps. 'Oh, yes. There was this car. It was parked a short way up the street, facing us — a black Zodiac saloon. Looked new.'

'Anyone in it?' David shook his head. 'Did you note the registration number?'

'I'm afraid not.'

'But you must have seen it. It'll be floating around somewhere in your subliminal. Try to isolate it.'

David tried. The attempt was unsuccessful.

'It may come to me later,' he said. 'Things do. In fact, I've a vague notion that it was familiar in some way; the number, not the car. But what's all this about, sir? What makes you think the woman has been kidnapped?'

Morgan selected another acid-drop and shook his head in reproof. The bald patch on top of his round head gleamed in the electric light. He had done his best to cover it with the hair remaining to him, but there was not enough to do the job properly.

'Your father would never have been so slow, David. He was a real newspaperman. Use your intelligence, boy. You left the woman standing on the pavement.

41

But she didn't go up to her flat, and she hasn't been to work to-day; her flat-mate assured me of the first, the salon of the second. So where is she? Where would she have gone of her own volition at one o'clock in the morning and wearing evening dress?'

'A boy-friend may have been waiting for her. Perhaps the Zodiac was his.'

'Why didn't she change first? It wouldn't have taken long. But, granted he was too impatient for that, where has she been all day? Wandering around London in a dance frock?'

David shrugged. 'O.K., so she's been kidnapped. Although I can't think why. She's no sex kitten, and who'd pay a ransom for Nora Winstone? But why have you been roped in? Why can't M Division handle their own dirty work? It isn't as though the woman was important.'

Morgan smiled. It was a warm, attractive smile, even when forced. He had practised it before the mirror many times; partly because he was a vain man, and partly because he knew that a disarming smile was one of the most useful attributes in the business.

'That's where you're wrong, my lad. Right now Nora Winstone is one of the most important women in the country. To the police, anyway.' The smile faded. 'Does the name Dyerson ring a bell? Police Constable Frank Dyerson?'

'I can't say it does. Should it?'

'It should. It was front-page news over the week-end. Dyerson was shot dead by a young thug down by the river late Saturday night. A thug who apparently goes by the odd name of Bandy. Remember?'

David did remember. 'Where does Nora fit in?'

'She was a witness to the shooting. The only one we have.' Morgan frowned. 'Or had.'

'Was she, though!' David whistled. 'But wait a minute, sir. Is that right? According to the papers there were three witnesses. No names mentioned, of course, but I'm sure they said three. What about the other two? And wasn't there a night watchman? Can't he help?'

'Not a hope. The poor chap was

knocked out before he even knew the brutes were there. He's still in hospital.' Morgan crunched the thin acid-drop sliver to powder. 'The other two never showed up.'

'And Nora did?'

'Nora did. It was she who told us there were others. A young couple canoodling in a doorway, according to her.'

'Didn't she give you their names?'

'No. She said they were strangers to her.'

'And you think that's why she was kidnapped? Because she could identify the gunman?'

The superintendent helped himself to another acid-drop before replying.

'Because he *thinks* she could identify him,' he said slowly.

David sat up smartly. 'And can she?'

Morgan frowned. 'It seems doubtful. She says she dropped her spectacles just as Dyerson shone his torch on the man's face. She couldn't distinguish the features, she says.'

David exhaled in exasperation. 'I don't get it,' he said. 'First you tell me the woman's important, now you as good as say she isn't. How come, sir?'

The superintendent shifted uneasily in the swivel chair. Why the devil couldn't they provide him with a padded seat? Comfort was due to his age if not to his rank. At forty-eight the flesh was less resilient.

'Of course she's important,' he said testily. 'Every copper in the division — in the whole command — is sweating blood to put this lot in the cooler. But at the moment we're up a gum-tree. Right at the ruddy top. There isn't a smell of them — not even the faintest whisper of a smell. And that's odd, you know, because there's usually *something* in these cases. Crooks in general don't hold with coppers being shot, it unsettles the atmosphere. If it weren't that they seem to have unloaded the loot successfully I'd say we were dealing with new boys.' He banged his fist on the desk — purposefully, not in anger. 'We'll get them eventually, of course. Sooner or later someone will talk out of turn. My fear is that when that happens we may not have enough evidence to hold them. And that's why I said Nora Winstone is important.'

To David it seemed that the superintendent was rambling.

'How?' he demanded impatiently. 'What use is she if she can't identify the man?'

Morgan leaned back and surveyed his godson through narrowed eyes.

'Ask yourself what she was doing in that alley on Saturday night, and there's only one answer. She was spying on the other two. There's nothing else she *could* have been doing.' He coughed. 'Not alone, anyway. So they could not have been the strangers she said they were. She must have known at least one of them.'

'Then why deny it?'

'Search me. Maybe she didn't want to involve them, or maybe she was just plain scared. Scared for herself, scared for them — I wouldn't know. But I do know one thing. If I could have gone to her and told her that I had the gunman in the cooler and that all I needed to put him away for keeps was someone to identify him, she'd have played ball one hundred per cent. If she couldn't identify the chap herself — and she heard his voice, remember — then she'd have told me who could. If she knew, that is.' Abstractedly he scratched his head, exposing more of the bald patch. Then, realizing what he was doing, he hastily smoothed the hair back into place. 'Don't ask me why, but Constable Dyerson's murder really got under that woman's skin.'

David's interest was now fully roused. He nibbled nervously at his fingers, the sharp, wolfish teeth biting into the hard skin round the nails. Snowball would really go for this. Not just the kidnapping — the dailies could have that — it was the unseen drama behind it that Snowball would expect him to disinter. That could be tricky. But at least he was in on the ground floor.

'How come this Bandy creature got wise to Nora if he didn't see her and the newspapers didn't publish her name?' he asked.

'She may have talked. We warned her not to, but you know how women chatter. Perhaps she failed to appreciate the danger.'

'Nora Winstone isn't a chatterer. I should know.' But there was nothing to be gained in pursuing that line of inquiry. They could only guess at the answer. 'Is there no chance of finding the two other witnesses without her?' he asked.

'There's always a chance. We're working on it. But it will take time, and that's something we're short on.'

Morgan could stand the chair no longer. His posterior had gone to sleep, there were pins and needles in his legs. He drew up the zip of his trousers, fastened the buttons, and stood up. Supporting himself with one hand on the desk, he stamped his feet to restore the circulation.

David stood up too. He said, 'With all due respect, sir, aren't you putting the cart before the horse? What use is a witness until you have a suspect to be identified?'

'A hell of a lot of use. To start with, we need a description of the man. Nora Winstone couldn't give us that. Polished shoes, tight jeans, an impression that he was young — that was as far as she could go.' Morgan ceased stamping and began to massage the seat of his trousers. 'But that's not all. This Bandy creature will have read the papers, he'll know that Nora isn't the only ace in the pack. He needs the other two. He'll try to extract their names from Nora; and, since his methods of extraction will undoubtedly be more persuasive than ours, he'll probably succeed.'

David knew what he meant by persuasion. He said, 'I suppose it has occurred to you, sir, that they may not be content merely to hold Nora? That when they've got what they want they may — well, eliminate her?'

Morgan looked suddenly tired. When he could he shaved twice daily, but to-night his chin and cheeks were dark with stubble.

'You're too right it has. And the others too if they find them before we do.'

David hesitated. Unless he were angry he seldom ventured to criticize his godfather to his face. But he ventured now. He said slowly, 'Was it wise, sir, to allow the newspapers to publish the fact that there were witnesses to the shooting? Wasn't it hazarding their lives unnecessarily?'

The superintendent did not take criticism easily. A vain man, he was apt to lose his temper when his actions or decisions were questioned. Now he looked more sad than angry, the grey eyes were clouded.

'I've asked myself the same question, David. We hoped to panic them into a false move. But I don't know. If only Nora Winstone had kept her mouth shut . . . '

He began to pace slowly up and down the room, hands buried in his pockets, head bowed. David had no great affection for his godfather, but he felt sorry for him now. He said cheerfully, 'It's easy to be wise after the event. Pardon the cliché, but we deal in them.'

Morgan made no comment. For a while he continued his pacing, pausing eventually in front of a large wall-map of M Division area. David joined him.

'Exactly where did the shooting take place, sir?' he asked.

Without hesitation Morgan put a well-manicured forefinger on the map. David guessed that he had studied it many times before.

'Just there.'

'Rotherhithe Street,' David read aloud. 'I don't know it.'

'It runs for miles along the south bank.' The finger moved round the bend of the river to Limehouse Reach. 'Mostly warehouses, with the occasional pub. And when the pubs close of a night it's more or less deserted.' Abruptly the superintendent turned away from the map. Putting a hand to his mouth, he yawned widely and long. Tears came into his eyes, and he knuckled them away. 'By Themis, but I'm tired! Time to call it a day, I think. You'd better cut along, David.'

David suppressed a smile. Some years back the superintendent, dipping into a book on Greek and Roman mythology, had discovered that Themis, daughter of Uranus, had represented in Homeric poems the personification of the order of things established by law, custom, and equity. She was, he had thereupon decided, the only right and proper deity for a policeman to swear by — since when he had sworn by no other.

'Suits me,' he said. 'I'll ring you if I remember the registration number of that Zodiac. It will probably come to me in the small hours.'

'In which case you can save it till the morning,' Morgan told him. 'And watch that blasted editor of yours. I don't want his dirty finger messing up this pie. Give him the facts and tell him to stick to them.'

'Snowball's not greatly interested in facts,' David said doubtfully.

'I know he's not. Which is why I don't trust him. And if he tries steam-roller tactics you can tell him I said so.'

Inspector Nightingale, the divisional detective inspector, a man of the superintendent's own age, less formidable in bulk and with a grey, egg-shaped face that appeared to have cracked in several places, was talking to the station sergeant in the main office. Morgan introduced them to David. They chatted for a few minutes, and then David, anxious to be gone, said brightly, 'Well, I'm off. Nothing else, is there, sir?'

'Just one little thing.' The superintendent's eyes were suddenly steely, the tired look had gone; his voice, hitherto *legato*, was now *staccato*. 'Why did you call to see Nora Winstone at her flat this evening? I don't think you told me.'

From the very start of the interview David had been anticipating this question, had even pondered his answer. If he mentioned the diary he would have to hand it over, and he did not wish to do that until he had had a chance to peruse it in private. Morgan had said to watch Snowball, that he did not trust him. Well, David did not trust him either. But, cynical and unscrupulous though he was, Snowball knew his way around; he would not stick his neck out regardless. He would be content to bide his time, waiting for the full story to break; and when it did he would expect David to be ready with all the intimate little details, the scandal and the sob-stuff that *Topical Truths* regularly fed to its readers. Maybe some of those details could be found in Nora

Winstone's diary.

As the interview progressed he had allowed the diary to slip from his mind, so that now, when the question came, he was unprepared. He said, with a slight stutter in his speech, 'D-didn't I? I suppose it d-didn't seem important, sir.'

'Important or not, I'd like to know.'

David fingered his tie. The knot had slipped farther round his neck than usual, and he pulled it straight.

'I just thought she might like to come out for a drink,' he said hopefully.

Morgan stared at him. 'Really? Getting low on girl-friends, aren't you?'

David flushed. He knew Morgan did not believe him, but he refused to be provoked into the truth. He said shortly, 'I felt sorry for her. Can I help it if I'm human?'

Morgan let him go, watching him thoughtfully as he walked across the big office and out into the hall. But Nightingale was watching the superintendent. He knew that look. When David had gone he said, 'What's up, Super? Something bothering you?'

Morgan rubbed his chin, scraping across the bristles.

'I don't trust that young man,' he said. 'He's my godson, but I don't trust him. He's selfish and obstinate, and he's got big ideas.' As an afterthought he added, 'And he wears his hair too long.'

'Nothing wrong with ideas.'

'Not if they're the right ones. But ever since that Shere Island job he's seen himself as God's gift to journalism. It has blunted his sense of responsibility as a citizen. Maybe he doesn't realize it, but that's how it is. He'd do his grandmother if he thought there was a story to it.' Morgan sighed. 'Well, his grandmother's dead, which may be lucky for her. But he's got a godfather, and I don't want him to do me.'

'You think he wasn't sticking to the truth?'

'I think he was monkeying with it, to say the least. However, David's my problem. What's new with you, Warbler?'

The D.D.I. grinned. It gratified him to hear his nickname on the lips of his superior. It showed that Morgan had not forgotten their days on the beat together.

'Nothing on the Bandy gang. But we've collected another headache. A stiff. Big one, too; they found him in the river. Someone stuck a knife in his back.'

'H'm! People are getting a darned sight too careless with knives these days. Has he been identified?' Nightingale shook his head. 'Well, he's all yours. But I've been thinking about those missing witnesses. You know — the young couple. If, as Nora Winstone says, they were canoodling, then it's a dead cert they are locals. Or the girl is. One doesn't pick a spot like Rotherhithe Street for a cuddle unless it happens to be handy. And it could be that their reluctance to come forward is because cuddling is something they shouldn't have been doing — if you see what I mean.'

The D.D.I. did see. 'Naughty, naughty, eh? Marriage lines getting crossed?'

'Something like that. It's worth considering, anyway. See what your chaps on the spot can pick up in the way of local gossip. Could you manage a house-to-house inquiry?'

Nightingale looked doubtful. 'The immediate neighbourhood, perhaps. We're too short-handed to go far afield. That would take time.'

Morgan nodded. 'We're short on time. I'll see if I can help.' He put a hand into his pocket and pulled out an acid-drop. 'I wish I knew for sure how Nora Winstone came to be in that alley on Saturday night.'

'I could make a guess.'

'Don't. I know how your unhealthy mind works.' He sucked hard, the hollow in his cheek coming and going. 'Obviously she was keeping an eye on the other two. But why? Who were they that she should be so interested in their love-making?'

'Perhaps the man was her husband.'

'Perhaps. It might help if we could trace him. See what you can dig up at Somerset House. And we may as well release her name to the Press. Just the bare news of her disappearance; no mention of kidnapping, and certainly no reference to Dyerson's murder. We don't want our missing witnesses putting two and two together, or they'll grow even more reluctant.' Morgan yawned. 'A pity we haven't a photograph.'

'You're sure there are other witnesses? That she didn't invent them?'

'Why should she? However, I'm not sure of anything right now except that I'm off home to bed.' Morgan yawned again, and walked over to the main desk to collect his bowler and umbrella. 'Good night, Warbler. Enjoy your stiff. Ring me if anything fresh crops up.'

'It'll be a pleasure,' the D.D.I. assured him.

★　★　★

It was while waiting at the traffic lights in the High Street that David saw the name-plate on the wall — Long Lane. It led to Rotherhithe — he had noticed that when studying the map with Morgan — and acting on impulse he turned right with the green. It was just after eleven o'clock. He would take a look at the scene of the crime, see it as Nora Winstone had seen it.

There was the suspicion of a slow puncture in his off-side rear tyre, and he drove slowly, uncertain of the route but sure that he had to keep heading east. Long Lane led into Abbey Street, and presently he came to crossroads and turned right into Jamaica Road and knew that he was nearly there. The district had a less impoverished aspect than he had anticipated; wide streets, modern shops and houses, and blocks of flats that looked as though they had only recently been completed and occupied. True, some of the side-roads were less imposing, particularly those to the south. But it was the riverside that interested him, and he dropped into second gear and drove still more slowly, looking for Cathay Street. Marigold Street, Cherry Garden, West Lane, Cathay Street. He turned left and left again, and stopped the Alvis opposite the police-station to consult the map.

Paradise Street. Who had suggested such exotic, lovely names for such an unlovely district? Had he hoped that their appeal might offset the squalor and wretchedness which, David suspected, had characterized Rotherhithe when the streets were originally christened? He put the Alvis into gear, took the first turning right, and found himself in Rotherhithe Street.

It was much as the superintendent had described it; deserted now, but no doubt busy enough by day. A disorderly street, that narrowed and widened at will; a street of warehouses and small factories, of dumps and yards and offices; a street with less than its fair share of windows; a street for things, not for people. The tall buildings hemmed it in, towering broodily, the glow of the city behind them.

He abandoned the Alvis and wandered slowly east, seeking the alley where Nora had stood. Between Cathay Street and Rose End, Morgan had said, and nearer the latter. He went as far as Rose End, a narrow cul-de-sac with blackened little villas on the west side and the blank wall of a warehouse opposite. Then he turned back. This was a cobbled stretch, with macadam at either end. Here, then, was where Constable Dyerson had died.

He stood in the mouth of the alley and peered across the narrow street. In that archway, perhaps, the young couple had stood, presumably unaware that they were being watched, and certainly not anticipating the tragedy that was about to impinge on their lives. At the other end of the alley was the river; he could see the lights of Wapping beyond it. There had been a wind on Saturday night; now the air was still. The sound of traffic along Jamaica Road came to him clearly.

The sliding doors of the warehouse beyond the alley were closed, the padlock was new. David went back to the car and bent to examine the suspect tyre, noting with relief that the pressure was holding. But there was something else. The number plate caught his eye, and he became aware that it was familiar to him in a way it had not been familiar before. He stood for a few moments staring at it, and wondering how that could be; but the solution eluded him, and presently he dismissed it as unimportant, and climbed into the Alvis and drove off. The cause of this new familiarity continued to tantalize him, however, and he kept turning it over in his mind. Enlightenment came with Westminster Bridge. He realized that the last three figures of his own number formed the registration number of the Zodiac he had seen near Nora Winstone's flat.

4

Elsie Sheel was a thirty-five-year-old blonde; plump, highly coloured, and friendly. She was still in pyjamas and dressing-gown when David arrived the next morning; sleep was heavy in her eyes, her hair was unbrushed, her face devoid of make-up. But she offered no apology for her appearance. She stood in the doorway, fastening the cord about her waist and blinking her eyes at him, and demanded to know his business.

'You got me out of bed,' she accused, 'and it's only just gone nine.'

'I'm sorry,' David said. 'But this is urgent. It concerns your friend Nora.'

She stopped blinking. 'Have they found her? Is she all right?'

David shook his head. Hastily he introduced himself and explained that it was he who had been with Nora on the Tuesday evening and had brought her home, magnifying that brief acquaintance into a ripe friendship. She would be more expansive, he thought, if she believed that.

A gently sympathetic smile engulfed her plump face as she opened the door wide for him and slopped back into the room. With the corner of her dressing-gown she swept crumbs from the deal table, and, lifting a cushion from the floor and depositing it in a frayed wicker chair, invited him to sit down.

'Nora and me, we've only been sharing the flat a few weeks, so I don't know her real well,' she explained, sinking her body into the only other chair. It too was of wicker, and creaked loudly in protest. 'It was my sister Glore what was with her before. But she married an American boy and went to the States, and Nora couldn't manage the flat on her own, like. So Glore asked me if I'd team up with her, and I said I would. But you being an old friend — well, I guess I know how you feel.' She sighed breathlessly. 'What do you think they'll do to her, Mr Wight? They won't — well, you know?'

David was not sure that he did. With

more certainty than he felt he said, 'She'll be all right. They just want to keep her away from the police, I imagine.'

He could see what Morgan had meant about the flat being cell-like. The room in which they sat was tiny. The deal table filled most of it; a white-wood cupboard stood next to the gas-cooker, and beyond the cooker was the sink, a single tap suspended above it. The two wicker chairs were the only other pieces of furniture, and there would hardly have been room for more. There were no rugs on the worn and ugly linoleum. The design on the wallpaper had disappeared with age, there were damp brown patches filling one corner of the ceiling.

'Poor Nora.' Elsie sighed heavily. Remembering the duties of a hostess, she said, 'I'll put the kettle on. I never eat breakfast; just a cup of tea. I expect you could do with one too, eh?'

While she busied herself at the stove he inquired casually if Nora had ever spoken to her of himself. He knew that that was unlikely, since until two days ago Nora had not even known his name; but the question helped to stress the implied friendship between himself and the missing woman.

'I can't say as she did. But then Nora isn't one for talking about her friends. Very quiet, she is. Keeps herself to herself, like.'

'Doesn't she even discuss her husband?'

She swung round at that, china-blue eyes wide in her round, doll-like face.

'She told you about him, did she? Well, I never! She must have took a fancy to you.'

'She just mentioned him,' David said modestly. 'What's he like?'

Elsie had returned to the stove. 'I never met him,' she said, after carefully counting three spoonfuls of tea into the pot. 'He never come here. I couldn't even tell you his name. It just come up once that she had a husband. I think they was separated or something.'

Elsie, it seemed, was no mine of information where Nora was concerned. 'Are her parents alive?' David asked. 'They ought to be informed — although I dare say the police will do that.'

The kettle started to sing. Elsie poured the boiling water on to the tea-leaves and placed the pot on the table, covering it with an ancient woollen cosy. 'They don't know where they are,' she said, fetching cups and saucers from the cupboard, her mules slapping noisily. 'I couldn't tell them. I don't know nothing about her family. Would you like a biscuit?'

He declined the biscuit. 'Any brothers or sisters?'

'I tell you, I don't know.'

She seemed distressed by her ignorance. David said, 'I suppose the police looked through her things, didn't they? They would have got the addresses of any relatives from her letters.'

Elsie shook her head. 'She didn't get any letters. Not while I been here. Sugar?'

As he sipped his tea David wondered about Nora Winstone. At the start he had thought of her as just an unfortunate woman who had been sucked into tragedy through no fault or design of her own. But was there more to it than that? The more he learned — or failed to learn

— about her, the more mysterious she became. She had a husband who was not a husband, she received no correspondence, she was so reticent about her family that not even the woman who shared her home could tell him one solitary fact about them. And Morgan's shrewd guess at the reason for her presence in Rotherhithe Street, even if correct, still left much unexplained. Did Elsie know the answers?

Elsie did not. 'She never said where she'd been,' she told him. 'I didn't know it was Rotherhithe, not until I seen it in the papers.'

'What did she say?'

There Elsie was on more knowledgeable ground. She had been asleep when Nora had returned that night, but Nora had awakened her, had wanted to talk. Distressed and shaken by the tragedy she had witnessed and by the subsequent ordeal at the police-station, for once her habitual reserve had deserted her. She had poured it all out; the van emerging from the warehouse yard, the clang of the closing gates, the policeman's torch dancing on the cobbles as he came pounding down the street, the dreadful certainty of what was about to happen as for a brief moment the two men had confronted each other; and then the shot and the crumpling body, and herself running to the dead man's side as the noise of the van's engine had faded into the night.

It all happened so quickly, Nora had said; just a brief, violent tragedy and then silence. There was no sound of opening windows, no voices, no hurrying feet. Rotherhithe Street was as still and as silent as the body on the cobbles, and when she was certain that the policeman was dead and that there was nothing she could do for him she had collected her spectacles and had run to the police-station at the junction of Cathay Street and Paradise Street. And there she had stayed until, the questioning over, they had brought her back to the flat in a police car.

Elsie Sheel sighed as she concluded her story, and refilled her cup and David's. He did not stop her. The tea was hot and strong, with no resemblance to the sticky brew he had suffered at the police-station. He said, 'Did she mention that there were others there at the time? A young couple?'

'Not then she didn't. She was too took up with that poor man being murdered.' She sipped with great refinement, little finger exaggeratedly crooked. 'But it was all in the papers the next day. Or was it Monday? I couldn't get it out of me mind. As I told Paul, it's the first time I've ever been that close to a murder, like — me living with someone what had actually seen it happen.'

'Paul? Who's Paul?'

'Paul Brenn-Taylor. He's often in the Croc of a morning. Of course, I didn't mention Nora's name, like. Paul's all right. But the others was listening, and you never know, do you?' David agreed that you did not. 'Nora said the police warned her to be careful, that if this Bandy got to know about her she might be in danger. She said I wasn't ever to tell anyone. And I haven't.' There was a hint of tears in the blue eyes. 'But they found her just the same, didn't they? I wonder how.'

David thought he could tell her. If Bandy or one of his gang had chanced to be in the Crocodile when Elsie Sheel was enlarging on her particular interest in the crime, they would not have needed Nora's name to find her. The knowledge that she shared a flat with Elsie would have been sufficient. But he did not explain this to Elsie; there was nothing to be gained by adding to her grief. He did, however, ask about Paul. A Paul Brenn-Taylor had been head of his house while he was at school; a tall, authoritative youth whom David, from the wide gap of two years, had both admired and feared.

Elsie received the news with surprised delight. Her emotions were transient.

'Well, I never! It's a small world, that's what I always say. And he's ever so nice. A bit sarcastic like, but that generous you wouldn't believe. Such a shame he's got only one arm.'

'One arm? How did he lose the other?'

She did not know. A car accident, perhaps. 'He doesn't talk about it,' she said. 'Seems to embarrass him, like.'

David realized they were straying from the purpose of his visit.

'Damned bad luck,' he said. 'He was a fine wing three; captained the school fifteen. I'll give you my phone number; you must ask him to get in touch with me. But tell me about Nora. How did you come to learn of the two other witnesses if not from her?'

'Well, like I said, it was in the papers. You could have knocked me down with a feather. Of course, I asked her about them when I come home, and she said yes, she had seen a young couple. But she didn't know who they was, she said.'

'And did you ask her then what she was doing over in Rotherhithe?'

Elsie shook her dull blonde head.

'I would've if I'd thought. I suppose I just forgot.'

David was sadly disappointed. He had not expected much from Elsie, but he had expected something. Had Morgan fared any better? He was wondering how to take his departure when Elsie said sharply. 'How did *you* know she was the woman in the papers? Nora didn't tell you. She didn't tell anyone. She said so.'

She was sitting bolt upright, staring at him suspiciously across the table. David gave her a disarming smile. 'The police told me,' he said. 'I called to see Nora last night, while they were here. They wouldn't let me come up, but they asked a lot of questions. I was at the police-station for hours.'

Her body sagged a little, but she did not relax completely. She said, 'You're asking a lot of questions yourself. Why? What are you after?'

'I told you, I'm a friend. I want to help Nora.' He pushed the hair back from his eyes in a characteristic gesture. 'You see, in a way I feel responsible for what has happened. If I hadn't been in such a hurry to leave when I brought her home Tuesday night — if I'd waited until she'd gone in, perhaps even come up with her . . .'

He shrugged, leaving the sentence unfinished. But it was enough for Elsie. She put out a plump hand and gently touched his where it lay on the table.

73

'You don't want to blame yourself,' she told him. 'It wasn't your fault. If they hadn't got her Tuesday they'd have got her some other time.' The hand withdrew; reluctantly, it seemed to David. 'Mind if I call you David?'

'Please do.'

She accepted the cigarette he offered, puffing at it vigorously once it was alight. The stale lacquer on her nails made her hands look dirty. 'Anyways, I don't see as how you can help her now. Do you?'

'Not clearly. But I can try. I'm a journalist, you see. We get to hear things.'

'Really?' She was more intrigued by his profession than by its possibilities. When he told her the name of the magazine on which he worked she squeezed herself from the creaking chair to rummage under the white-wood cupboard. Triumphantly she produced several copies of *Topical Truths*. 'I take it every week,' she told him delightedly. 'I must've read everything you've written.'

He was young enough to feel flattered.

He had spent some time persuing Nora Winstone's diary. It had not told him much, but on the day after Constable Dyerson had been shot Nora had written, 'Must warn Bill against Bandy.' That was all; there was no further reference to the tragedy, no exposition of her personal reaction. That one jolt to her memory was all she had confided to paper. Why? To David the answer was obvious. Bill, whoever he might be, was important to Nora. So important that she would not trust his safety to memory. But when he asked Elsie about Bill she shook her head. Nora had never mentioned the name, she said. 'Who is he?'

'I don't know,' he confessed. 'From what Nora said I gathered he was someone close to her. Unfortunately she didn't say enough for us to trace him. A pity — he might have been able to help.'

'I don't see how anyone can help,' she said. 'Only the police.'

* * *

The offices of *Topical Truths* were on the top storey of a tall building near the Holborn end of Fetter Lane; adequate without being spacious, and sufficiently dark to demand electric light for most of the working day. Staring out of the window at the traffic below, David reflected gloomily that it would be as good a place as any from which to commit suicide. Naturally optimistic, he was pessimistic now; he had banked on Elsie Sheel and Nora's diary for information, and both had failed him. The diary had proved the greater disappointment. He had risked incurring his godfather's wrath by concealing it, only to find that it contained little more than a long list of addresses and telephone numbers. So far as he could see there was nothing in it for him, nothing in it for Snowball. The hot scoop he had eagerly anticipated looked like being a frost. On the way to the office he had telephoned Morgan to tell him what he had remembered of the Zodiac's registration number, and had been tempted to mention the diary. Fear, not cupidity, had stopped him. Morgan would flay him alive for concealing material evidence, no matter how sterile that evidence might prove to be.

He turned to look at his editor. Snowball was still poring over the diary, had been poring over it for the past ten minutes, making numerous notes on a memo pad. He was a skinny, wizened little man, with long, bony fingers and a mop of dirty white hair. It was the hair that had earned him his nickname; thick and unruly as David's, but cut to form an enormous puff-ball that dwarfed the wrinkled face beneath. Like David, he was indifferent to his appearance. He sat now in his shirt-sleeves, tie loose and collar unbuttoned, frayed braces precariously supporting his trousers by one button only at two out of the three points of suspension. As usual, his bifocals were nearer the tip of his nose than the bridge.

'Getting anywhere?' David asked. 'Personally, I'd say it's a wash-out. What ought I to do? Hand the damned thing over to Morgan, or keep it and pretend it never happened?'

Snowball sucked hard on his pipe; it had gone out, and he placed it on the desk beside him. The office stank of the strong tobacco he always smoked.

Without looking up from the diary he said, 'You don't need me to tell you what you ought to do. Whether you'll do it is another matter. What was the name of that darky?'

He had a harsh, rasping voice, surprisingly strong for such a little man. David said, 'I don't know. Nora called him George. Why?'

Snowball ignored the query. 'A list of addresses and telephone numbers as long as your arm, and all of 'em male. Is she that kind of a woman?'

'I wouldn't know. We didn't get that far.'

'H'm! Well, George doesn't get a mention. There's no William either. So who's this Bill she refers to? He's the boy we want.'

David shook his head. 'Search me. But I agree he's important. He was important to Nora too; so important that she wouldn't trust his safety to her memory.'

'Then why isn't his address in the book, along with the others?'

'Because it was too familiar to be forgotten, I imagine.'

Snowball grunted. 'Could be. Or maybe it's here and we haven't recognized it. Well, whoever he is — husband, boy-friend, brother — we have to find him. That sticks out a mile.'

David eyed him with disfavour. It would help, he thought, if he could learn to like the little man. But he found that difficult.

'How do you propose we do that?'

'Look for him, of course. There's this list of names in the diary; I'll put young Oliver on to that. Routine stuff. He can't mess it up, though he'll do his damnedest, bless him!'

'And me?'

Snowball took up his pipe and lit it, releasing a pungent cloud of smoke. He said, between puffs, 'There's a Robert Lumsden on this list. Only name in the Rotherhithe area. He's yours.'

'Thank you very much.'

The editor scratched his head. He was always scratching it. David suspected that he never washed his hair, that it was alive with fleas. Sometimes he fancied he could even see it move.

'That mysterious young couple Morgan mentioned. The Winstone woman must have known them; why else would she be spying on them so far from home? Her home, I mean; the couple are more likely to be locals. And if Robert Lumsden is a pal of hers he may be a pal of theirs. Find out.'

Just like that, thought David. Find out! Without concealing his annoyance, he said sharply, 'And where does that get us?'

'Oh, be your age, David! Your friend Morgan's no fool. I doubt if this Bandy creature is either, or he'd be in the can by now. Both will be looking for the missing witnesses, though with different ends in view. Well, you find them first. At least you have some sort of a lead, damn it!'

In David's opinion a list of addresses and a man's Christian name was not much of a lead. He had hoped to find in the diary sufficient juicy material for a typical *Topical Truths* story which, suitably embellished, could be published as soon as Morgan gave the word. He had been prepared also, if Snowball thought it advisable, to follow up any direct leads which the diary might give. He had not contemplated a wild-goose chase round Rotherhithe such as his editor now proposed.

'What about the diary?' he asked.

The editor picked it up, tapped it thoughtfully on the palm of his hand, and pushed it across the desk.

'Hang on to it until we know where we're going. After that . . . ' He shrugged his thin shoulders. 'Suit yourself, my boy. It's your neck that'll get wrung, not mine.'

'Thanks,' David said bitterly. 'Any more helpful advice?'

Snowball stood up. His legs were short in proportion to his torso, so that he looked even shorter standing than sitting.

'Yes. If Lumsden's a wash-out you might try a house-to-house investigation.' David started to protest, but Snowball cut him short, flapping his long, bony hands, the nails of which were packed with grime. 'Not the whole district, you fool. Just the vicinity immediate to the crime.' A large goitre disfigured his neck, and he had a habit of pressing it with his fingers when deep in thought. He pressed it now. 'T.V., huh? They've all got 'em these days. If you come up against someone who hasn't, switch to radio.'

'T.V.?' David frowned. 'I'm not with you.'

'Programme investigator. For the under-thirties, say; that should include anyone who could reasonably be described as young. When did that cop get himself shot? Saturday? Then ask what programme they watched Saturday night. But it's the ones who didn't watch that matter. Find out what outside attraction took them away from the set. And get their names. Don't forget you're looking for a youth whose Christian name is Bill or William.'

You had to hand it to Snowball, David thought, with grudging admiration; a scoundrel, but a knowing scoundrel. The old boy's assumption that Bill was the male half of the missing couple was sound; and although Bill himself might not live in Rotherhithe, his girl almost certainly did. David wondered how

Morgan and the gunman would set about looking for them.

'It's a common enough name,' he said. 'What do you suggest I do with him if I find him? Tell him what has happened to Nora, try to get his co-operation? Or do I hand him over to Morgan?'

'If he reads the papers he'll know what's happened to Nora. It won't cheer him any if you tell him why — if he doesn't already know, that is. He'll realize this Bandy means business; and if he was scared of offering himself as a witness before he'll be even more scared now. No, I don't think I should mention the Winstone woman. And forget the police. For the present, anyway.'

David was puzzled. He had assumed that the object of the exercise was to find the missing couple, warn them and get their story, and then hand them over to Morgan with the compliments of *Topical Truths*. That would be something of a coup, the biggest they had had since Shere Island. What was Snowball up to? What was at the back of that sneaky mind of his?

'I'm just playing canny,' Snowball told him, grinning. There was little mirth in the grin. His teeth were brown except where the gaps showed, and the gaps were plentiful. He was always about to have the remainder of his teeth extracted and dentures fitted, but so far he had never got around to it. 'Morgan can't use witnesses until he has a suspect.'

'He most certainly can. He needs a description of this Bandy creature. Nora couldn't provide that.'

'All right. We'll get the description and pass it on.'

'How?'

'There are ways,' Snowball said enigmatically. 'You let me worry about that. But hand that couple over now, and Morgan will just sit on them — weeks, maybe months. Produce them at the crucial moment, and you've got drama. And it's drama that makes news.' The grin faded. 'Now get busy and find them.'

'And sit on them myself? What happens if the thugs catch up with us? It could be unpleasant.'

'I'll take care of that. Your job is to find

them.' The telephone rang, and he grabbed at the receiver and rasped an acknowledgment. Then he handed it to David. 'For you.'

The caller was Brenn-Taylor. David was both surprised and flattered. He had not really expected Brenn-Taylor to contact him, and certainly not so soon; they had had little in common at school, and were unlikely to have much in common now. Perhaps it was another instance of distance lending enchantment to the view.

'Elsie gave me your message,' Brenn-Taylor said. He had a silky, languid voice with the merest suspicion of a lisp. 'Nice to know you're still around. We must have a bite together some day. Do you working lads get time off for lunch, or is it pie and beer at the local?'

Normally it was pie and beer. But, as Snowball had intimated, David would be unlikely to get results in Rotherhithe until after working hours. For once he had leisure to spare.

'I could manage lunch to-day,' he said. 'Are you free?'

Yes, Brenn-Taylor said, he was free. 'Meet you in Kettner's around twelve-thirty. Pink gin or sherry? I'll have them lined up.'

David chose the gin, and hung up. Snowball was drumming impatiently on the desk. The dancing fingers, knuckle-bones triumphant, touched the diary and seized on it.

'Hang on to that,' Snowball said, handing it to him. 'What Morgan doesn't know can't hurt him.' He scratched energetically at his hair, so that the mop seemed suddenly alive. 'Can't hurt you either, eh?'

★ ★ ★

It was strange, thought David, how little some people changed. He had not seen Paul Brenn-Taylor for ten years, yet he recognized him immediately. The dark, wavy hair, already greying at the temples, was more carefully trimmed and brushed, his teeth were more yellow, he had filled out and was perhaps an inch or two taller; otherwise, apart from the missing left arm, he was much the same. Brenn-Taylor had always been a neat dresser, he remembered; now, with the money to indulge his tastes, he looked immaculate. He was not a handsome man. His brown eyes were slightly asymmetrical, his large, transparent ears projected almost at right angles from his head, his lower lip protruded aggressively. Broad but round-shouldered, his thin legs accentuated by the narrow trousers, he would have looked top-heavy had not the large feet restored the balance.

'Nice to see you, dear boy,' he said, in the affected drawl David remembered so well. At school David had been wary of that drawl; it could sharpen without warning into incisive abuse or vitupera-tion. He remembered, too, the way Brenn-Taylor had of peering at the person he was addressing, as though he were short-sighted — which he was not. 'A little late, aren't you? I took the liberty of ordering lunch; hope you don't mind. We'll down these and eat.'

That too, thought David with some resentment, was typical of Brenn-Taylor as he had known him. But he did not protest. Instinctively he was again the fifth-former, acknowledging the inalienable right of the prefect to give orders. As the lunch progressed the relationship softened; rapport came with the wine. Yet even the wine could not entirely dispel David's feeling of subordinancy. It was uncommon to him, and he fought against it. But it was still there at the end.

The lunch was excellent — glazed paupiettes of sole, roast duck with orange salad, bananas au rhum, a ripe stilton. They drank Chablis with the sole, a fine Clos de Vougeot with the duck, cognac with their coffee. It was Brenn-Taylor who at first did most of the talking. He had travelled extensively, knew a number of celebrities, and possessed a fund of good stories. Listening to him, David grew increasingly envious. 'What do you use for money?' he asked eventually, as the anecdotes piled up.

'Just money. An aunt in the States left me her all when she died, dear soul. I belong to what are vulgarly known as the idle rich. More idle than rich, perhaps — but I get by.'

'Lucky devil.'

Brenn-Taylor glanced down at the empty sleeve. 'I could be luckier.'

It was the first reference either man had made to his injury. Encouraged by the Burgundy, David said, 'I'm sorry about that, Paul.' That made another first; they had not used Christian names before. 'Skip it if you like, but — well, how did it happen?'

Paul shrugged. 'The usual. A damned drunk losing control of his car.' He lifted his glass to gaze reflectively at the light through the rich redness of the wine. 'I'm resigned to it now, but it took some getting used to. Put paid to a lot of youthful dreams.' He sipped at the wine. The drawl was back in his voice as he said, 'Tell me about yourself, dear boy. Elsie tells me you're mixed up in crime. How come?'

David told him, careful to say no more than Paul might have learned from Elsie or the newspapers. That, he reflected sadly, was little enough. There was only the diary. Although the Press had not connected Nora Winstone's disappearance with the murder of Constable Dyerson, Elsie undoubtedly had.

So had Paul. Listening to David, he had only toyed with the bananas au rhum. Now, when the waiter had removed his plate, he said, 'A pity Elsie's so garrulous. It's done her friend a power of no good.'

With that David agreed. 'How well do you know the regulars at the Crocodile?' he asked.

'You might say we're on excellent drinking terms. Respectable types, most of them. I'd be surprised if they included this Bandit fellow.'

'Bandy, not Bandit. Though Bandit would be more appropriate. I presume he's called Bandy because — ' David's hand, its nicotine-stained fingers conspicuous against the white tablecloth, paused half-way to his glass. 'Hey, Paul! There wouldn't be a bandy-legged coot among them, would there?'

'Not as I've noticed, dear boy. But then I've never actually studied their pins.' His lips parted in a wry smile. 'You're sitting pretty, aren't you? Find the missing witnesses, take them along to the Croc, and let them unmask the criminal. They know him, he doesn't know them. It's a cinch, dear boy.'

David echoed the smile. 'Always provided Bandy happens to be among those present.'

Yet it was a new and fascinating prospect, and during the silence necessitated by the presence of the coffee waiter he savoured it. Not only to find the missing couple, but to expose the gunman as well — that would indeed be a feather in his cap. The gloom that had descended on him in Snowball's office had been lightened by the excellent lunch. Now he was even enthusiastic.

There was just one snag. He first had to find his witnesses.

'And that, dear boy, will be like looking for needles in a haystack,' was Paul's comment. He lit an enormous cigar, taking pains to ensure that it was evenly alight. 'I wish you luck. Another brandy?'

'Thanks.' At the start of the meal

David, while appreciating Paul's choice of food and wine, had pondered uneasily on the cost. Now he no longer cared. 'But at least this Bandy creature will be faced with the same problem. Unless Nora Winstone has given him a lead.'

'I doubt if he'll even bother to try,' Paul said. The lisp was more pronounced now; David suspected the brandy. 'Why should he? Witnesses aren't dangerous unless they're prepared to come forward and testify. Apparently these two are not.'

'But they won't be allowed to remain in obscurity. Not if the police can help it. And not if I can help it — although they don't know about me, of course.' David sipped appreciatively at the cognac. He was not certain where the change had occurred, but now it was he who had taken charge of the conversation. Realization of the switch gave him a childish feeling of pleasure. 'To my mind he just *has to* find them. And I shudder to think what will happen to them when he does.'

'Then don't think, dear boy.' Paul finished his coffee and replaced the cup with an air of finality. 'Mind if I rush off?

I have a date with an angel who objects to being kept waiting.'

'Don't they all?'

'Yes.' He beckoned to the waiter. 'How about you? Off to Rotherhithe on your quest?'

'Not directly. A short kip back at the flat wouldn't come amiss.' David waved a hand over the table, narrowly missing the bowl of flowers. 'I'm not used to so much hoggery midday. And they'll all be out at this hour. Down there they work.'

Paul insisted on paying for the lunch. As they parted at the entrance he said, with more earnestness than he had so far shown, 'I envy you, David. It must be pleasant to have a purpose. Count me in if you need an assistant at any time. And I mean that.'

Surprised, David felt that he did.

He did not return to the flat. Instead he went to a cinema where, between snatches of uneasy slumber, he watched the screen and reflected on Paul Brenn-Taylor. At school a difference in age and position had prevented friendship between them. Paul had clearly enjoyed his authority; scorning popularity, he had run the House with what David and his friends had considered to be unduly harsh efficiency. They had disliked and feared him. Yet to-day, ten years later, the two of them had lunched together like old friends. More surprising still, Paul, who to David had seemed to have everything that can make life agreeable, had professed envy of him, David.

To David it was incomprehensible.

It was half-past six when he left the bus in Jamaica Road, and walked down St James's Road to the address written in Nora Winstone's diary. But Robert Lumsden was out, and the woman who opened the door to him could not or would not say when he would be home. She was a stiff, uncommunicative creature; David's discreet probing discovered nothing more of her lodger than that he occupied a ground-floor room and was often away. When he inquired about Lumsden's job she took fright and shut the door on him.

He went back to the church and

strolled down Jamaica Road to Cathay Street. On his previous visit he had been impressed by the signs of prosperity and progress in the streets and buildings; now he was impressed by the people. They were well dressed and looked prosperous, they had emerged from depression and poverty as Rotherhithe itself was emerging. In ten years time, he thought idly, Rotherhithe might well rival Islington as a fashionable residential area, as Islington was already rivalling Chelsea.

Cathay Street was less impressive. It was also profitless so far as his quest was concerned. The few residents he spoke to were friendly and co-operative; but most of them were elderly, and it seemed that none of the younger men had been christened William. Many of them had been out on the previous Saturday night, as they apparently were on most Saturdays, but David did not bother to inquire into their activities. Quite clearly none of them had been cuddling a girl in Rotherhithe Street.

One interview aroused his interest. The door was opened to him by a lush brunette with spiky eyebrows, and wearing a yellow polka-dot frock that seemed too flimsy to contain her ripe figure. She had all the curves that he liked to see, and none of those he did not. In her cheerful cockney voice she told him that her name was Judy Garland.

'It sounds familiar,' he said, smiling back at her.

' 'Tain't my real name. That's Christine. But 'most every one calls me Judy.' She looked him up and down. Apparently she liked what she saw, for she said, 'Want to come in?'

David decided that he did. He was becoming tired of doorsteps. The small parlour was clean and gay, and so crammed with furniture that there was little room in which to move. In one corner stood a twenty-one-inch television set.

He explained the ostensible reason for his visit. Miss Garland was intrigued. 'Fancy them wanting to know a thing like that.' She pushed him into a chair, but did not sit down herself, preferring to lean against the table. 'I get kinda itchy if

I sits for long,' she explained. 'That's why I don't watch the telly much. But Mum and Dad, they watch it all the time. Never stop. Have a beer?'

He had a beer. So did Miss Garland, blowing her way through the froth and gulping down the liquid with gusto. Then she took a deep breath that stretched the bodice of her frock almost to bursting. 'I'm a sucker for beer,' she said. 'Better'n all that hard stuff. P'raps that's why the boys like taking me out. I mean — well, it costs less, don't it?'

'That wouldn't be the only reason,' he said.

'No,' she agreed cheerfully. 'I know what they're after, all right. You got a girl? Steady, I mean?'

He hastily disclaimed such a possession, and led the conversation back to television and Saturday night. No, she said, she had not been watching; as on most evenings, she had gone out. Where? Oh, they'd had a drink at the Angel and then gone to the flicks.

'And after that?'

Some of her vivacity departed at the

question. She did not respond to his knowing look. 'That's my business.'

'Of course it's your business,' he agreed hastily, anxious not to offend. 'Yours and the boy-friend's. What's his name? Tom? Jack? Bill? He's a lucky fellow, whoever he is.'

She shook her head. Unless she were an accomplished actress those names had no particular significance for her. David's disappointment was tempered with relief. It would not have been pleasant to think of Judy Garland as a target for a gunman.

She soon recovered her vivacity. They finished the beer, and when, somewhat reluctantly, he left, it was with an invitation to call any time he happened to be passing. 'Can't promise beer,' she told him gaily, 'but there's always a cuppa.'

He thanked her. 'Be seeing you.'

Half-way down the street a man was gazing up at one of the houses. He did not appear to show any interest in David, but as the latter reached the corner he noticed that the man was staring after him. David paused to stare back. Even when the man had turned and walked away he continued to stare. He was puzzled. Not so much that the man should have shown interest in him, but that he could be so certain he had seen him before and not remember where.

There were ten houses in Rose End, merged into a whole whose united front differed from the wall across the road only by the uniform insertion of doors and windows. Their roofs were of slate, their bricks a dirty grey from which most of the pointing had crumbled. Separating each front door from the narrow pavement was a single step, its stone worn almost hollow by generations of feet. The grey pall that had descended over the docks that May evening intensified the general air of gloom pervading Rose End. David, surveying it from Rotherhithe Street, felt the gloom enter into him also.

He decided to start at the far end, where the road narrowed abruptly into a footpath that led to Paradise Street. At the second house he tried it seemed that his luck was in. After listening to his opening spiel, the woman who had answered the door shouted over her shoulder, 'Bill! You there?' There was an answering shout from inside the house, and she called out, 'Come here! There's a gentleman wants to see you about the telly.'

Bill Brandon was a tall, gangling youth, good-looking, but with a sad, vacant expression. Yes, he said, he watched the telly; watched it most nights of a weekday. But when David asked about Saturday he couldn't remember. 'Ma!' he bawled. Then, discovering that she was standing immediately behind him in the tiny hall, he grinned. 'Was I in or out Sat'day evenin', Ma?'

'You was out,' she told him. 'And goodness knows what time you come home. It was gone twelve when I went to bed, and you wasn't in then. If your Dad were here — '

'Well, he ain't.' The youth turned to David. 'I was out, mate.'

David gave what he hoped was an ingratiating smile.

'At the cinema? The local? We're trying to discover, you see, how these counter-attractions affect our viewing figures.'

Bill Brandon shrugged. 'Just out,' he said laconically. 'You know — with the lads.'

David had to leave it at that.

One other resident aroused his compassion, if not his interest. She was a girl of about Judy Garland's height and build, but there the resemblance ended. Where Judy was all curves, this girl was all lumps. Her hair was a mousy brown, and she stood awkwardly, as though her legs or her feet pained her. But it was her face and her voice that troubled him. Her face was one continuous twitch; eyebrows, cheeks, nose, lips — they were all part of it and never still. She had difficulty too in forming her words. She did not stutter; the words, or at least the syllables, came out whole. But there were long, agonizing pauses while her mouth worked desperately to frame them.

In a doorstep interview that seemed endless he learned that her name was Mina Einsdorp, that she was twenty-one, that both her parents were out, and that there was no television-set in the house.

Hastily he switched to radio. Yes, they

had a radio, but they did not listen often.

'Did you listen Saturday evening?' He could not see her as the female half of the couple in the archway, but he had to go on. 'You, not your parents.'

She shook her head. It was easier than talking.

'Were you out?' A nod this time. 'Mind telling me what you did? We treat all answers as confidential, of course.'

'The — the — ' He thought she would never make it. 'The cinema.'

He had expected that. 'And after? A café, perhaps?'

It seemed that speech was becoming more difficult, the pauses between the words were longer. But eventually he learned that she had gone for a walk. And then, because the questions had ceased and she was able to be done with words, for a brief moment her face was still, and she smiled at him. It was a pleasant smile, and it seemed to David that it was at once familiar and unfamiliar. Then the twitches recommenced, and the smile faded.

The interview had depressed him, and his calls on the other residents of Rose

End were brief and unfruitful. I may have missed something, he thought, as he trudged back to St James's Road, but I don't greatly care. This sort of lark is not for me.

Robert Lumsden opened the door himself; this time it was his landlady who was out. He was a good-looking young man in the late twenties, with a mass of curly ginger hair and a cheerful, freckled face. David said, 'Sorry to bother you so late, but you were out when I called before. I'm trying to trace a lady named Nora Winstone. Mrs Nora Winstone. Do you know her?'

'Can't say I do. Should I?'

David was uncertain how to continue. Lumsden appeared to be telling the truth, yet what was his name doing in Nora's diary if the two were unacquainted? While he hesitated, Lumsden said, with a faint burr to his voice that David could not place, 'You intrigue me. Come in and tell me more.'

His room was untidy but clean. An iron bedstead stood against one wall, a large wardrobe and a chest of drawers filled another. Under the window was a long table, littered with sketches and paintings, and with all the paraphernalia of a line and watercolour artist. There were sketches and paintings on the bed, more on the mantelshelf and on top of the chest. To David's untrained eye few of them appeared to be finished.

Lumsden grinned at him. 'Sorry about the mess. Wasn't expecting visitors.' There was only the one chair, and he swept a pile of clothing from it. 'Sit down. I'll take the bed.'

David preferred to stand. He said, 'Are you a professional artist, or is this just a hobby?'

Lumsden flapped a hand at the mantelshelf. There was paint on the dark-blue jersey and grey flannels.

'If you mean that sort of stuff, it's a hobby. I'm a commercial artist by trade. Now, what's all this about? I've never even heard of a Mrs Winstone. Why come to me?'

'Because your name and address are in her diary.'

'They are?' There was no mistaking his

genuine amazement. 'Well, what do you know? Who the hell is she, anyway? I don't get it.'

David did not get it either, and he decided not to be too explicit until he did. He said, 'I happened to find a diary that belonged to her. As it has your name in it I thought you might be able to give me her address so that I could return it.'

'Sorry, no dice.' Lumsden scratched his head in perplexity. 'Where is this flipping diary? Let's have a look at it.'

'I left it at home,' lied David.

He went across to the mantelshelf and examined the water-colours more closely. The scenes were familiar. One of them was painted from across a sandy cove, with the rocks piling up into a forbidding headland and the ocean rollers breaking over them. As art it was no great painting, but it was photographic. He said, 'Isn't that Poldhu, near the Lizard?'

'It is. Thanks for the recognition; it does something for my ego. I've done quite a lot of painting round that area. My aunt runs a caravan camp between Poldhu and Pendwara, and I spend some of my holidays there.' He grinned. 'I'm not all that keen on the place, but it's cheaper than paying for lodgings.'

'You're a Cornishman, aren't you?' David said. He had placed the burr now.

'I was born there. Got it out of my system now, though. Do you know that part of the world?'

David grinned back at him. 'My uncle has a pub in Pendwara. I get cheap holidays too.'

It was nearly midnight by the time he returned to his flat. He had decided that, in recompense for a tiring and somewhat depressing evening's labour, he would indulge himself with a decent meal in town on the expense account. Paul had given him a taste for good food. Snowball was sticky over expenses, but he could be persuaded; and this was an occasion for persuasion. He sat drinking in a pub near Leicester Square until closing time, and then went on to a favourite restaurant near by and took his time over fillet steak and mushrooms, followed by cheese and biscuits and coffee.

His flat was on the ground floor of an

elderly Georgian house in a quiet Fulham street, and consisted of a large bed-sitter with an alcove partitioned off to form a minute kitchen. The Alvis was parked outside, and as always he made sure that she was properly tucked up for the night before he mounted the wide steps to the front entrance. He was tired, and glad to be home. All that walking! He just wasn't used to it.

At first he thought the lock was broken, or that he had the wrong key; the key entered the lock smoothly enough, but it would not turn. It was not until he had fiddled in the dark for some irritating seconds that he thought to try the handle and found that the door was unlocked. It did not perturb him; he had left the flat unlocked before. He ran his finger over the wall to the switch, flicked it down, and shut the door behind him.

He stared round the room in amazement. Disorder was complete. Drawers had been pulled from the chest, their contents littered the floor. Suitcases had been opened, his desk rifled, and his papers scattered in confusion. There were underclothes soaking in the wash-basin, a further pile on the floor beside it. The wardrobe doors were open and his suits had slid from their hangers.

And on the bed, feet and hands tied and a handkerchief bound over her mouth, lay a girl.

5

'Susan! What the hell's been going on?'

Without waiting for an answer he ran to the bed and began to free her feet. Not only were they bound together, they were also tied to the bedpost. When there was no response to his query other than a vicious jerk of the nylon-clad legs he looked at the girl in hurt surprise; then, realizing his error, he moved to the head of the bed and removed the handkerchief from her mouth. Even then she did not speak, though her lips moved. He fetched a glass of water, and put an arm round her and held her while she sipped. From the expression on her face swallowing was clearly a painful business, but presently she turned her head away and held out her hands.

'My wrists, darling.' Her voice was a croak. 'They hurt.'

He untied them. A host of questions was on his lips, but he refrained from speaking them; she needed time in which to relax, to compose herself. As she rubbed her chafed wrists he stared in dismay round the room, brows knit in angry concentration. Then he bent and began to massage her ankles.

'Thanks, darling. That'll do.' She swung her feet to the floor and sat up. Her auburn hair was ruffled from restless tossing, and she pushed and patted it into place. Her voice was still hoarse, and she picked up the glass and sipped again. 'Pass me my handbag, will you?'

'What happened?' David demanded, obeying.

'What do you think happened?' Her grey-green eyes surveyed him scornfully from beneath pencil-thin eyebrows. 'Either you've been burgled, or some of your friends have an odd sense of fun.' She bent to examine her face in the mirror, wrinkling her small nose in disgust. 'My, but I look a mess!'

He watched her as she applied lipstick and powder, combed her hair, and rearranged the casual auburn lock that hung tantalizingly over her forehead. He had known Susan Long since they were children together, and he accepted her presence in his flat as he would have accepted the presence of a sister had he had one. He was a self-centred young man, and his primary emotion now was irritation, not solicitude. But he was also aware that his irritation was ill-timed, and he did his best to suppress it.

Susan stood up and twisted the waist of her frock so that the full skirt hung evenly, and bent to smooth the pleats. But there were still pins and needles in her legs, and she flopped back on to the bed with a grimace. David said, 'What's the matter? They didn't hurt you, did they?'

'No. They were not exactly gentle, either.' She crossed one leg over the other and rubbed it vigorously. 'I think you might have asked me that before.'

'Sorry.' He stared round the room again. 'How many of them were there?'

'Two. At least, I think there were two. I never really got a proper look at them.'

He sat down on the bed beside her. 'What happened? What were you doing here, anyway?'

'What do you think I was doing? I came round to see you because I was bored. When I found you were out I thought I might as well do a spot of washing and tidy the place up. It usually needs it.'

'You made a good job of it,' he said, kicking at a suitcase.

Susan laughed. It was a gay, infectious sound.

'I did too, though I don't blame you for doubting it. And I darned some socks and put your undies in to soak.' She peered over at the wash-basin to see if they were still soaking. 'Then I began to feel sleepy (I was on the set just after seven this morning, although it was quite unnecessary. They didn't start filming till after lunch), so I switched off the light and lay down on the bed for a nap. And that's where they found me. I must have forgotten to lock the door.'

'What time was this?'

'When they arrived? I don't know — although I seem to have been lying there for hours. I woke up to find them rolling me over on to my tummy. I never even saw their faces. They trussed me up and gagged me, and one of them — he had a queer, squeaky sort of voice — told me to keep my head buried in the pillows. So I did — they didn't sound as though they would take kindly to argument. I could hear them moving about and opening and shutting doors and things, and then they left. They couldn't have been here long. Ten minutes at the most.'

'Did they say anything before they left?'

'To me? Not a word.'

David went over to the wardrobe and started to put his suits back on the hangers. 'They've made a mess of these,' he said in disgust.

Susan laughed. 'Is that possible, darling?'

He ignored the comment. 'I can't understand what they were after. There's nothing here worth pinching. You know that.'

'I know it, yes. But did they?' Susan stood up and stretched. She had a plump, well-rounded figure. Stretching displayed it to perfection, but the demonstration was wasted on David. 'Is there anything to eat? I'm starving.'

'Help yourself. There's bacon and eggs. And coffee. I could do with a cup of coffee myself.' He slammed the wardrobe door shut. 'I'll clear up some of this mess.'

Ten minutes later he joined her in the small kitchen and plumped himself down on the solitary chair. 'So far as I can see they've taken nothing,' he said. 'Or nothing of the slightest value. There may be the odd handkerchief missing; I wouldn't know about that. They must have been loco.'

Susan winced as drops of hot fat spluttered from the pan on to her hands. She had wrapped a towel round her waist. 'Have you rung the police?' she asked.

'I'll do it later. How's that coffee coming along?'

'Nearly ready. Sure you don't want anything to eat?'

'I might manage an egg.'

They ate their meal in near silence; Susan was too hungry to talk. When she had finished she gave a satisfied sigh, wiped her mouth and fingers (her fingers were short and stubby, and she wore her nails long and pointed to disguise the fact), and said casually, 'Why were you so late coming home this evening? A girl?'

As a rule they met once or twice a week, although it was Susan who usually arranged the meetings. More often than not it was also Susan who paid for their entertainment. But they had not seen each other since the week-end, and David realized that the girl knew nothing of the events of the past two days. So he told her. Susan could be trusted to keep her mouth shut. She had been his confidante before.

She was both thrilled and horrified. 'Things happen to you, don't they, darling?' she said. 'First that dreadful business at Shere Island, and now this. Do you know Nora Winstone well?'

'For heaven's sake, Susan! Haven't I just told you I don't?' As always, he resented the thinly veiled reproach that invariably crept into her voice when she asked about other women he had met. 'I've danced with her a few times at the Centipede, and I took her home Tuesday night because it seemed the decent thing to do. I don't *know* her at all.'

Susan eyed him fondly. Despite the many years she had known him, it was only recently she had decided she was in love with him. That, of course, put no restraint on David; he was completely unaware of her love, and showed no sign of reciprocating it. Despite that (or perhaps because of it), she was always suspicious of, and uneasy about, the other women in his life; although few but herself would regard him as a good catch, she reflected, noting the stubble on his chin, the crumpled collar and the crooked tie, the way his dark hair flopped untidily over his eyes. But then his untidiness was an essential part of David. No, it was his selfishness and his obstinacy that might make other women reject him. And financially he was a complete loss. Even as a more or less unknown actress her earnings were greater than his.

Susan smiled to herself. With so many short-comings, it was strange that she should want him for herself. Yet he had many endearing qualities. He was cheerful and amusing and very good company; he never bore resentment or shirked an issue; and when sympathy was really warranted he could be truly sympathetic. Above all, she found him exciting; and to Susan boredom was the cruellest enemy of all.

'You don't suppose the two events are connected?' she asked. 'The kidnapping, I mean, and this place being burgled.'

'Broken into, not burgled. No, of course not. Why should they be?'

'I don't know, darling. But if this Bandy creature (do you think he's a jockey?) decided you were one of Mrs Winstone's boy-friends he might want to know more about you. You drove her home. And I bet you kissed her good-night.'

'Only out of politeness. She's not my type.' David considered the suggestion. 'Still, could be. I'll ring Morgan in the morning.'

'Why not now?'

'At this hour? No, thank you. The old buzzard's language would probably fuse the whole telephone system.'

'You could leave a message for him at the police-station.'

'That's true. It would save time in the morning.'

The desk sergeant at M Division headquarters suggested he should dial 999 and report the matter to the local police. David accepted this suggestion, although he had no intention of complying with it. 'But it's important that Superintendent Morgan should also be informed,' he added.

The sergeant was impressed. 'I could get him at his home, sir, if it's really urgent.'

'No,' David said hastily. 'Just see that he gets the message first thing to-morrow.'

He offered to run Susan home in the Alvis, and was relieved when she refused. But he walked with her to the Fulham Road.

'Ring me this evening, darling,' she said, as she climbed into the taxi he found for her. 'Before, if there's any news.'

He promised to do that.

Walking slowly back to the flat, he pondered Susan's suggestion that Bandy might be curious about him. It was an unnerving thought; from what he knew of that gentleman his curiosity could be dangerous. David preferred his own interpretation; that a couple of casual crooks had believed the flat to be unoccupied, had found the door unlocked, and had walked in on the off-chance of picking up something of value. It was a decent neighbourhood, and the houses looked prosperous. And yet — well, why had they taken absolutely nothing? The electric razor, for instance, or his new suit. They were worth a few quid, surely. And there was a pair of gold cuff-links in the stud-box.

Footsteps behind him caused him to stop and turn; thinking of the gunman had made him jumpy. But the footsteps had stopped too. A shadow — was it a shadow? — moved, and he called out, 'Anyone there?'

He was unhappy about his voice. It sounded creaky. Then the shadow came forward and became a man; a slim man in a light-blue suit of exaggerated cut, and wearing pointed shoes. Under the turned-down brim of the hat his face was dark, there was the greater darkness of a small moustache.

'You David Wight?' the man said.

The words were slurred, as though painful to utter. Yet the voice struck a chord in David's memory, and he moved closer. As the man looked up David saw the jagged scar that split his forehead.

'I know you,' he said. 'You were at the Centipede on Tuesday night. With Nora Winstone.'

'That's right,' the man said. 'I'm her husband.'

6

This just isn't my night, David decided wearily as he led the way back into the flat and switched on the light. First Susan, and now this chap. But although his body was tired his mind was alert. Winstone might be the link he had been seeking. If anyone could provide information about Nora's family it must be her husband.

'Take a pew,' he said. And then, 'Hey! Been in the wars, haven't you? Who did that?'

'That' was a heavily damaged face. Winstone's right eye was half closed, the skin around it bloated and discoloured. His full lips were split and swollen and twisted, his cheek bruised and cut. With that jagged scar across his forehead he was not a pretty sight.

'Bandy done it,' he said, his good eye narrowed in a scowl.

'Bandy!' This was better than David

had expected. 'You know him? You've actually met him?'

Winstone shrugged his narrow shoulders. He did not look comfortable on the chair, and it occurred to David that the man might have suffered other, unseen injuries. But he was too impatient for news to worry about his visitor's state of health.

'I met him,' Winstone said. 'Man, I sure met him. But I won't say I know him.' He fingered his bruised cheek, and winced. 'He don't do this while I'm looking at him.'

To David, all West Indians were alike. He could have passed this man in the street unrecognizing were it not for the scarred forehead and the odd little chevron of a moustache. Yet now as he looked at him he saw in him an individual, not a race; and Winstone, he suspected, was not a happy individual. Whatever life had been for him before, of late it had not been kind. True, he looked prosperous enough, with his light-weight suit and his expensive shoes, his silk shirt and his gaudy tie. But there had been that business at the club, and now this . . .

'You look as though you could do with a beer,' he said. 'Hang on a minute.'

The beer and the glasses were in the kitchen; he had no fridge, and in the summer the beer was usually warm. But the May night was cool, and so was the beer. Winstone drank it painfully, displaying a gap in his teeth that had not been there before. There was still a plentiful supply of gold.

He said, 'You want to know about Nora?'

David nodded. 'I certainly do. How did you come to tangle with this Bandy?'

It was not a pretty story. They had picked him up in the small hours of Wednesday morning, Winstone said, while he was walking home from the club where he worked; three men in a car, and all masked. 'Picked him up' was a literal description of what happened, for previously they had jumped him from behind and knocked him out. He recovered his senses in the car, but not for long; the men saw to that. He had no idea where they took him. He had a vague memory of being dragged up some stairs, and then he was in a small room with several other men, also masked. They poured spirits down his throat, sat him on a chair, and slapped his face until he seemed reasonably alert. After that they started to question him.

'About your wife?' asked David.

Winstone nodded. 'They seem to think I know about Nora, but I don't. I don't read no papers, you see. So then they tell me. They say they got Nora in the house, and that we both getting the treatment if we don't play ball. It don't take no guessing to figure what they mean by that. Man, them are real mean guys!'

David believed him. 'What did playing ball include?'

They had asked him first about the two other witnesses to the shooting; who were they, what were they doing in Rotherhithe Street? 'I tell them I don't know nothing about no shooting, that this is the first I hear. So then they rough me up a little and ask me again.' Winstone fingered his jaw and took another sip at the beer. 'What can I do, man? Like I said, I don't know nothing. They rough me up some more, and say to go in and knock some sense into Nora. She being stubborn, they say; she won't talk. And if she don't talk soon, they say, there's going to be trouble for both of we. Real trouble.'

'Did you see Nora?'

Yes, he had seen her. She was in an adjoining room, with a mattress on the floor and a chair and a table, and the windows boarded up. They had handled her roughly, but they had not yet beaten her up the way they had him; her face was grey and lined without its make-up, but it was not bruised or marked. She was still in the black velvet dress she had worn at the Centipede, although now it looked bedraggled and creased, and was torn at one shoulder. She wore no shoes, there were more ladders than thread in her stockings; her blonde hair was no longer piled high on her head, it had fallen raggedly about her shoulders. She had shown no emotion at seeing him, Winstone said. Perhaps what she had been through had drained her of emotion.

'What did she say?'

Winstone shrugged. With him it was an habitual gesture. It seemed that his mobile shoulders could not be still for long.

'Nothing. She talks, but she don't say nothing them guys wants to hear.'

'Did you try to persuade her?'

Yes, he had tried. He was frank about that. He had tried because he was scared, because he valued his life more than justice or the lives of two unknown people. He had tried to make Nora see it the same way. But Nora was stubborn; his pleading had been unavailing. On one point, however, she had seemed to make sense. Her one chance of survival, she said, was to deny them the information they needed. The treatment might get rougher, but only she could tell them the names of the other witnesses, and they would keep her alive until she did. Then they would kill her, as they would kill the others when they found them. She must hope that the police would find her before that happened.

'She's brave,' Winstone said, with a sad little shake of the head. 'Real brave. And hard. Man, I never see a woman so hard. I reckon nothing won't make her talk if she don't want.'

'But didn't she tell them about losing her spectacles?' David protested. 'Didn't she explain that she was no danger to them because she couldn't identify the murderer?'

'She tell them. They just don't believe her. They think she lying to save her skin.'

David shuddered. Nora Winstone meant nothing to him personally, but it was horrible to think of any woman, and particularly a woman he knew, in the clutches of men like Bandy and his gang. They had not needed to kill Constable Dyerson. They had killed because it had been the easiest, not the only, solution to their dilemma. Or perhaps it was simply that men like Bandy preferred to kill.

'What then?'

'They let me go,' Winstone said. 'They put me in the car with a sack over my head, and dump me on Wimbledon Common. By the time I get the sack off they gone.' He sighed deeply. 'Man, am I glad!'

David stared at him. 'They let you go?'

'Sure. I'm here, ain't I?'

'Yes, of course.' It had been a stupid question. 'Have you been to the police?'

The vestige of a grin showed on the twisted lips. Light glinted on the gold teeth. 'Me and the police, man, ain't exactly like that.' He held up two fingers, one crossed over the other.

'What has that to do with it?' David was angry now. He banged the glass down on the floor and pushed nicotine-stained fingers through his unruly hair. 'It's your wife we have to think of. Are you going to leave her with those brutes just because you're scared of the police?'

The grin vanished. Winstone said earnestly, 'I ain't scared of them, Mr Wight. I don't like them, but I ain't scared of them. I just want to do best for Nora. That's why I'm coming here.'

'Oh!' David was slightly mollified. 'But why me? Why not the police?'

Winstone took the cigarette he proffered, lit it and gave a few abortive puffs, then put it down carefully in the ashtray.

With a mouth like his smoking was little pleasure.

'Because Bandy says not. He says if the cops starting to interfere Nora going to get killed.' David gave an impatient click of the tongue. With or without Winstone's help, the police would interfere should the opportunity occur. 'And why you want me to go to the police? I don't know where Nora is, and I don't know what they guys look like. So what I tell the cops? That Nora still alive? Man, I can do that on the telephone.'

David frowned. The argument was reasonable, but was it based on truth? Could Winstone really give no more information than that? He said, 'Are you sure that's all? You may not have seen the men's faces, but how about their voices, their physical appearance?'

'They all sound the same under masks,' Winstone said. He took another painful puff at the cigarette, and eased his body in the chair. 'Look the same, too. Some shorter than others, but so's most guys, ain't they?' He frowned. 'They was young, mostly.'

'Well, that's something. Anything more?'

'One of them have the top of a finger missing.' Winstone held up both hands, flexing the long brown fingers before his eyes. After a pause he said, 'On the left hand.'

He put his hands back in his lap. David saw that there were little flecks of foam at the corners of his mouth, and wondered if the man were nervous. He said again, 'But why me? What am I supposed to do?'

Nora had mentioned his name, Winstone said, and that he was a journalist, and the name of his paper. She had told him this when he had asked her about the kidnapping, and to Winstone it had seemed to offer a forlorn chance of saving her. Newspapers were powerful. If the editor were to offer a reward . . .

'It's not that kind of a paper,' David said sadly. 'Not that kind of an editor either, unfortunately.'

Winstone looked dispirited. To cheer him David outlined briefly the task that *Topical Truths* had undertaken — to find the missing witnesses and put them under police protection. He said nothing of

Snowball's professed intention to hold them until it suited him to produce them; it was an intention of which David had disapproved at the time, and which now seemed to him both dangerous and immoral. It was imperative that once they were found they should be adequately protected. To David it also seemed important that their safety should be made public. 'It will show the brutes that killing your wife will solve nothing. They'll probably release her and try to skip the country.'

He spoke with assurance, although he was not himself assured. But the West Indian nodded eagerly. He said, 'Man, that makes sense. You let me help you? I like to make trouble for they guys.' He fingered his cheek and lip. 'Like hell I do!'

The man's eagerness carried conviction, yet David hesitated to accept his offer. Was that because of colour prejudice? he wondered guiltily. Winstone's face bore eloquent testimony to the treatment meted out to him by Bandy and his gang; he had every cause to wish to get even with them. There was no reason to doubt that he was Nora's husband, or his desire to rescue her. Even if they had not been living together they were certainly on friendly terms, or Nora would not have invited him to the Centipede.

Yet caution persisted. 'I'll be glad of your help when things start moving,' he said, standing up and flexing his muscles. 'How do I contact you?'

Winstone stood up too. 'You know the Seventy-Seven Club?' David nodded. 'I play with the band.' Then he grinned. 'Man, maybe I better contact you. With a face like this I can't do no trumpet-playing. And maybe I change my digs, in case Bandy decide he want to see me again.'

David gave the man his telephone number, watched him write it down. The West Indian's fingers were long and supple, but he wrote laboriously. David wondered what sort of an education he had received; the bare minimum, he suspected. He wondered, too, why Nora had married him and why they had separated, and the reason for his mistrust of the police. Had Winstone a criminal record? But even had he felt justified in putting all these questions, this was no time for them. It was three-thirty in the morning.

He said, 'Can you help me to trace your wife's relatives? What do you know of her background?'

Winstone, it seemed, knew nothing. Nora had been the singer with the band when he had joined it, and they had gone on from there. She had never spoken of her family or her past.

'And the young couple? Did she tell you nothing about them? She knows them, doesn't she?'

'Sure, she knowing them. She not denying that.'

Winstone had picked up his hat and was twisting it round and round between his long brown fingers. David said desperately, 'Didn't she mention any name at all while you were discussing them? Not even a Christian name?'

'Not the girl. But she worrying about the man, I think. She say his name Robert.'

David stared at him. 'Robert? You mean Bill, don't you?'

'Robert,' the other said firmly.

He left with the promise that he would inform the police by telephone that Nora was alive. With that David professed himself content. He could give Morgan the further facts himself should he consider it necessary.

Tired as he was physically, he found his mind too active for sleep. When Winstone had gone he threw himself on the bed and thought about Robert. Presumably Nora had been referring to Robert Lumsden. Why then had Lumsden denied knowing her?

'I could have sworn he was on the level,' he said aloud to the ceiling. 'Shows what a ruddy fine detective I am.'

After a while he undressed and put on pyjamas, climbed into bed, and switched off the light. But it was some time before he slept. For if Winstone were right — if Robert was the man in the archway — then who was Bill? And why was it Bill, not Robert, whom Nora had been so anxious to warn?

7

As the door closed behind the finger-print experts Superintendent Morgan seated himself in the best armchair, carefully hitched up his well-pressed trousers, and looked across at David. But the picture of elegance was incomplete. For once he was unshaven. The massive chin and the heavy jowls were dark with stubble.

'It may interest you to learn that I have not yet had breakfast,' he announced. 'What's the state of the larder?'

David was on the bed. The arrival of Morgan and his minions had awakened him from a heavy sleep, and he had returned to the bed, after donning dressing-gown and slippers, because there he was out of the way. Drowsily he had answered his godfather's questions and watched the men at work, waiting for the moment when they would go and he might return to sleep.

Now it seemed that sleep was not for

him. He rolled off the bed, drew the dressing-gown cord tighter about his waist, and stood up.

'Susan scoffed the last of the bacon and eggs,' he said, yawning and stretching. 'I can manage coffee and toast. Any good?'

'It will fill the far-flung corners, no doubt,' his godfather told him.

Being bachelors, they were used to fending for themselves; Morgan in particular prided himself on his cooking. The toast was crisp, the coffee smooth, the milk miraculously unburnt. When the meal was ready they took it into the living-room and made themselves comfortable.

David was too tired to be hungry. Watching Morgan wolf his way through the toast, he asked idly, 'How are things going, sir?'

Morgan shrugged. 'They aren't. Even the dabs we've picked up here will get us nowhere if we're dealing with new boys. And we may be; they seem a strange mixture of the clumsy and the clever.' He sipped at the coffee. David expected him to elaborate, but he did not. He said, 'Not entirely new, however. Remember that warehouse job in Southampton some weeks ago, when the night watchman was shot? That was the same mob.'

'How do you know?'

'The bullets were fired from the same gun. Pass the butter, please, will you?'

David passed it. He wished he could hand over his troubles as easily. At that hour and after only three hours' sleep his morale was low, and it seemed to him that he was overburdened with troubles. He had said nothing to Morgan of the diary, nothing of Winstone's visit; and he knew that these omissions, and that of the diary in particular, were inequitable and dangerous. In addition to that cryptic reference to 'Bill' the diary contained the name and address of Robert Lumsden; and if Winstone were to be believed Lumsden could well be one of the missing witnesses. Yet what would Morgan say if he were now informed that his godson had possessed the diary for over forty-eight hours without revealing its existence? David's imagination boggled at the thought. In comparison, the concealment of Winstone's visit seemed almost innocuous. Provided the West Indian honoured his promise to give the police what little information he could over the telephone, no vital evidence was being withheld. The visit itself was of no moment.

'You're not eating, David. Off your oats?' Morgan took the last piece of toast from the rack and reached for the coffee-pot. 'More coffee? Sure? Well, I may as well finish it. In this game it is as well to eat when one can. There's no knowing when there will be time for another meal. When did Susan leave?'

'Around one-thirty, I think. Can't remember exactly. The old thought box hasn't had its ration of sleep.'

'Six hours should be plenty for a lad like you.'

David had spoken without thinking, but it was too late to rectify the blunder. To prevent the Superintendent from pursuing that line of thought he said, 'So really you're no nearer to this Bandy chap than you were on Wednesday?'

Morgan finished the coffee, wiped his

lips delicately with his handkerchief, and returned the handkerchief to his breast pocket.

'Not so that you'd notice it. Are you? I'm told you've been sightseeing down Rotherhithe way of late.'

David's weary brain slowly absorbed the implication. So he had been right; the man in Cathay Street had been watching him. He had thought afterwards that he might be one of Bandy's men; the knowledge that he was a policeman was both reassuring and disconcerting, although it did not explain his conviction that the man's face was familiar.

'All part of the job,' he said airily. Since he could not deny the insinuation, he must proclaim the innocence of his motive. 'I had a look round the district, spoke to one or two of the natives. When the story breaks we want to be ready with our sob-stuff.' The sigh he gave was strictly for the superintendent's benefit. 'I can't say it was a fruitful visit. No one seemed particularly interested. But I'm relieved to hear it was one of your chaps who was dogging me. I had a nasty suspicion it might be Mr Bandy.'

'Yet you kept your suspicion to yourself.'

'I'm sensitive to ridicule.'

Morgan grunted. 'You weren't too sensitive to mention last night's visitors.'

David was beginning to wish he had been. Had Susan not rushed him into action he might have seen the wisdom of silence. Too much contact with the police was unhealthy.

'That's entirely different,' he said. 'Whatever their purpose, they most certainly weren't coppers.'

'H'm! And since nothing was stolen, what do you suppose that purpose was?'

'I've no idea. Have you?'

'I can guess. I think Bandy must have got it into his head that you and Nora Winstone were more than casual acquaintances, and decided he would like to know more about you. You may remember that the same possibility occurred to me.' David did remember, and glowered at him. 'You'd best watch your step, my lad. If he decides you're a nuisance you could be in trouble.'

'I'll watch it.'

'You do that.' Morgan heaved his big body out of the chair and brushed the crumbs from his suit. As he walked across to the wash-basin he said, 'Incidentally, don't get any fancy ideas about your own importance. My chap wasn't in Rother-hithe just to keep an eye on you. I've got better uses for him than that.' Fingering his chin, he peered into the mirror and frowned at what he saw. 'Mind if I borrow your razor? It'll save a visit to the barber.'

'Help yourself.'

While Morgan shaved, David cleared away the breakfast things and washed up. He was not troubled by his godfather's warning, since he knew it had been prompted by a mistaken suspicion that he and Nora were friends. Even if Bandy had formed the same opinion, the search of the flat would have disclosed nothing to confirm it.

When he returned to the room Morgan was replacing his collar and tie. David wondered what size he took in collars; with such a thick neck he must have his shirts made to measure. That would not

141

worry the elegant superintendent. Clothes were his extravagance.

'Time I was off,' Morgan said, carefully adjusting his bow tie. 'Matters may become interesting if either of your visitors last night proves to have a police record.' Satisfied with his appearance, he turned away from the mirror and reached for his jacket. 'But I'm afraid it's all China to the Isle of Wight that the blighters wore gloves, and that all those lovely prints Davis has collected will turn out to have been made by you and Susan, or some other legitimate visitor. However, we can but hope.'

David stared as though mesmerized at his godfather's broad back. Winstone! Winstone had been his most recent visitor, had sat in that chair, had handled the ashtray and drummed his fingers on the glass-topped table. Winstone's prints would be fresh and plentiful.

And Winstone had hinted that he had been in conflict with the law! There would be specimens of his finger-prints at C.R.O.!

Tongue-tied by indecision, David nibbled

furiously at his nails as Morgan buttoned his jacket and collected his bowler and umbrella. 'You must have a meal with me some time soon,' Morgan said, smoothing his hair back over his ears. 'We'll fix an evening. Are you returning to bed or are you going slumming? It'll be nice down by the river.' A slight frown spoilt the placidity of his expression as he considered his godson. 'I suppose you couldn't find time for a hair-cut?'

David rushed into confession. It was now or never, and it could not be never.

'I — I'm afraid I've slipped up, sir. I forgot to mention that I had another visitor last night. He arrived soon after Susan had left.'

'Forgot?' The well-trimmed eyebrows lifted perceptibly. 'I doubt that, David, knowing you. However, go on. Who was your visitor?'

'A West Indian. The chap who was dancing with Nora Winstone at the Centipede Tuesday night. He says he's her husband.'

'Does he, though!' Morgan replaced hat and umbrella on the table, gripped the lapels of his jacket in a manner that made David think of a prosecuting counsel about to cross-examine, and fixed his godson with an accusing glare. The music had gone from his voice. 'Well, that's a lie, for a start. There's no record of such a marriage at Somerset House.' He took a deep breath. David, it seemed, was to be his Ephialtes in this business. This was all he needed to make the nightmare complete. 'For the moment we'll forget your forgetfulness. What was the gentleman's business with you?'

David told him. He could not understand why the West Indian should have lied about marriage to Nora, but the lie did not alter the basic facts. He did, however, omit to mention that Winstone played the trumpet at the Seventy-Seven Club. Although Winstone had said he was unlikely to be performing for the next few days, it was possible that he might be found at or through the club. For the present, David decided, it would be better to keep Morgan and Winstone apart.

Morgan sat down. David sat down also, feeling slightly weak at the knees. He can't really *do* anything, he told himself; nothing more than a ticking off. But he recognized the look on his godfather's face, and knew that the ticking off when it came would be severe and unpleasant.

'And you intended to keep this to yourself,' Morgan said. It was a statement, not a question. 'For possible use in that scandal sheet of yours, I suppose.'

'No,' lied David. 'But Winstone didn't leave until around four this morning, so that I just wasn't with it when you arrived. I'm sorry. I never intended to hold out on you.'

The superintendent released his lapels and waved a well-manicured hand in a non-committal gesture. Dismissal? wondered David hopefully. Or disbelief?

'I've no time now to discuss the ethics of your behaviour, David; but I'll find time later, believe you me.' He took a notebook from his hip pocket, perched himself on the table, and began to write busily. The notebook was slim and bound in soft leather, so that the fit of his trousers should not be impaired. 'You say he mentioned someone named Robert.

145

Didn't he give any clue as to who the chap was or where he could be found?'

'None at all.' That at least was true.

'And Winstone wants to help, does he? How do you contact him if he left no address?'

'I don't. He said he'd be on the move for the next few days, but he's going to get in touch with me.' So much truth went to David's head, and he said earnestly, 'I've given you all the information I can, sir. Winstone may have lied about his marriage — I wouldn't know about that — but I'm sure he was telling the truth otherwise. He'd certainly had a real bashing. I imagine his reluctance to talk to you in person was because he has a police record. He hinted as much. However, you'll be able to check that from his finger-prints. They should be plentiful. He sat in that chair and — '

'So that's it!' Morgan snapped the notebook shut. His bull neck and freshly shaven cheeks were red with anger. 'That's why you suddenly came clean. You realized that Winstone was one man we might be able to put our finger on,

146

and that when we did he would probably involve you. Forgot my foot! Why, you unscrupulous young . . . '

His voice faded as the telephone rang. To David the sound was a welcome one. He sprang up quickly and lifted the receiver to his ear.

The call was not for him. 'Inspector Nightingale, sir,' he said.

Morgan snatched the receiver from him. The scowl was still on his face as he listened, but David learned nothing from the conversation except that his godfather was in a poor humour and that he would be returning to the Borough High Street immediately. He considered that last piece of information the most satisfactory he had heard for some time.

Slowly Morgan replaced the receiver on its cradle, his hand lingering on it as though reluctant to let it go, grey eyes narrowed. David did nothing to disturb his reverie.

'They've found the car,' Morgan said eventually. The anger had gone from his voice, replaced by melancholy. 'It was abandoned near St Albans.'

David stared at him. 'Car? What car?'

'The Zodiac with a registration number similar to yours.' There was the rustle of paper as Morgan's hand went to his pocket. He popped an acid-drop into his mouth, gave it a preliminary suck, and said grimly, 'It seems your coloured friend was lying when he said Nora Winstone was alive.'

'You mean — they've found her body?'

'No. Her scarf. Elsie Sheel has identified it. It was in the back of the car, tucked down behind the cushion.'

'So what does that prove? That they used the car to kidnap her? We'd guessed that already.'

'It goes further than that, I'm afraid.' The little hollow appeared in the superintendent's cheek as he sucked venomously at the sweet. 'It seems that the rear seat of the car — the carpet too — was soaked with blood.'

8

'My money's on Morgan,' Snowball said. 'If he says Winstone's a liar, that the woman is dead and that Winstone was never her husband, then it's a hundred to one he's right.' He hunched his thin shoulders and spread his arms in a semitic gesture. 'You watch your step with that darkie, my lad. Don't trust him. You could be in trouble if you do.'

'I'll watch it,' David said. After an almost sleepless night and a roasting from his godfather he was in no mood to be criticized, and this was the second time that morning he had been told to 'watch his step.' 'I'm not the trusting kind. But I still say Morgan could be wrong.'

'So could you.' Snowball leaned back in his chair, hooked his thumbs under his braces, and regarded David quizzically over the top of his bifocals. 'Or isn't that a premise you are prepared to accept?'

David lit a cigarette, flicking the lighter viciously.

'You and Morgan haven't seen Winstone's face. I have. He took a beating all right; no doubt about that. So why shouldn't the rest of his story be true? He and Nora could have got hitched abroad, couldn't they? And what does blood on the car cushion prove? That someone got hurt, maybe killed. But it doesn't have to be Nora, does it?'

'The right car and the right scarf — but the wrong body?' Snowball's jacket was draped over the back of his chair, and he turned to fumble in the pocket for his pipe. 'That's a hell of a coincidence, isn't it? My money's still on Morgan.'

David scowled. He was not defending Winstone so much as trying to justify himself. He had voiced an opinion, and an innate stubbornness drove him to uphold it.

'Why? Take this marriage business. Why should he say they're married if they're not? What does he gain by it? Why not just say they are friends — lovers, if you like? He'd expect me to believe that, I'd seen them together at the club. Why lie if the truth is more credible and the issue isn't affected?' He inhaled too deeply and broke into a fit of coughing. Spluttering and thumping his chest, he went on, 'As for insisting that Nora is alive when he knows she isn't — again, why? He's representing himself to me as a man thirsting for revenge. Wouldn't that sound even more credible if his wife were dead?'

Snowball's pipe was now in full blast. His hazel eyes were clouded as he peered at David through the fog of smoke.

'You have a point there, David. It doesn't clinch your argument, but I admit you have a point.'

'Two points,' David said triumphantly. He waved a hand to dissipate the cloud between them. 'And here's another. Winstone mentioned this chap Robert. Where did he hear the name if not from Nora? And how could that be if Nora were dead?'

The editor took his time in answering, fingering the goitre as he considered this. 'It's not an uncommon name,' he said eventually. 'Maybe he just threw it at you as bait. He was not to know you would connect it with a particular individual.'

'Well, I do. And if Lumsden turns out to be one of the missing witnesses we'll know Winstone's on the level. Fair enough?'

'I suppose so,' Snowball admitted grudgingly. 'But don't ride your judgment too hard. It could come a cropper.' Just like the old buzzard, thought David, to shove a sting into the tail when he's beat. But Snowball had not finished. He brought his head down and his body forward, to rest his forearms on the desk. Spectacles in hand, he pointed them at David. 'And go easy with Morgan. He may be your godfather, but don't let that fool you. Morgan's essentially a copper, and a zealous one. If he catches you trying any more fast ones . . . ' He broke off, lifted a skinny hand, and slapped it down hard. 'Wham!'

David jumped at the sound. He said cheekily, 'I didn't think you cared, sir.'

Snowball grinned, showing the gaps in his gums.

'You're dead right I don't. But if

Morgan cracks down on you he may crack down on me, and that I do not want.' The grin vanished. 'You need to get smart, my lad. You don't think fast enough, or you'd never have landed yourself in that fix this morning.'

'You try thinking fast on three hours' sleep,' David told him. But he knew that the criticism was justified, and his tone was only a moderate grumble. 'Did Oliver get anywhere with that list of names?'

'Not far.' Snowball replaced the spectacles on his nose and searched through a pile of papers until he found what he wanted. 'Three of them — Willson, Cayley, Grant — admitted to knowing her. Very cagey with their answers, however; been out with her a few times, they said, but couldn't supply any background. Didn't know she was married. The rest — ' he flipped the paper with the back of his hand, 'like your friend Lumsden, they'd never even heard of her.'

David tugged at his tie with one hand. With the other he scratched his backside.

'Doesn't that strike you as odd? Why

should strangers be listed in her diary?'

'It doesn't follow that they're strangers. She could be the kind of woman a respectable man doesn't admit to knowing.'

'That isn't true of Lumsden. I'll swear the name Winstone meant nothing to him.'

'You're an expert on character, aren't you?' There was a sneer on the little man's cracked lips. 'Well, she could have other names. Her kind often do.'

'What do you mean by 'her kind'?'

'Nothing. I'm not starting another argument.' Snowball puffed furiously at his pipe until the bowl glowed, and reached for a pile of manuscript. 'Now clear off down to Rotherhithe and get results. That's what I pay you for, don't I? I can get arguments for nothing.'

★ ★ ★

Bill Brandon was no more communicative on the second visit than on the first, but he appeared unresentful of David's persistency. This time David got inside the house; it was raining heavily, and Mrs Brandon was out.

'She don't take to you chaps,' the youth told him. He waved a grimy hand round the small, scantily furnished parlour. 'Once she got a whole pile of stuff on the knocker, and then the firm come and took it back. The money weren't coming in reg'lar enough, they said.' He seated himself on a wooden chair. 'A pity. Them armchairs was real comfortable.'

He sounded cheerfully unconcerned at the family misfortune. David wondered how much he had contributed to it. He said, 'I'm not on the knocker.'

'I know. You're on the telly. You told me.'

'I'm not that either.' David had thought about this. In his rôle of television investigator he could invent no excuse for this second visit, certainly none that would permit the questions he wished to put. So he had decided to abandon it. For Bill Brandon, at any rate, he would be himself. 'I'm a journalist.'

'You are?' The youth's vacant face became almost animated. 'Then why all this guff about the telly?'

'That's what I'm here to explain.'

But he did not explain. He spoke only the threshold of truth; of the theft from the warehouse, the shooting of Constable Dyerson, and the search for the men who had killed him. He said nothing of Nora or the missing couple. They could be introduced later if Bill's reaction appeared to warrant it. 'I adopted the guise of T.V. investigator because I wanted to meet the people. You know — the human touch.'

'You mean we'll be in the papers?'

It was not the reaction David had expected, but it had possibilities. It pointed a line for him to take.

'Could be. Not all of you, of course. Just those with something to say. Preferably something dramatic.'

But Bill Brandon had nothing dramatic to offer. At the time of the murder he had been 'out with the lads'; it was not until the next day he had heard the news. 'There was a chap said it was a woman what done it,' he said. 'A blonde. He seen her at the nick.'

David offered him a cigarette. Casually

he said, 'A woman, eh? Sounds interesting. Did your pal recognize her?'

'She used to live down Bermondsey way,' he said. 'That's where he come from. He didn't know her name, he said; just seen her around. And he ain't a pal of mine, mister. I just bumped into him in a caff.'

That, David thought sadly, disposes of that. He did not even ask the name of the 'caff.' An unknown youth who lived down Bermondsey way and had seen a blonde in the nick was too slender a lead to follow.

It was raining heavily as he walked down Rose End to Rotherhithe Street. He had his head down and his coat collar up, so that it was with something of a shock that he bumped into a man strolling slowly towards him. David muttered an apology and hurried on, his spirits as depressed as the weather. Clearly Bill Brandon was not the Bill of Nora's diary; he had neither the guile nor the intelligence to play a part. Only Robert Lumsden remained. And if Lumsden failed him there was no lead left to follow.

It was as he turned the corner into Cathay Street that he realized he was being followed. Previously he had heard the soft footfalls without their significance being apparent. Now they were. He looked quickly over his shoulder. Yes, the man was there, a discreet distance behind. David was almost certain it was the man he had bumped against in Rose End; a thin, insignificant little fellow in a long blue raincoat that almost swept the ground. The turned-down brim of his trilby obscured the upper part of his face; only the squashed nose and the pointed chin were visible. Morgan's scraping the barrel, he thought grimly. Or was this an attempt to merge with the surroundings?

He had intended to pay a call on Judy Garland; now he hurried past the house, all thought of social dalliance gone. The man would have gained nothing from his sleuthing so far; Morgan was welcome to Bill Brandon. But he was not welcome to Robert Lumsden. Not yet. Somehow the man must be lost before St James's Road.

A taxi came cruising down Jamaica

Road. It was heading east, and without pausing to wonder at his good fortune David broke into a run, waving his arms and shouting. He reached the corner as the taxi skidded to a halt, and was about to instruct the driver to turn and make for St James's Road when he changed his mind.

'Just keep going,' he said. Morgan's watchdog might have a police car handy. 'I'll tell you where to turn off.'

As the taxi moved away the man appeared at the street corner. The fact that his quarry had escaped him did not seem to disturb him; he stood irresolute for a few seconds, and then turned and walked back down Cathay Street. Delighted at his success, David turned from the window and relaxed, filled with an impish glee at having outwitted a professional. That luck had been with him did not dilute his pleasure.

The driver took him round by Southwark Park and into St James's Road from the southern end. David stopped him some distance short of the house, in case Morgan's sleuth had managed to pick up the trail again. But the precaution was unnecessary. There was no sign of the little man in the blue raincoat.

As usual, Robert Lumsden was out. Without disguising his chagrin, David asked the woman when she expected him to return.

'I don't,' she said frigidly. 'He comes and goes as he pleases. It's none of my business. But if he's home before midnight I'll be surprised.'

David wondered whether he should leave a message asking the man to ring him, but decided against it. It was not a matter one could discuss easily over the telephone, and there was always tomorrow. If tomorrow should also prove abortive he must think again.

He was cooking a couple of chops for his supper when Morgan telephoned. As he recognized his godfather's voice a little tingle of dread ran down David's spine, and then dissolved.

'David?' The voice had lost its bite, the harmony was back. 'Rees Morgan here. You told me that, according to Winstone, one of Bandy's gang had the top of a finger missing. Did he say which hand or which finger?'

David smiled to himself in relief. Apparently his sins were forgiven, if not forgotten. And did the query indicate that Morgan was now less certain of Winstone's duplicity?

'The left hand,' he said. 'I don't think he mentioned which finger. Why?'

'Just trying to sort out the possibles.' There was a pause while Morgan turned to talk to someone beside him. When he spoke to David again his voice was even more mellow. He said, 'Been down by the river this afternoon?'

'You should know,' David said. The other's unexpected affability encouraged him to ask, 'Didn't he tell you I gave him the slip?'

'Didn't who tell me?' The bite was returning. 'What the hell are you talking about?'

David sensed the warning, but he could not stop now.

'Your tail. Isn't that the word? Little chap in a blue raincoat; not the one who was tailing me yesterday. He picked me up in Rose End, and followed me to Jamaica Road. That's where I lost him. Managed to hail a cruising taxi.' David grinned to himself at the memory. Emboldened by his godfather's silence, he said, 'Weedy little runt. He must lower the average height of the Force quite considerably.'

Morgan said quietly, 'I told you, David — no one tailed you yesterday. One of my chaps happened to recognize you while he was making inquiries in the district; he'd seen you with me Wednesday night.' So that explains the familiar face, thought David. 'But he wasn't there to-day. None of my chaps was. If someone tailed you that someone wasn't a policeman.' There was a slight pause. 'You can draw your own conclusion from that.'

The conclusion David drew was not encouraging. 'Bandy?' he suggested.

'I imagine so. You're interfering, and he wants to know why. You'd better let me have a description of the man. Incidentally, there are no weedy little runts in the Force. You should know that.'

The chops were overcooked by the

time David returned to them, the potatoes a watery mess. But even had they been perfect he would not have enjoyed them. Morgan had taken away his appetite. It had been annoying to believe himself under police surveillance. To know that he was being shadowed by a ruthless gunman was unnerving.

It was not, David decided, an evening on which to sit at home and brood; he would do better to go out. A few pints of beer might restore his ailing spirits. Yet to drink alone was not to be convivial. He needed a companion, and on impulse he rang up Paul, though with little hope of finding him at home. Paul, he knew, was accustomed to dining out. But luck was with him. Paul was not only at home, he was happily disposed to an evening's drinking.

They met at Finch's in the Fulham Road. Finch's had been David's choice. He was in no mood for a quiet saloon bar and a table in the corner. He wanted life and bustle and noise and variety, and Finch's could usually offer those.

At first they talked in generalities, or

discussed the drinkers around them. Hair was much in evidence. Worn long, it stood out like a fringe over the men's collars or fell, undraped and apparently uncombed, around the women's shoulders. There was a profusion of jeans and hairy-looking sweaters, a few beards. The more conventionally dressed customers, David and Paul among them, pointed the contrast without looking out of place.

'How goes the Quest?' asked Paul, as they started on their second pint. He spoke the word 'quest' with a capital Q, as though it were a crusade or a pilgrimage.

'Not too well,' David said. It was a topic he would have preferred to forget for the evening, but he could not avoid the direct question. 'Still, I suppose I must be warm. Bandy wouldn't bother to have me tailed otherwise.'

'Tailed, eh!' Paul gave a low, elegant whistle. 'Does he look like taking the offensive?'

'I don't think so. But it's unnerving, to say the least.'

'You can say that again, dear boy.' Paul drank deep, his prominent lower lip seeming to scoop up the beer. 'Incidentally, I was in the Croc at lunch-time. So were most of the regulars. No bandy legs there, I'm afraid, and I don't think I missed a pair. How is your revered godfather progressing?'

'I wouldn't know for sure. Not too happily, I suspect.'

'And Elsie's friend? Mrs Winstone, isn't it? Any news of her that I can pass on? As a friend of yours, Elsie expects me to be bursting with information.'

'There's news,' David said, 'but I wouldn't pass it on.' He told Paul of the bloodstained car. 'Elsie would almost certainly jump to the same conclusion as Morgan.'

'She would indeed.' Paul bent to peer at him over the rim of his glass. 'But not you, eh? Does that mean you have inside information, or are you naturally optimistic?'

'A little of each,' David told him, and was glad that his friend did not press for further detail.

It was ten o'clock when they finished their fourth pint and decided they had

had enough beer for one evening. They were both in a quietly convivial mood. The prefect / middle-school relationship which had marked their first meeting had gone, and it seemed to David that he and Paul had been buddies for years. Certainly he could not have chosen a more suitable companion for that particular evening. Paul's stories, his dry comments and biting wit, had been just what he needed.

Out in the Fulham Road David said, 'Care to come back to my place for a quick one? It's not far.'

'I don't think so, dear boy.' Paul smiled toothily, a trifle unsteady on his large feet. 'Unaccustomed to quantities of beer as I am, I feel that a quick one might be disastrous. Let us leave well alone. But I'll walk you back with pleasure. Exercise is what I need.'

David welcomed his company. As they turned from the lights of the Fulham Road into the street in which he lived, his troubles seemed to come crowding back on him. Between the pools of light thrown by the street lamps there was only the red glow from behind curtained windows to relieve the darkness, and in every doorway, behind each area wall or parked car, he half expected to see a little man in a trilby hat and a long blue raincoat. The expectation did not frighten him, but he found it disconcerting.

Outside the flat stood the Alvis. It needed only a slight show of interest from Paul for David to unhook and draw back the cover. 'Nineteen twenty-five,' he said proudly, patting the bonnet. 'Not bad, eh?'

Without any great show of enthusiasm Paul agreed that it was not bad at all. Dutifully he listened to technical detail and further praise, and admired what the night permitted him to see. But as David replaced the cover he drawled, 'Not for me, dear boy. One has to drive to enjoy a car like that. As the perennial passenger I'd loathe it.'

From the foot of the steps David watched his friend's progress up the street. Silhouetted against the lights of the Fulham Road, Paul walked slowly, the fingers of his right hand drumming idly against the low area walls as he went. David had always understood that the loss of an arm could upset a man's balance, but it did not seem to have affected Paul. His movements were as assured as his manner. He had learned to live with his disability.

Or had he? David wondered, climbing the steps. Maybe he had adjusted himself physically. But as a boy Paul had not been noted for his tolerance; beneath the suave exterior of the man did bitterness still rankle? One could not blame him if it did. Despite his wealth, Paul must be missing much in life that was good.

David paused to look back at the night and fumble for his key. Then something solid descended on the base of his neck, and abruptly he lost consciousness.

9

He struggled back to reality with the sensation that his head was held firmly in a vice; his ears were being squeezed together, and he felt that at any moment the pressure would become so great that his head would explode. The total darkness became a semi-darkness, a nebulous expanse out of which form and structure gradually emerged, unstable and vacillating as reflections in a ruffled pool. It took time for them to harden. When they did he became aware that he was still on the steps of his flat; the rough edges were biting into flank and neck, forcing his head sideways at a painful angle. There was a drumming in his ears, and he sat up slowly and put a hand to his head to contain the pressure. Only when the drumming had subsided did he venture to turn his neck.

His first fully conscious sensation other than pain was of surprise that this could happen to him on the threshold of his own home, little more than a hundred yards from a main London thoroughfare. Then he remembered Constable Dyerson, and surprise turned to thankfulness. At least he was still alive. One hand pressed to the nape of his neck, from whence most of the pain seemed to emanate, he gripped the stone balustrade with the other and pulled himself up.

It took him some time to find the key and fumble it into the lock; but already his brain was clearing, and once in his room he went directly to stare at himself in the mirror. There was no blood, no visible bruise. The back of his head was sore under his gently probing fingers, but it seemed that he had suffered no serious injury.

Only when he had bathed his head in cold water and swallowed a couple of aspirins did he begin to consider *why* he had been attacked. Had it been a bungled attempt at murder? Surely not; since his assailant had not been disturbed he would have had all the time he needed to finish the job. Robbery was also out; his watch was still on his wrist, his wallet intact in his breast pocket. That left only intimidation. Yet how could such an assault influence the victim's conduct if he were left in ignorance of its source? Surely some form of warning, either preliminary or coincident, was a necessity. Or was Bandy assuming that he was David's sole enemy, and that David knew it?

His head ached abominably, the stiffness in his neck seemed to be getting worse. Deciding that he was in no condition to wrestle with what appeared to him now as an insoluble problem, that it would be better left till the morning, he began to undress. Normally this was a speedy process, with the discarded clothing flung over the back of a chair. Tonight, because each rapid movement sent pain shooting through his head, he took it more leisurely, easing his arms gently out of jacket and shirt, keeping his head up as he bent carefully to remove shoes and socks and trousers, emptying his pockets (something he normally did only when changing his suit) in a subconscious desire to delay each enforced action for as long as possible. Then, arrayed in pyjamas and dressing-gown, he went into the kitchen to heat some milk for a night-cap.

Watching the saucepan, he wondered whether he should telephone Morgan. But what could Morgan do? Without a description of his assailant, what could anyone do? The news would only increase Morgan's suspicion that he was in possession of information denied to the police, and he had no wish to antagonize his godfather further.

He took the milk into the living-room and collected cigarettes and lighter from the small pile of articles he had taken from his pockets. Lighting his cigarette, he surveyed the pile. And it was then he realized that something was missing, and knew the reason for the assault.

They had taken Nora Winstone's diary.

★   ★   ★

His head was still sore when he awoke the next morning, but the stiffness had gone from his neck and he felt surprisingly fresh. Obviously a cure for a hangover, he decided, although not to be recommended except in extreme circumstances.

He did not dawdle over dressing or breakfast. Lumsden's was the only name in Nora's diary that could immediately be connected with Rotherhithe, and Bandy would waste no time in going after him. Lumsden was elusive, but he might choose that morning to be available. David had to find him first.

He spent most of that Saturday in pubs and cafés, drinking glasses of beer and cups of tea and coffee that he did not want, and consuming a number of equally unwanted meat pies. In the intervals between eating and drinking he made frequent calls at the house in St James's Road. But it seemed that Robert Lumsden spent no more time at home on a Saturday than he did on a working day, and David's anxiety grew with each fruitless visit. So did the landlady's irritation. At first she had been in an unusually friendly mood, informing him that her lodger had not returned home the previous night until well after midnight, but had been up and away again before seven that morning. By mid-afternoon it needed heavy work with the knocker to bring her to the door at all.

As the day wore on some of the urgency left him. It seemed that Bandy had not reacted with the anticipated speed, for according to the woman there had been no other callers. By six o'clock David decided he had had enough of Rotherhithe. Lumsden was probably out for the evening.

On his final visit he left a note with the landlady. The message it contained was urgent, but purposefully vague. He had cause to believe, he wrote, that Lumsden was in great personal danger, and urged the man to telephone him early the next morning. 'It's very important,' he told the woman. 'Put it on his mantel-shelf so that he will see it when he comes in.'

'If he's in a state to see anything,' she said. 'Which sometimes he ain't of a Saturday.'

David went back to Fulham and rang Paul's number. But Paul was out, and as an alternative he tried Susan. 'I'm minded to take you out to dinner,' he told her. 'I need someone to talk to.'

'It's an effusive invitation, darling,' she said. 'But of course I accept. Am I paying?'

He grudgingly accepted responsibility for the bill. 'But nowhere expensive, mind. This is on me, not the expense account.'

They went to the Yellow Duck, a small restaurant near Sloane Square. It had a bar; the food and service were good, the prices reasonable but not cheap. Susan was pleasantly surprised; she had not expected anything so affluent. When David called for the wine list instead of offering the usual choice between light ale and lager, she expressed her surprise vocally.

'I changed my mind about the expense account,' he told her. 'I think I can work it.'

The restaurant was partitioned into alcoves, discreetly lit and with softly padded benches for seats. David had chosen a corner alcove, where provided they spoke quietly they were unlikely to be overheard. He did most of the talking. When they were together Susan was accustomed to the rôle of confidante, and even welcomed it. Particularly over a meal. She enjoyed her food, and it was pleasant to be able to eat and listen instead of being expected to eat and talk.

Susan chose a Dover sole after the soup, David a steak. He was not averse to talking with his mouth full, and he did so almost incessantly. But somehow with David it did not seem to matter; it was all part of his general untidiness, his immaturity. His sharp pointed teeth masticated rhythmically and fast, the words pouring out of the wide mouth; he was apparently in such a hurry that the pauses necessitated by swallowing were cut to a minimum. But as the wine took effect he became more relaxed, teeth and tongue moved more leisurely. There were even intervals in which Susan was expected to comment, although when she did so he did not listen. He used the intervals to collect his thoughts for a fresh spate of words.

They were sipping coffee when he eventually came to a stop. It was the first time Susan had heard the whole story — or the whole story as David knew it — and she was disturbed by what she heard. Nora Winstone aroused her sympathy, Bandy her abhorrence. But her main reaction was one of fear for David.

'You mustn't go on with it, darling,' she protested. 'It's far too dangerous.' She was about to add that the danger was unnecessary, that the search could be continued more efficiently by the police. But prudence stopped her. She knew her David.

He was playing with his coffee-spoon. Now he waved it in a gesture of defiance and disapproval.

'Rubbish!' he said flatly.

'It isn't rubbish. They search your room, follow you around, and finally assault you. Or is that final? What happens next? I hate to think.'

'Now you're being melodramatic,' he chided her. But his voice was kind. It was not unpleasant to be mistaken for a hero. 'They knocked me out last night for the same reason as they searched my room and followed me around; they wanted information. Now they've got the diary they'll probably leave me alone.' He smiled indulgently, and rapped Susan's knuckles gently with the spoon. 'Stop worrying. Did Morgan take your finger-prints, by the way? He said he'd need them.'

'Someone did. And don't try to change the conversation. Doesn't Mr Morgan think you ought to stop?'

'I don't know what he thinks. I haven't asked him.'

She sighed. 'I can't understand what you've got against him, darling. I think he's sweet.'

'Not to me he isn't. When I'm with him I just freeze up inside. He treats me as though I were still in short knickers; every time he offers me one of those dreadful acid-drops I want to scream.' He replaced the spoon in the saucer. I must buy him some pumicestone, Susan thought, eyeing the nicotine-stained fingers — although he probably won't use it. 'I think he considers himself *in loco parentis*, though the Lord knows why he should. He doesn't approve of me, and I still have a couple of uncles left.'

'He's on the spot. They aren't.'

'You're too right he's on the spot. Right now I wish he'd get lost. Having him breathing down my neck gives me the willies.'

'It's Bandy who's breathing down your neck,' Susan reminded him. 'Not Mr Morgan. You might be safer if he were.' She took a final sip at her coffee and looked at her watch. 'However, it's your neck. Now tell me how you propose to entertain me for the rest of the evening. It's only nine o'clock. Can't we go somewhere and dance?'

'Where?'

That David had not immediately vetoed the suggestion was proof to Susan that he had not properly assimilated it. He was away off with his thoughts — in Rotherhithe, probably, she thought resentfully, remembering the smirk on his face when he had told her of Judy Garland. That was one thing about David she thoroughly disliked. He never spared her the attractions he found in other women.

'Couldn't we go to that club of yours? The Centipede? Put it on the expense account, if that's what worries you. Tell Snowball you've been making further inquiries about the Winstones.'

Abstractedly he shook his head, twirling the thin stem of the wineglass between long, bony fingers. Then suddenly the abstraction was gone. He put down the glass, sat bolt upright, and stared at her with a glint in his eyes. Susan was good to look at; even David had admitted that, though seldom to her. Her red hair gleamed in the soft light, the simple black frock revealed the creamy whiteness of her neck and throat and the curves of her supple figure. But it was not her looks that claimed his attention now. She had given him an idea.

'Lady, you get your wish.' There was no room in the tiny alcove for swift movement, but he got to his feet and slithered awkwardly out into the passage. 'Grab your coat while I pay the bill. We're going dancing.'

'At the Centipede?'

'No. The Seventy-Seven.'

Susan had started to rise, her back propped against the wooden partition. Now she slid down on to the bench again, her grey-green eyes glowing at him.

'The Seventy-Seven? Darling, isn't that rather out of your class?' She had been to the club with other escorts, but never with David. 'Can *Topical Truths* afford such extravagance?'

'It'll have to.' He grabbed her arm impatiently. There was no tenderness in his hold as he pulled her from the alcove. 'This is a must.'

The Seventy-Seven was in Greek Street, and occupied two large basements knocked into one. The accent was on comfort, service, and discretion, and all were excellent. At one end of the long room was a bar, at the other a small stage on which a four-piece band — piano, tympani, trumpet, and guitar — played smoothly, the music sweet, the trumpet muted. The guitarist was also the singer; a West Indian, he had a pleasant tenor voice that excited neither himself nor his audience. The music, the lights, the softly padded chairs, the quiet voices of the waiters, provided an atmosphere inspiring indolence rather than energy. To Susan, a self-professed sybarite, it was pleasantly seductive and synthetically romantic; she fitted into it snugly. David, with his crumpled suit and his unruly hair and his air of impatient haste, did not. She knew he had not brought her there from choice. This was undoubtedly business.

David ordered drinks, the bill for which made him shudder. He had asked for and been given a table near the band, and he sat listening to the music and watching the musicians. The room was not crowded, and only a few couples were dancing; there was no abandon in their movements, they shuffled lethargically round with bodies fused. Susan would have liked to dance too, but she knew that David had other ideas. Maybe he would ask her later. She smiled to herself at the thought of David cutting loose among the slowly moving couples. He was a galvanic dancer, all arms and legs and sudden twists and turns.

Gazing round the room, she said, 'There's your friend Paul.'

David twisted in his chair to follow her gaze. Paul was at the far end of the room. He wore a dinner jacket, lapels softly rolled, a maroon cummerbund about his middle and a maroon tie at his neck. He had not seen David, and was reclining languidly in his chair, eyes half closed, his large feet thrust far under the table, a fat cigar trailing between thumb and forefinger. His companion, a tall brunette in a red sheath dress that plunged in a deep V to her waist, had her back to David. She was incredibly slim. Her hair spiralled tightly above the crown of her head, so that she looked like a finely pointed pencil.

A magnum of champagne was on the table between them.

David turned back to Susan. 'You never told me you knew Paul.'

'Didn't I? Everyone knows Paul. One meets him at most parties.'

'Not me. Perhaps I go to the wrong parties. Who's the girl with him?'

'Mary Halliday. You know — the model.'

'Never heard of her.'

Sipping abstractedly at his whisky, David concentrated once more on the band. They kept an even tempo with a well-defined beat, and Susan's feet were tapping to the music. She said, 'You're not exactly attentive, darling. Do you always sit and gaze at the band when you take a girl out?'

He stared at her blankly. Then his mouth split in a wide grin.

'Sorry. But this is where Winstone plays the trumpet. Didn't I tell you?'

'No.' She looked at the trumpeter. 'You said he was coloured.'

'That isn't Winstone, stupid. Winstone's away for a few days — until he gets his face remodelled.'

'Then why are we here?'

'To ask questions. Morgan thinks he's a fraud, I say he's genuine. I want to know which of us is right, and I'm hoping some one in the band can tell me. That chap with the guitar is the one I have my eye on.'

The guitarist was a tall, rangy man with a narrow head and body, his hair black and woolly, his cheeks sunken. Susan thought he looked hungry, but David was less interested in his appearance than in attracting his attention. It seemed that the man's eyeballs had only two positions; upward when he was singing, downward when he played his instrument. He took no apparent interest in the people for whom he was performing.

As the dance ended David saw Susan smiling past him, and turned. Paul was coming towards them across the floor. He took a direct course, heedless of the dancers whose progress he impeded.

'Hello, there!' Paul nodded to Susan and clapped David on the shoulder. 'Didn't know you frequented this dump, dear boy. Never seen you here before, have I?'

'Never been here before,' David told him.

'That would seem to explain it.' His tone was solemn, his thin lips mobile. As he lifted his hand to beckon the hovering waiter his feet shifted quickly to restore the balance. Susan suspected he was not entirely sober. 'Mary and I are moving on, or I'd ask you to join us. But you'll have a drink with me first.'

Without asking what they were drinking he nodded to the waiter. David said, 'Is this a favourite haunt of yours?'

'I find it more soothing than some.'

He did not sit down. They chatted for a few minutes, with Paul revealing intimate details of some of the couples as they danced past. Few, according to him, had the moral right to be together, a fact which caused him amusement rather than concern. Then, looking at his watch, he said, 'That waiter's damned slow. Mind drinking to absent friends? My wench will be fretting.'

Mary Halliday showed no sign of fretting when he rejoined her. She gave him the full model smile, leaning intimately towards him as he helped her up. David noticed that it was the head waiter who escorted them to the door, bowing obsequiously as he held it open. Paul completely ignored him. He saluted David, blew Susan a kiss, and sauntered out.

When the waiter arrived with champagne David grinned happily. 'Typical Paul,' he said. 'The grand gesture, and ruddy generous too.'

'Typical,' Susan agreed. 'I'm not so sure about the generosity. I think it's egotism. Makes him feel important.'

'You've got green eyes.'

Susan laughed. 'Maybe I have. And it's all second hand at that. But he's supposed to be terribly spoilt. Comes of being an only child, I suppose.'

'I'm an only child,' David reminded her.

Which adds weight to the theory, thought Susan. She said lightly, 'Maybe your parents were more sensible. Paul's suffered from the same disadvantage as himself.' She sipped at the champagne and gurgled in her throat. 'Ummm! Here's to Paul. May he go on being an egotist if this is the way it takes him.'

The champagne inspired David to abandon the subtle method of approach for direct action. As the band finished a number and laid down their instruments he stood up and walked the few paces to where the guitarist sat. The man's eyes were shut; presumably this was the third position — the non-playing, non-singing position.

'May I have a word with you?' David asked.

The man's eyes opened lazily; they were large and rather pink. 'Go right ahead, man,' he drawled. 'Ah'm listenin'.'

The eyes were closing again as David said quickly, 'It's about George Winstone.'

The dark lids checked and shot up, the long, drooping body suddenly tightened. But the voice was still lazy as he said, 'How's about him?'

'Doesn't he usually play the trumpet here?' The man nodded. 'Why isn't he here to-night?'

'He's sick.'

'How sick?' The man did not answer. 'Did you know his wife is in trouble?'

For a brief moment the man regarded him. Then his gaze shifted, to rove round the room. There was movement among his fellow musicians, and he said, 'Ah'll come to yo' table after the next number.'

Adding, as an afterthought, 'Whisky sour.'

David ordered a double whisky sour and poured more champagne for himself and Susan. He was in a hopeful mood. The seed had been sown, and it seemed that the fruit might ripen. The guitarist had acknowledged Winstone as a member of the band, had not denied that Winstone was married or that his wife was in trouble. At least that part of Winstone's story was not a lie.

'Sounds promising,' he told Susan. 'He's not the loquacious type, but the whisky may help.'

If the whisky loosened the West Indian's tongue it did not make him more informative; he talked round Winstone and then, somewhat guardedly, about him, but what he said was not what his listeners wanted to hear. Even leading questions were nudged gently aside.

'You say you know he took a beating,' David said. 'Do you know why?'

The guitarist shrugged. 'His wife went with another man. It happens.'

That was one way of putting it, thought Susan. She did not like the man. He talked to David, but his eyes were on her, and she objected to the look in them. It was encompassing rather than appreciative.

David was uncertain how to proceed. If that was the explanation Winstone had given it would be unwise to refute it. He was there to obtain information, not to dispense it.

'Winstone came to see me last night,' he said slowly. 'He asked me to help him get his wife back. I'd like to do that. Can you tell me the other man's name?'

The pink eyes moved reluctantly from Susan to David. 'No,' he said, after an interval. 'George didn't say.'

David was in no doubt that the man was lying, but he was puzzled as to why. Was it fear of Bandy, suspicion of his questioner's integrity, or merely uncertainty of what Winstone would wish him to say? David decided that he too would play safe.

'I'm handicapped by knowing so little about them,' he said. 'Perhaps you can help me there. How long have they been separated?'

The question fared little better than the others. The guitarist had joined the band about six months previously, when Nora had been the vocalist. Then Nora had left and he had taken over her job, and a few weeks later Winstone had announced that he and Nora were no longer living together. 'She still comes here sometimes,' he said, finishing his drink. 'Once a month, maybe.'

David ordered another whisky sour. 'Are they considering a divorce?' he asked.

The man did not know. Nor could he tell them anything of Nora's family. He seemed to have lost all interest in the topic of George Winstone, and his eyes were again embracing Susan. They were large, magnetic eyes which she found difficulty in avoiding, and she was glad when he uncoiled his long body from the chair and stood up.

'Got to be getting back,' he said. 'Thanks for the drink, man.'

'One last question.' David stood up too. 'Where can I find Winstone? He forgot to give me his address.'

'Maybe he ain't got one,' the man said, avoiding David's eyes. 'Could be.'

He nodded to Susan and loped back to the stage.

An indeterminate victory, thought David. It enabled him to crow over his godfather and Snowball, but it carried him no farther in his inquiries.

Susan said, 'Well, thank goodness that's over. May we dance now?'

They danced. David's energy was somewhat below par, but it was sufficient to clear all but the most determined shufflers from the floor. Susan enjoyed it. She would have preferred his arms tight about her, his cheek against hers. But that was a hold she had not yet experienced with David, and it was fun to indulge occasionally in the uninhibited antics that constituted his almost primitive form of dancing. Even the band seemed to respond to him. The music grew hotter, the trumpet was no longer muted.

Her cheeks were flushed when eventually they sat down. She said breathlessly, 'That was fun. Do we go now, or do we wait for them to throw us out?'

'A load of fairies like this lot?' He waved a contemptuous arm to indicate the other customers. 'I'd like to see them try. We'll cut a few more capers first.'

They cut a few more capers. Susan began to enjoy them less. With the wine he had drunk at dinner (Susan's share of the bottle had been meagre) and the whiskies and champagne since, David's footwork was less sure. He was also perspiring freely; drops of sweat trickled down into his eyes, his hair hung lankly over his forehead, his hands were moist and clammy. After their third spell on the floor Susan said weakly, 'I can't take it like I used to, darling. Isn't it time we went home?'

He agreed that it was. Although pride would not let him admit it, either by words or a slackening of tempo, he was more than ready to quit; he was unused to violent exercise, and his headache was returning. As they came up the steps into Greek Street he drew in great gulps of the night air, sweet and moist after the rain.

'We'll walk to Piccadilly and take the tube from there,' he said. 'Do us good after the fug down there.'

She would have preferred a taxi, but she did not argue. She clung to his arm and prayed that her feet would carry her the distance. David, she knew, liked to walk untrammelled. But he could not have it both ways. She would never make it unaided.

Half-way down Shaftesbury Avenue he said, 'If Lumsden doesn't ring in the morning I'm sunk. Or do I go down to Rotherhithe and sit on his doorstep, waiting for him to come home?' He looked up at the sky. There were no stars visible. 'A bleak prospect. It will probably rain like hell.'

Susan said, 'Why concentrate on the man? Can't you find the girl? You said yourself she must live close by, or they'd never have chosen a place like that in which to park.'

'I've tried the girls. The only two who admit to being out late that night and who showed any guilt reaction were Judy Garland and the Einsdorp girl. I don't think it was the first, and I'm damned sure it wasn't the second.'

'Why not?'

'Because of her voice. And the twitches. She just couldn't make a boy-friend.'

Susan sighed; partly in sympathy, partly from weariness.

'Poor thing! Fancy having to go through life handicapped like that. It must be sheer hell. Was it an accident, do you think?'

'Probably. She might not be bad-looking if her face would keep still, but it won't.' He fumbled with his free hand for a cigarette. 'Mina. That's an unusual name, isn't it?'

'Ummm! Probably a diminutive.'

'Could be. Short for Wilhelmina, perhaps. Wilhelmina Einsdorp. What a mouthful! I suppose it's Dutch, but that doesn't make it any easier.'

'I was at school with a girl named Wilhelmina,' Susan said. 'She wasn't Dutch, she was Irish. We used to call her Bill.'

David grunted, feeling for his lighter. 'You'd need to shorten it to something. Mina or Bill, it — Oh, no!'

He stopped so abruptly that Susan

nearly fell forward on her face. David clutched her and swung her round. Eyes shining, he looked down at her ecstatically. Passers-by eyed them curiously, but David ignored them.

'Susan, you're a genius!' He was beside himself with glee. 'Bill! Why the hell didn't I think of that myself?'

It was a pity, thought Susan, as she was enveloped in his embrace, that he had to choose Shaftesbury Avenue in which to kiss her. She would have preferred less publicity. But she did not protest. A kiss from David was always welcome, no matter where it took place.

The embrace over, they walked on. There was a new liveliness to David's step, so that Susan was almost running. Breathlessly she said, 'I don't want to quench your enthusiasm, darling, but aren't you taking a lot for granted? Even supposing your Mina is also known as Bill, how can you be sure she's the right Bill? You said yourself she couldn't make a boy-friend.'

'Well, I was wrong. I don't know how she managed it, but a boy-friend she's got. Or had. And I suspect it's Robert Lumsden.'

'I still don't see how you can be so sure.'

'Because of the likeness.' Genially he patted the hand on his arm. 'Remember I told you there was something familiar about her? Well, now I've got it. If that girl isn't related to Nora Winstone in some way I'll eat my hat.'

10

As the telephone bell jangled into his dream David stirred uneasily, turned on to his stomach, and buried his nose in the pillows. But the bell went on ringing, and suddenly he was wide awake.

'Lumsden!'

He had forgotten to put the telephone by the bed. Flinging the blankets aside, he went quickly across the room and picked up the receiver. But the caller was Paul, not Lumsden. Paul had had a new Jaguar delivered the previous day, and he wanted to take it down to the coast. He was, however, without a chauffeur; the man had been given the day off. Would David care to drive the car for him?

'Sorry,' David said, not without regret. 'No dice. I have to work.'

'On a Sunday? Don't journalists have a union?'

'It's the Winstone case,' David explained. 'I've a new lead, I think. Can't afford to ignore it. Thanks for the champagne, by the way. It went down well.'

'Think nothing of it, dear boy. Well, be seeing you. Sorry you can't make it to-day.'

David went back to bed, but not to sleep. It was only eight o'clock, but already he was wide awake. He lay thinking about Lumsden, and considering what he should say to the man when he rang. He must not be too explicit. Lumsden's anxiety must be aroused, but it must not be satisfied. Not over the telephone. The man had to be convinced that to confide in David was his wisest course, that *Topical Truths* had his best interests at heart and was prepared to pay for the privilege of safeguarding them. If fear could not persuade him cupidity might.

But to ensure success a meeting was imperative.

At eight-thirty he got up and dressed and had his breakfast. For the next hour he sat by the telephone, reading the Sunday newspapers but assimilating little of what he read. By ten o'clock, when Lumsden still had not rung, he knew that expectancy was not to be fulfilled. Either the man had not read the note, or he intended to disregard it.

Yesterday, when Lumsden had been his sole hope, such a disappointment would have filled David with gloom. It would have meant that his assignment had come to a full stop. But now he had Mina. He went out into the sunshine, stripped the cover from the Alvis, gave the brasswork a final, loving polish, checked oil, water, and tyre pressures. He was fed up with trains and buses. To-day he would spoil himself and take the Alvis. It would be some compensation for having to pass up the opportunity to drive Paul's Jaguar.

He drove down to Rotherhithe at a steady pace, enjoying the envious glances of enthusiasts and small boys and the curious stares of the uninitiated. Arrived at St James's Road, he parked the Alvis and walked the remaining fifty yards to the house. Lumsden was almost certain to be out. But at least it might be possible to discover whether the man had had his note.

'I'm sorry,' he apologized to the woman. 'It's me again. I suppose Mr Lumsden is out?'

'He's more than out,' she told him. 'He's gone. Left this morning.'

'Gone?' This was something he should have anticipated. 'Gone for good, do you mean?'

'He didn't say so, but I shouldn't be surprised.' There was a look on her face he had not seen there before, a look of curiosity mingled with apprehension. 'Said he was off for a holiday, be away about a fortnight. But he took all his things. What's left is mostly rubbish.'

'Did he say where he was going?' She shook her head. 'I suppose he got my note?'

'He got it.'

She hesitated, her mouth open as though about to say more. Then it closed with a snap, and without another word she went back into the house and slammed the door. David guessed what was bothering her. She must have read his note, or Lumsden had told her its content, and she had assumed it was the cause of her lodger's sudden departure. No doubt she was also wondering what the danger that threatened him might be.

She could be right about the note, he thought, as he walked back to the Alvis. It could have panicked Lumsden into immediate action, so that he upped and bolted without waiting to telephone. Or perhaps there had been no need to telephone. Perhaps he had already recognized the danger.

It was Mrs Einsdorp who opened the door in Rose End to him. She was a little woman, with a grey, lined face and thinning, straggly grey hair. Her eyes were red, and David wondered if she had been crying. He wondered too at her age. She must be well over sixty, he thought. How did she come to have a daughter as young as Mina?

She shook her head when he asked to speak to the girl. Mina, she told him, was away. She had left early that morning.

David was disappointed, but not surprised. Assuming that Mina and

Lumsden were the missing witnesses to the murder of Constable Dyerson, then it was natural to suppose that if one disappeared the other would go also; and since it was unlikely that they had received separate intelligence of the danger threatening them, Lumsden must have warned the girl. Had they gone together?

He said, 'Your daughter's full name is Wilhelmina, isn't it?' She nodded. Confident now that he was on the right track, he went on briskly, 'It's important that I get in touch with her at once, Mrs Einsdorp. May I have her address?'

There was no doubt she had been crying. She did not ask his business with the girl, but shook her head wearily, the tears beginning to well in her tired eyes.

'She didn't leave no address,' she said, and sniffed. 'She just went. Early this morning it was, before I was up. There was a letter she wrote . . . ' She fumbled in her apron pocket. David hoped he was about to be shown the letter, but it was a handkerchief she produced. With it she dabbed at her eyes and blew her nose. 'It was on the kitchen table when I come down. Said she'd be writing in a day or so, and not to worry. But it didn't say where she'd be.'

'I'm sorry,' he said gently, his disappointment fading before her obvious grief and the knowledge that, if the couple were lost to him, they were also lost to Bandy and the police. 'Perhaps I should explain why I'm here. I'm a journalist, and it happens that my magazine is interested in your daughter. We know quite a lot about her. In fact, I may even be able to tell you the reason for her sudden departure.' She looked at him in bewilderment, and he smiled reassuringly. 'May I come in for a few minutes? I think you and I should have a little chat.'

She took him into the small front room, but because she did not sit down herself he felt compelled to stand. A photograph in an ornamental wooden frame on the sideboard caught his eye; it depicted a young man in a stiff high collar standing erect and unsmiling behind a young woman seated on a chair. The young woman was holding a baby.

Presumably this was the Einsdorp family; he could see the resemblance between Mrs Einsdorp and the young woman in the photograph. Yet on the mount, written in a faded, spidery hand, was the date — July 1924. That, according to David's reckoning, made Mina's age to be thirty-eight!

So the baby was not Mina. Mina had said she was twenty-one. She might be a few years older, but she certainly wasn't thirty-eight.

He said, 'Mina isn't your only child, is she? Haven't you an elder daughter? Nora? Nora Winstone?'

She sat down then. She sat as though she were unused to sitting, her meagre body perched on the edge of a hard wooden chair, her roughened hands in her lap. The apron looked too big for her, concealing almost entirely the blue blouse and skirt beneath. The woollen stockings were wrinkled, the fur on her slippers had moulted.

Yes, she said, she had another daughter. Nora had left home at sixteen, and her visits since had been very infrequent.

'Sometimes we don't see her for months. Only the name's not Winstone, sir; it's Einsdorp, same as ours. Dad's parents were Dutch, you see. But Nora mostly uses her stage name. Desnay, it is.'

She spelt it out for him, and he thanked her. 'Is she married?' he asked.

Her reddened eyes looked at him quickly, and then fell. 'No,' she whispered. And then, louder, 'No, she never married.'

That puzzled David. Had Nora kept her marriage a secret from her parents, knowing they would not approve? Since she had left home so young and visited them so seldom, it seemed unlikely that their approval could be important to her. Or was the old lady lying? Was that the cause of her confusion? Had she refused to accept the fact that she had a coloured son-in-law?

Although now plagued by a new problem, he at least had the answer to an old one. Robert Lumsden had denied Nora Winstone, but no doubt he, together with others listed in the woman's diary, would have admitted knowledge of Nora

Desnay. Come to think of it, he had two new problems, not one. If Nora had been so cavalier in her treatment of her parents, why should she be so devoted to her young sister that she was prepared to suffer Bandy's anger and brutality to ensure the girl's safety? At the time Nora left home Mina could only just have been born. And since then? Just a few very infrequent visits, and apparently no other contact. How could sisterly love and devotion grow and flourish on such sparse acquaintance?

David thought he had the answer. He said gently, 'I don't want to seem impertinent, Mrs Einsdorp, but are you being entirely truthful? Don't you in fact have only the one daughter? Mina is Nora's child, isn't she?'

She sat so still that at first he thought she had not heard him. But he did not repeat the question; he moved to a chair and waited patiently. Presently a shudder convulsed the frail body, and he wondered uneasily if she were crying again. But when she looked at him the red-rimmed eyes were dry.

'Yes,' she said. 'She's Nora's daughter.' And added inconsequentially, 'Nora calls her Bill.'

He got the whole unhappy story from her by degrees. The family had been living in Bermondsey then. Mr Einsdorp had inherited some of the strict Calvinistic principles of his Dutch forebears, and had subjected his daughter to a stern discipline — a discipline against which Nora, spoiled and petted and protected by her mother, had secretly rebelled. The rebellion had terminated in the discovery by Mrs Einsdorp that Nora was pregnant; although she had kept the discovery from her husband for as long as possible, two months before the baby was born he had turned the girl out of the house, and had told her not to return. From that day to this, said the old lady, he had neither seen her nor spoken to her.

'But she visits you,' David objected. 'You said so just now.'

'She comes when he's out. He works nights, you see.' Mrs Einsdorp shook her head. 'I think he knows. But he won't see her, not even after all these years. To him

208

it's just like she's dead. Nora says she don't want to see him neither. She's hard, same as her Dad. Yet it seems like she's fond of him; always asks how he is.' She sighed. 'Well, blood's thicker'n water, they say.'

He nodded impatiently. 'And the baby? Mina?'

It was Mrs Einsdorp who had persuaded her husband to adopt the baby. It was not the child who had sinned, she had pointed out; Nora could not look after it herself if she had to earn a living, and the only other solution would be to put the child in a home. Was he prepared to let that happen?

Mr Einsdorp was not. After considerable argument he had agreed to adopt the child, but only on the understanding that she was to be brought up as their own daughter, and that Nora should have no say in the upbringing. He had even insisted on choosing the baby's name.

David had wondered why Nora should have chosen to refer to the girl as Bill instead of adopting the diminutive by which she was generally known. Here, perhaps, was the explanation. It was an expression of rebellion against her father's dictatorial attitude.

'You mean Mina doesn't know Nora is her mother?' he asked, aghast.

'She calls her Auntie,' she said simply. 'I'm her mother.' Her tired eyes rounded. 'You said you was a reporter, didn't you? You won't go putting all this in the papers? Dad wouldn't never forgive me.'

'We won't print a word without your permission,' he assured her. And meant it. 'You may not realize it, Mrs Einsdorp, but you and your family are badly in need of help. That's why I'm here — to help you. However, we'll go into that later. When did you move to Rotherhithe?'

'Soon after Mina was born. That was Dad's idea. He didn't want the neighbours to know, you see.'

David did see. 'And that unfortunate affliction — the impediment in her speech, the twitching in her face? Has she had that from birth?'

'Oh, no, sir. She was a lovely little thing. That come after the accident.'

The accident had occurred when Mina

was fifteen, and was working in a local factory. The building was old, and much of the woodwork rotten. A board had given way as she was coming down a flight of stairs, and she had tripped and fallen, injuring her spine. 'In hospital for months, she was,' the woman said, with a deep sigh. 'Months. And when she come out . . . ' She dabbed at her eyes. 'It's her nerves, you see. She won't never get any better, the doctor says.'

David expressed his sympathy. 'It sounds like negligence on the part of her employers. Did she get compensation?'

'The judge give her seven thousand pounds.' She mentioned the sum as if it were of no interest, as insignificant as a few pence. 'But she weren't allowed to spend it. She has the interest, of course, but she don't get the rest till she's twenty-one.'

She's twenty-one now, thought David. Had the old woman forgotten?

Seven thousand pounds. A man could go far with money like that. Had the same thought occurred to Robert Lumsden? Had seven thousand pounds blinded him to Mina's impediment and the ugly twitches in her face, sparking an interest which was purely mercenary on his part, however romantic on hers?

He said, 'It's a tidy sum. Money can't compensate for injuries like hers, of course, but it must help. How did your daughter take it? Nora, I mean.'

'She was proper upset about the accident. Down at the hospital 'most every day, she was. Mina means a lot to Nora. But she was pleased about the compensation. She always wanted Mina to have the best; most weeks she'd send money for me to spend on her. I had to hide it from Dad, or he'd have made me send it back.'

David could believe that. Nora Winstone might have an unorthodox code of morals but he suspected she also had a form of honesty and sincerity. As for the Calvinistic Mr Einsdorp . . .

'What time does your husband go to work, Mrs Einsdorp? I suppose right now he's asleep upstairs?'

She sat up straighter, her eyes rounding. She had the most expressive eyes he had seen in an old woman.

'Of course he ain't,' she said, staring, her fingers twisting and kneading in her lap. 'He's in hospital. I thought that was what you come about.'

'I'm sorry. I didn't know. Nothing serious, I hope.'

'His head's broke.' The fingers were suddenly still, there was a sharpness in the quiet voice that had not been there before. 'Some young thugs done it. They broke into his warehouse — Saturday before last it was — and beat him up. Come on him from behind — never give him a chanst, he said.' As an afterthought she added, 'They killed a policeman. It was in the papers.'

David was too startled for immediate comment. Morgan had told him of the night watchman, but he had never given the man another thought. Was there a connexion here, or was it just coincidence that Einsdorp should have been injured in a raid witnessed both by his daughter and his granddaughter? At least it explained the anger that Morgan had sensed in Nora. It had been generated not so much by the murder of Constable Dyerson as by the assault on her father.

'I'm sorry,' he repeated mechanically. 'He's getting better, I hope.'

'That's what they tell me at the hospital. I hope they're right.'

With something of pride she detailed the injuries her husband had suffered. David was not particularly interested, but by the time she had finished he had recovered his wits once more. He said, 'I'm sure they are. And it's about the warehouse job that I'm here, Mrs Einsdorp. Your daughter Nora came down to visit you that evening, didn't she?'

Yes, she said, Nora had been down. But she never gave previous notice of her visits, and Mina had been at the cinema. It was after midnight when the girl returned, and by that time Nora had left. 'I never did find out what made her so late,' Mrs Einsdorp said, frowning. 'The police come about Dad, you see. They took me to the hospital. And when I come back — well, I was that worried I never thought to ask.'

'Was she upset when she came in?'

She thought for a while, her eyes closed in concentration.

'I can't remember.' As the implication of his question occurred to her she opened her eyes wide. 'Why should she be upset? We didn't know about Dad till the police come.'

He told her then. Quietly and unemotionally, softening the highlights as much as he could to ease the pain he must cause her, he told her how her granddaughter had been with a man in Rotherhithe Street that night, how Nora had watched the couple from the shadows, and how all three must have witnessed the murder of the policeman. He told her how Nora had gone to the police, and how, as the result of her action, she had been kidnapped and was being held by the gunman; and he tried to explain, without being too melodramatic, the danger that threatened Mina. But he did not mention Winstone, nor Robert Lumsden by name. Nora's marriage was her own affair; if she chose to keep it secret from her parents it was not for him to reveal it. As for Lumsden — well,

Lumsden's association with the girl still had to be confirmed, however sure of it he might be in his own mind. Perhaps the confirmation would come now, from the woman.

Apart from an occasional exclamation of pain or alarm or momentary disbelief she listened to him in silence; her tiny body seemed to shrink as she leaned farther and farther forward from the edge of the chair, her head performing in a series of little shakes as though she were a bird with a freshly caught worm in its beak. Her fingers played nervously with the apron, screwing it round and round and then releasing it. And all the time her eyes seemed to grow larger, eventually to fill with tears.

'But why didn't Mina tell me?' she wailed between sobs. 'And she didn't. Not a word. Not even when the police come about Dad. And Nora . . . ' She sobbed louder. 'What will happen to her, sir? What'll they do to the poor girl?'

'Nothing, I hope.' He tried to sound cheerfully optimistic. 'They will probably hold her until the hunt has died down and they can clear out of the country. Then they'll let her go.' He went over and patted her awkwardly on the shoulder. He had little experience of coping with tears of grief. 'It's worrying for you, I know, but you mustn't lose heart. What we have to do now is to ensure they don't get hold of Mina and Lumsden as well. That's the best guarantee of Nora's safety.' He paused, aware that he had spoken Lumsden's name and that she had accepted it without comment. 'You know Robert Lumsden?' he asked.

She nodded her bowed head. Content, David went back to his chair and waited, allowing her time to recover.

Presently she dabbed at her eyes with the apron and sat up.

'They been going steady best part of a year,' she told him in a watery voice. 'Dad don't like him; he thinks he's after her money, you see. So does Nora. But I don't know; he's a good-looking boy, and ever so polite.' She dabbed again at her eyes, ending with a hearty sniff. 'Mina's ever so in love. He's the only boy she's had, you see, since the accident, and it meant a lot to her. He took her to the pictures every Wednesday, regular as clockwork.' Mrs Einsdorp heaved a deep sigh. 'Well, it's done now. I just hope she'll be happy, that's all.'

David was not sure what it was that was 'done.' He presumed the woman was referring to the fact that Lumsden and the girl had gone away together, and he said, 'You told me she had left a note for you, Mrs Einsdorp. May I see it? It may give some indication of where to look for them.'

She stood up, her body bent at first and straightening slowly. 'It's in the kitchen,' she said. 'I'll get it.'

She was, he thought, the most docile creature he had ever interviewed. She had accepted and answered his questions almost without comment, had never queried his right to put them. Did he have a right? he wondered. Perhaps not. But at least he was there to help her. That he was also helping himself was immaterial.

When she shuffled back into the room she was wearing spectacles. 'It don't say where they went,' she said, handing him the note. 'But read it if you like.'

He did like. He was a better judge than the woman, he thought, of the value of any information it might contain.

'Dear Mum,' he read. 'This is just to tell you that Robert and me have gone away together. We were married last Monday, but we kept it a secret because we thought Dad might try to stop us. Now we're off on our honeymoon. Robert says not to tell you where we're going, so I won't. But I'll write to you soon. And not to worry, dear. I know Dad doesn't think Robert is right for me, but he doesn't know him as I do. I love him, and I'm ever so happy. Your loving daughter, Mina.

'P.S. I hope Dad is heaps better. Tell him not to be mad at me, and give him my love.'

Marriage. He had not expected that, although it was certainly logical. How else could Lumsden gain control of the girl's money? David read the note again, looking for something that was not there. Mina wrote only of a honeymoon; there was no mention of what David had supposed to be the true reason for her flight. Was she then unaware of the danger that threatened her and her husband, or was the omission intentional, made to spare her supposed parents further grief?

Well, marriage did not alter the situation as it concerned him. The couple still had to be found.

'Quite a surprise, eh? I hope they'll be very happy.' He handed back the note with a friendly smile. 'I should do as she says, Mrs Einsdorp, and try not to worry. Mina will be all right; she has a husband to look after her now. I see she promises to write. When she does you must let me know at once. And remember to keep the envelope. She may not give her address, but the postmark would help us to trace her.'

He tore a page from his notebook and wrote down his telephone number. She looked at it doubtfully.

'I don't know as that's right,' she protested. 'Wouldn't it be better to tell the police? I mean, they'd look after her, wouldn't they? They'd see as she didn't come to no harm.'

It was the first time she had sought to deny him. Surprised, he could summon up no valid argument with which to refute her.

'We'd look after her too, Mrs Einsdorp,' he said weakly. 'A newspaper is a powerful instrument.' That would tickle Snowball's fancy, he thought, and wondered what possible power could be wielded by *Topical Truths* under such circumstances. 'Naturally we would inform the police as soon as we found her.'

'I don't know,' she said again. Mrs Einsdorp could be stubborn. Turning the paper over and over between her fingers, she said, 'I'll ask Dad. He'll know what's best. I'll do like he says.'

From that decision he could not budge her.

★ ★ ★

Snowball lived in a small semi-detached house in Beckenham. Perched on a step-ladder, he was busily clipping the front hedge when David drove up in the

Alvis. From the road only his head was visible, a great white puff-ball balanced on top of the yew. Then the puff-ball vanished, to reappear at the front gate.

'Is this possible?' he demanded, as David approached. His spectacles glinted in the afternoon sunlight, so that in place of eyes there were two white caverns. 'Is an employee of mine actually working on a Sunday?' He held the gate wide. 'Come in, come in. Now you're here you can mow the lawn.'

From anyone else David would have accepted this threat as a feeble attempt at humour. But not from Snowball. Snowball might well expect him to do just that. He said quickly, 'Something has cropped up which won't keep till to-morrow. The lawn will.'

'That so?' Snowball removed his spectacles and plucked reflectively at the goitre. 'Well, I suppose I'll have to listen.'

They sat in deck-chairs on the back lawn, and David told him of his visit to Rotherhithe, becoming unhappily aware that in the telling the tale seemed to lose much of its importance and urgency.

Snowball thought so too. He said tartly, 'Very dramatic, David. But if you don't know where the couple are, then all we can do is wait until the girl writes to Grannie. So where's the urgency?'

David had no answer to that, though he had racked his brains for one throughout the journey down to Beckenham. The urgency was there, but he lacked the inspiration to cope with it. He had hoped that his editor might be more successful.

'It's useless to wait,' he said. 'When the letter arrives the old woman will go straight to the police. That's for sure.'

Snowball clucked impatiently.

'Sit on her doorstep, waylay the postman. Be there when the letter arrives. A twice-daily vigil won't hurt you. Or do you suggest we advertise for them?' He levered himself out of the deck-chair. 'I'm going indoors to make a pot of tea. You sit there and soak up some sun. It may bring you inspiration.'

David lay back and closed his eyes. From the kitchen came the rattle of crockery; to have the old man waiting on him was a unique experience, and he intended to enjoy it. Pleasant, too, to relax in the sun. There was no garden at the flat, but here in this quiet suburban road it was almost like being on holiday. It reminded him of his uncle's pub down in Cornwall. There was the same small garden at the back, with a lawn and flower-beds and masses of rose-trees (odd that old Snowball should be a gardener), and a gravel path winding down to a green-painted shed with a tarred roof. The view was different, of course. Here there were only trees and the roofs of houses. Whereas at Pendwara . . .

He struggled awkwardly out of the chair, almost knocking the tea-tray from Snowball's hands. But he did not stop to apologize. He said excitedly, 'I've got it! I know where they've gone! Cornwall. Lumsden's aunt runs a camp near Mullion. It's the ideal spot for a bolt-hole. For a honeymoon too, come to that.'

The editor unfolded the legs of the tray and placed it carefully on the lawn.

'And you're thinking that a trip to the coast would make a pleasant break, eh?

All right. But watch your step, young man. Overdo the junketing, and I'm knocking it off your annual holiday. Now, then — do you take milk and sugar?'

11

To David Wight, packing was a comprehensive term. It included a final cleaning, polishing, refuelling, and checking of the Alvis, a cursory tidying of the flat, writing notes to whom it might concern, a telephone call or two and, finally, the jamming of a few necessary articles into a suitcase. This last occupied the least time of all.

Dusk was falling as he completed the first stage and carefully replaced the cover on the Alvis. As he snapped the penultimate fastener into place a voice behind him said quietly, 'Any news, man?'

David jumped and turned quickly. He had been so engrossed in his task that he had not heard Winstone approach. He said irritably, 'If you creep up on a chap like that you're liable to get hurt. News? Yes, of a sort. But I don't know that it concerns you.'

He turned to fix the last fastener.

Winstone said, 'I'm aiming to come before this, but things getting tricky. I got to be careful. Reckon I'm being watched.'

David grunted. 'You've got company, chum. It's almost traditional.' Then, realizing the implication, he glanced quickly up and down the darkening street. There were a few people about, but no loiterers, no suspicious-looking characters. 'Did you manage to give him the slip?'

'I guess so. Little guy in a grey suit and brown shoes. I seen him two — three times to-day. Seems like he always going my way.'

'Mine favoured brown shoes and a blue raincoat,' David said. 'I wouldn't know about his suit.' He walked round the Alvis, making sure the fasteners were secure. The street seemed to have emptied, the darkness was more opaque. He said, 'Better come inside. It may not be healthy out here.'

Obediently Winstone followed him into the flat. He no longer sported the light-blue suit and the pointed shoes of Thursday evening; they had been replaced by a black sweater, polo-necked and baggy, over narrow jeans, with rope-soled sandals on his feet. The injuries to his face were less conspicuous. Heavy scabs had formed on lip and cheek. His mouth still looked twisted, but his right eye was now open and the dark skin camouflaged much of the discoloration that remained.

David gave him a beer and started to tidy the flat, returning evasive answers to the West Indian's questions or ignoring them altogether. He was annoyed at the man's visit. The time when Winstone could have helped him was past. Now the man was only a hindrance.

His mood was too obvious for Winstone to disregard it for long. 'You don't want me here, huh? You don't trust me?' he asked.

David slammed a drawer home and turned to face him.

'Not exactly,' he said curtly, his mood tempering the truth. Morgan had provided several reasons for doubting the man; David had refused to accept them, and his visit to the Seventy-Seven had seemed to justify his refusal. Winstone himself, however, had not yet been challenged; how would he answer the superintendent's accusations? 'According to the police, most of what you told me on Thursday evening was sheer fabrication.'

It seemed that to Winstone police intervention was of greater moment than David's accusation. Or perhaps he did not appreciate that an accusation had been made. He said quickly, 'You told them I been here? Why you want to do that?'

David shrugged. 'No option. Earlier that evening my flat had been burgled, and the police were round here next morning collecting finger-prints. They must have found plenty of yours. Presumably they checked with Scotland Yard, and — '

'You think I got a police record? You wrong, man.' There was no jubilation in Winstone's voice, it was a statement of fact. 'I done things, but I ain't never been catched.'

'No?' Since only the police could

confirm or deny that statement, David let it pass. 'In that case you've nothing to worry about, have you? But the superintendent tells me there is no record at Somerset House of your marriage to Nora. Who's right? You or he?'

Winstone considered the question, watching the beer as he slowly swilled it round and round in the glass.

'We ain't married,' he said eventually. 'I'm willing, but Nora don't want it. She say she won't be tied to no man for good.' He looked up. 'And her right, I guess. Nora too restless, she changing man — job — home too quickly. We live together for six months, then she leave me. We don't have no quarrel. I do all I can to make her stay, but she just say she had enough, and walk out.'

'Then why tell me you were married?'

Winstone shrugged his slim shoulders.

'It seem like marriage to me. And if I say we just live together for a few months, you going to like that?' He took a quick sip at the beer. 'Man, you think I'm just another nigger living on white woman. That going to make you trust me, huh?'

David saw his point, and was inclined to accept it. But he had not finished yet.

'All right. But the police also say that Nora is dead. They found the car in which she was kidnapped. The back seat and the carpet were drenched in blood.'

Winstone stared at him. 'How they know it's the right car?'

'It was the one I'd seen outside the flat that night. I remembered the make and number. They also found her scarf in it.'

The man looked more puzzled than alarmed. He put the glass down on the table and with lean, supple fingers scratched his head.

'I don't know,' he muttered, as though talking to himself. 'Man, I just don't know. She was alive Wednesday morning, that I swear.' He stopped scratching. 'When they find the car?'

'I'm not sure. Thursday night or early Friday morning.'

'They don't find Nora's body?'

'They hadn't then. I don't know what has happened since, but I imagine not. It would have been reported in the newspapers.'

Slowly Winstone checked off the fingers of his left hand, crooking them one by one into the pinkly brown palm.

'Man, that's five days since they took her. Nobody going to tell me the cops can't find a body in five days.' The clenched fist was complete, and he bumped it several times on the padded arm of the chair. 'If there blood in that car it not hers. Couldn't be.'

'Then whose was it?'

Winstone shrugged, and cast his eyes up to the ceiling; in the lamplight they shone whitely. He seemed to think the gesture expressive enough, for he said nothing. David was inclined to agree with him; a plurality of corpses was certainly within the gunman's capability, the blood was not necessarily Nora's. And five days was a long while for a body to remain undiscovered.

He said, 'All right. But I'm trusting no one until I'm dead sure. Too many lives at stake, including mine. And now, if you don't mind, I've things to do.'

'You want me to go?'

'Suit yourself.' David had a guilty

feeling that he had been unfair. 'Pour yourself another beer and switch on the telly. There's no hurry.'

Winstone did neither. He sat leaning forward, the near-empty glass held between both hands, a frown puckering the jagged scar on his forehead as he stared unblinking at the carpet. To hell with him! thought David. Let him get on with it. I've enough worries of my own without shouldering his.

It had occurred to him that he should write to Lumsden at his lodgings in Rotherhithe; it was just possible that he had guessed wrong, that Lumsden had not taken the girl to Cornwall and might return while he, David, was away. So he told him what he had learned or guessed from his talk with Mrs Einsdorp, and that he had gone to Pendwara to find him. If Lumsden were to return in the meantime, he wrote, it was essential that he should get in touch immediately with the editor of *Topical Truths*. The safety of himself and his wife might depend on it.

He'll probably take no more notice of this than he did of my first epistle, thought David as he licked and sealed the envelope. He wondered what the landlady would make of it if curiosity should get the better of her.

He was writing a note to the milkman when the telephone rang.

'David? Oh, thank goodness!' Susan's voice was shrill. 'I've been trying to get you all day. I'd have come round to see you if I hadn't been so scared. I wasn't sure, you see, what they meant to do; even in broad daylight I didn't feel safe. And then when it got dark — '

'Whoa there!' Susan in hysterics was something new. 'Take it steady, can't you? What's all this about being scared? Scared of what?'

'The telephone call. He rang me this afternoon, just after lunch. And he said — '

'Who rang you?'

'Bandy.' David drew in his breath sharply. 'Or maybe it was one of his men. I don't know. But he said I was to tell you that if you didn't stop interfering in his affairs he would start interfering in yours. You wouldn't like that one bit, he said, and neither would your friends. And then he laughed — a fiendish laugh, David, really it was — and rang off.' Over the telephone he heard her sniff, but he did not think she was crying. 'I've been trying to get you ever since. If you hadn't answered this time I was going to ring Mr Morgan. I had to tell someone.'

'I've been here since seven,' David said. But that was immaterial. He must calm Susan down, try to make her feel secure. 'It's just a great big bluff, Susan; it shows they're getting jittery. They know they can't scare me off, so they're trying to add your persuasion to theirs. Don't be fooled by a simple trick like that.'

'I'm not fooled, I'm frightened. I'm frightened for myself and I'm frightened for you. When will you be round?'

David swore under his breath. He had enough on his plate without having to spend the evening trying to pacify an hysterical girl. 'In about three days time,' he told her. 'I'm off to the West Country early to-morrow morning, hot on the scent. Back by Wednesday at the latest. See you then.'

'Oh, no, you don't!' The hysteria was returning, but she checked it quickly. In a softer voice she said, 'David, please! After all, it was you who got me into this. Can't I see you for just a few minutes, darling? I'll not sleep a wink unless I do.'

He could have resisted anger, but not her pleading. And it was true that he was indirectly responsible for her present panic.

'O.K. I'll be along in about half an hour. Now, don't ring off. Winstone is here with me — you know, Nora's husband — and I want you to have a word with him.' Winstone had looked up quickly at the mention of his name and was staring at David. David stared back. 'I want you to listen to his voice and tell me if he was one of the men who tied you up Thursday evening.'

Winstone was on his feet now, but he did not obey David's beckoning hand. 'Frightened?' David asked.

The man shook his head. 'No, man. I never tied no woman up.' He took a few steps across the room. 'What you want me to say?'

'Anything that comes into your head. Tell her what Bandy and his mob did to you. No, better not. She's scared enough already.' He handed over the receiver. 'Tell her about your job in the band.'

In a few halting sentences Winstone told her. It was not an expansive description, but it sufficed. David said, 'Now tell her to keep her head buried in the pillows.' The West Indian looked his astonishment. 'Go on, tell her.'

Winstone told her. David took the receiver from him. 'Well?' he asked Susan.

'No, darling. Not like either of them.' She giggled nervously. 'I must say it was an odd conversation to have on the telephone.'

David hung up with a repeated promise to be round shortly. As he completed his packing Winstone said, 'You going to look for them two witnesses? You know where they are?'

'I may do.'

'You let me come with you? Like I say, I want to help.'

'No.' David wondered why he should be so emphatic in his refusal. A

237

companion on the trip could be an asset; but it had to be a companion he could trust, and he could not trust Winstone. Perhaps it was the man's colour, or the fact that by his own admission he had not always been law-abiding; or perhaps it was that suspicion once aroused was not easily allayed. To offset his bluntness he said, 'This isn't just a personal feud, you know. I'm working for a magazine, and my editor might disapprove if I co-opted an assistant.'

Susan lived in Bayswater. David took Winstone with him in the Alvis, and until leaving the car at Notting Hill the man continued to plead his cause. But David was adamant. 'Try shadowing your shadow for a change,' he suggested. 'If you're smart he might lead you to Nora.'

By the time David arrived Susan had regained her nerve, but she was unfeignedly glad to see him. He sat in her tiny flat, a large whisky in his hand and Susan squatting on a cushion at his feet, and listened again to the story of the threatening telephone call. The flat was sharply gay, with modern furniture and bright colours and an extravagant luxuriance of carpeting and curtains. There were a few ornaments in fine glass or china, one or two good prints on the walls.

David said, 'If Bandy meant to harm you he wouldn't warn you first. But he doesn't, of course. Not because of any scruples, but because he knows damned well it would be a gamble that couldn't pay off. No. He reckoned that a woman would be more easily bluffed into panic than a man.' Susan gave an indignant sniff. 'However, I'll let Morgan know. I expect he'll have someone keep an eye on you for the next few days.'

'You wouldn't care to keep an eye on me yourself?' she suggested. 'It'd be a lot cosier. I don't take kindly to strangers.'

'I told you, I'm off to Cornwall in the morning.'

'What part of Cornwall?'

'Near Helston.' That was enough for Susan. To keep her happy he added, 'When I get back we'll throw a party to celebrate.'

'*If* you get back,' Susan said. 'Your

friend Bandy may decide otherwise.'

The soft voice was tremulous. Despite her attempt at flippancy, he knew that tears were not far away, and that it was fear for him which prompted them. There was an unspoken pleading in the grey-green eyes as they gazed up at him from under that provocative auburn lock, a tenseness in the supple body so delectably outlined by the cotton frock, gay and deceptive in its simplicity. But he had to resist her pleading. He could not call off the hunt now.

'He won't,' he said confidently. 'I'm way ahead of him, and that's where I mean to stay. You'll see.'

Susan shifted her position, stretching out her shapely legs and tugging at the hem of her frock in a vain attempt to cover her knees. Planting both hands on the carpet behind her, she leaned back to regard him earnestly.

'And what then?' she demanded. 'What happens when you've caught up with the runaways? Do you hand them over to the police?'

'Probably. It depends on circumstances.'

'But you must, David. You've no option.'

'All right, I must.'

He leaned forward and ruffled her auburn hair. But Susan was in no mood for frivolity. She jerked her head away impatiently.

'It's time you grew up, David. This isn't a game; you're gambling with people's lives, your own included. Even if everything goes according to plan, there's more to follow. The police still have to catch up with Bandy, and until they do you won't be safe.'

He said cheerfully, 'We'll have clipped the blighter's wings. He'll either lie low, or try to skip the country. Either way he's out of business, and it will only be a question of time before he's caught.'

'And you will have been responsible. That's what frightens me. He may decide on revenge.'

David was touched by her concern, even a little perturbed by it. It was unlike Susan to indulge in pessimism. But as he drove back to Fulham his anxiety quickly evaporated; happy in the smooth running of the Alvis, exhilarated by the sharp crackle of the exhaust and the feeling of power under his feet, he was soon singing lustily. The Alvis would need to be at her best to-morrow. In the few months she had been his he had never taken her father than the home counties; Pendwara was nearly three hundred miles away, a stern test for the old bus. But he had no doubt she would make it. The treads on the rear tyres might be a little thin, but there was plenty of wear in them yet.

Outside the flat he tucked her up carefully, giving the bonnet a valedictory pat as he left her. The thought of the morrow cheered him. It would be good to get away from London, even better to know he had finished with Rotherhithe. And if all went well he would return with yet another scoop to his credit. Not, perhaps, as startling as Shere Island, but surely worthy of financial recognition by Snowball. As for Susan's gloomy foreboding of what might happen later — that was hooey. Revenge was a luxury that a crook in Bandy's position could not afford. Against his own kind, yes; that was traditional. But opposition from those within the law was what he would expect. It would not motivate revenge.

It was the lamp across the street that saved him. As he ran up the steps it glinted on moving steel, steel that shot upward and then swiftly downward. But David was ready. As the man lunged he leapt sideways, knocking the arm away and then turning and gripping it at the wrist with both hands. Exerting all his strength, he twisted it viciously. With a sharp cry of pain the man swung round, his back to David, his fingers opening to let the knife fall with a clatter to the stone paving.

'Not very clever,' David said, breathing hard. 'The best manuals tell you to bring the knife up, not down. It's quicker, and harder to counter.' He jerked his knee into the other's crutch and gave the wrist an extra twist. The man squealed shrilly. Exulting in his victory, David said, 'Tough as butter, eh? Now come inside and let's have a look at you.'

His exultation was his undoing. As he reached for the doorhandle he temporarily relaxed his grip on the other's wrist. The man brought his arm down sharply and swung round. Before David could defend himself a fist caught him flush on the chin and he staggered back, releasing his hold and banging his head sharply against the stone wall. His assailant did not wait for him to recover; he was down the steps in a flash, picking up the knife as he went. David could hear the padding feet vanishing into the darkness.

One hand to the back of his head, he moved away from the wall and stumbled down the steps to the street. The man had gone south, away from the lights of the Fulham Road. His footsteps were still audible, but David did not attempt to give chase. Never a fleet runner, he knew he would stand no chance of catching his assailant. And there was always the danger that the man might wait for him in the shadows, that a second attempt at murder might be more successful than the first.

He went back to the flat and examined his face in the mirror. His chin was sore, but there was no swelling. Gingerly fingering the back of his head, he could feel a lump forming. The skin was unbroken, but he knew he was in for a headache.

He poured himself a whisky and sat down to consider the situation. He had experienced no fear at the time of the encounter; but now that it was past his limbs felt weak and there was a fluttering in the pit of his stomach, and he knew that he was afraid. Danger was not a new experience. But suddenly to be faced with death when he had thought himself secure, to realize that he had become a man marked down for extermination, was a frightening prospect.

But David was stubborn. It occurred to him that he could call off the hunt, but he rejected that solution almost immediately; he could recognize fear, but he would not pander to it. And perhaps it was now too late to retreat. Perhaps he had gone so far that, even if he went no farther, his enemies would still consider him a threat to their security. He began to regret his summary dismissal of Winstone. The West

Indian might not be the ideal companion, but any companion would be a solace now. And who else among his acquaintances could take immediate leave of absence for a couple of days?

Paul. Paul had no ties. With his one arm he would not be much use in a rough-house; but a rough-house was not necessarily on the cards, and if they could leave London without being followed it could be disregarded entirely. From all other aspects Paul would be the ideal companion.

Paul received the telephoned invitation with caution. Yes, he was free. He had to be in Exeter on Wednesday, but he had no commitments until then.

'How do we go?' he asked. 'By train?'

'In the Alvis. Trains are out. We shall need transport when we get there.'

'You wouldn't rather we took the Jag?'

'No.' David knew that his blunt refusal was stupid, but he could not help it. The implied slight to his beloved Alvis was too great. 'For one thing, I'm used to the Alvis and I've never driven a Jag. For another . . . ' But he could not think of another, and he ended lamely, 'What's wrong with the Alvis, anyhow?'

'Nothing, dear boy. Don't think I'm trying to crab your lovely motor-car. It's just that I feel she isn't quite me.' Paul hesitated. 'What say we take them both? It would make it easier for me to get to Exeter on Wednesday.'

'O.K., we'll take them both.' It was the only compromise David's stubborn pride in possession would permit. 'I'll ring my uncle to-night and book you a room.'

'And one for my man, dear boy. You're not expecting trouble on the way down, are you? Not that I'd be much of a bodyguard.'

'I'm not expecting trouble at all,' David said. 'It's diplomacy we'll be needing, I hope, not brute force. I've had a bellyful of that this end.'

'Oh? How come?'

David told him. When he mentioned the telephone call Susan had received Paul said, 'They get around, don't they? But to threaten Susan — oh, very vulgar.' After a momentary hesitation he added, 'As a matter of fact they did one on me. I was advised, not very politely, that whither thou went I should not go. Or else!'

David was startled. He was also worried; he had never anticipated the gunman would spread his net so wide. But when, after sincere apologies, he suggested that Paul might prefer to forget about Cornwall, his friend strongly negatived the suggestion. 'No one tells me what I may or may not do,' he said.

The steely edge to his voice took David back ten years. Suddenly he felt estranged and diffident. 'I'm ringing Morgan to let him know about Susan,' he said. 'He may like to keep an eye on her. Do I mention you?'

'Heaven forbid!' The languor was back. 'The prospect of a large bluebottle buzzing around my doorstep fills me with gloom. Besides, I shan't be here.'

David rang Morgan at his home. Like David, the superintendent did not attach great importance to the threat against Susan, but he promised to keep an eye on her. Any lead, no matter how slim, that might conceivably lead him to Bandy was worth considering.

'This chap who tried to stick you,' he said. 'Can you describe him?'

'Not intimately. It was dark, and once I'd collared the brute he had his back to me. On the short side — about five foot seven — slim and wiry, and fast on his feet. Not well up in murder, I'd say. He wasn't so hot with the knife.'

'Don't count on that,' Morgan said. 'He may be more successful next time. And unless you're smart there'll certainly be a next time. Apparently you've reached the point where you're safer dead. Safer for him, that is.'

'It's an encouraging thought.'

'Isn't it? So stop playing the fool and tell me what you've been up to. They don't knife people for nothing. Not even journalists. You must have stumbled on to something. What is it?'

David thought that 'stumbled' was unkind. Yet it was largely true. He had stumbled on the diary, he had stumbled on Lumsden and Wilhelmina. If the police had had his luck, would they have been smarter? Perhaps. Even now, if he were to give them the facts, they would probably beat him to it. They had too many facilities for him to compete.

That, David decided, was unthinkable. He had risked too much to play second fiddle now.

He said blandly, 'I've no idea. I've been ferreting around and talking to a lot of people, but it doesn't seem to have got me far. If Bandy believes otherwise, then maybe I've been warm without knowing it.'

Morgan grunted. 'Maybe. And maybe you'll be warmer still. Now I've news for you. We've found Nora Winstone.'

'Oh!'

It seemed to David that the bottom had dropped out of his world. With Nora Winstone safe under police protection the urgency of his quest had gone. After what she must have suffered at the hands of Bandy and his gang, Nora would have lost her reluctance to talk. And once Morgan had the names of his missing witnesses it would not take him long to find them.

'That's great,' he said, trying to force

enthusiasm into his voice. 'How is she? Have you been able to get anything out of her?'

'Only a bullet,' Morgan told him. 'She's dead.'

12

David finished his packing in a state of rare anger. Five days ago Nora Winstone had meant nothing to him; he had spent just one evening in her company, and had been mildly relieved when it came to an end. Yet since then she had become something of a symbol in his life. He was not sure what the symbol represented — courage, tenacity, loneliness — but it was there, and he had lived with it. In many ways it had made Nora more real, more familiar, than the two people he was seeking.

And now she was dead.

Her death had more than an emotional significance for him. It meant that Bandy no longer needed her, that either with or without her aid he had discovered the identities of the other two witnesses. It meant that David and the gunman were now in direct opposition, which was why, as Morgan had suggested, Bandy had now decided to be rid of him. That decision had been only too clearly demonstrated. Yet there was also a mystery behind it. Bandy might know the identities of the people he was seeking, but how could he know where they had gone? Even had one of his men managed to penetrate to Lumsden's room — and according to the woman he had not — Lumsden's water-colours could not have held the significance for him that they had held for David. So why, after trailing him assiduously (if not very skilfully) for several days, should they seek to eliminate him at the moment when he might unwittingly lead them to the consummation of their search?

There were two possible answers to that question. Either they believed that David was as ignorant as themselves of the Lumsdens' whereabouts, but an interfering menace none the less, or they did not need him to lead them because, from some source with which he was unacquainted, they already knew where they were going.

David hoped fervently that the former

answer was the correct one.

The news of Nora's death had so shattered him that he had forgotten to tell Morgan of Winstone's visit that evening. Perhaps it was as well; it had spared him the lash of Morgan's tongue, and it was no longer important. But one thing was clear. According to the superintendent, Nora had been dead less than twenty-four hours when they found her. Winstone, then, had been telling the truth when he had said that Nora was alive. The blood that had soaked into the carpet of the abandoned Zodiac remained a mystery, but it had not been Nora's.

He was up early the next morning. It had rained heavily during the night, and a thin drizzle was still falling when he went out to the Alvis. He did not anticipate danger at that hour, but he was taking no chances. Opening the front door, he peered cautiously out into the street.

A man stood by the Alvis — a man in a long black raincoat and with a cap pulled over his forehead. He had his back to the house. David was about to retreat into the flat for further observation when he saw the dark woolly hair above the collar, and hesitated. And while he hesitated the man turned.

It was Winstone. He saw David and came eagerly up the steps to meet him.

'You going now?' he asked. 'Let me come with you, man. Please!'

David shook his head. 'I'm sorry. It just isn't on.' He motioned the other into the house. 'But come in for a minute. It's damp out here.'

The black raincoat glistened, the cap was soaking; water dripped on to the carpet. Winstone took a coloured handkerchief from the pocket of his jeans and mopped his face. He said, 'I not been home last night. There was a guy watching the house, and I don't want him following me this morning. Barney give me a bed.'

David did not inquire into Barney's identity. It did not concern him. He said, 'Is that why you want to come with me? To get away from trouble?'

Winstone looked at him. His gaze was expressionless. 'They kill Nora,' he said. 'I see it in the papers.'

'I know,' David said. 'I'm sorry.'

Winstone walked over to the window and stood looking out at the rain, hands sunk in his raincoat pockets. The bulky garment gave him an appearance of breadth, and as David took a last look round the room he paused to consider him. He no longer doubted the man's honesty of purpose. The lie about marriage had been excusable; everything else Winstone had told him had been proved true. In Cornwall there would be Paul; but after last night's attempt at murder it was possible that the journey itself might be hazardous, and on the journey he would be alone. Winstone had good cause to hate Bandy. How he would react to danger was problematical, but if he fought at all at least he would fight on the right side.

If only the man were not what he was — a West Indian, a self-confessed crook, and almost an illiterate — David would not have hesitated. Even so he did not hesitate for long. As he struggled into his raincoat he said shortly, 'O.K., you can tag along. Will you need any gear? We'll be away for a couple of days at least.'

Winstone swung round quickly. His teeth gleamed whitely in a mirthless smile.

'Man, that's fine. That just fine.' He patted the pockets of his raincoat. 'I got all I want. Where we going?'

'Cornwall.' David wondered if he knew where Cornwall was. 'Come on, let's get cracking.'

They took the A30 out of London. The rain cut down their speed. The single wiper operated from the top of the windscreen, and David's immediate vision was poor. There were no side screens; the rain beat in at them, and the hood was sufficiently elderly to have lost much of its tautness, flapping noisily above their heads. But the weather was not David's most urgent problem, although it conspired to confuse it. Even though Bandy might have guessed their destination, he could not be certain of their route; if he wanted to stay with them he would have to follow. The rain and the heavy London traffic called for all David's concentration; he had none to spare for keeping a close watch on the cars behind him. Every now and again a glance into the driving mirror would reveal a car which he thought to have seen there before, and anxiety and doubt would start to crowd him. Then the car would turn off or sweep past or be left behind, and he would breathe freely again. Winstone was little use as a watch-dog. David had told him to keep his eyes peeled for a possible pursuer; but there was no mirror on the near-side wing, and the celluloid rear window in the hood was yellowed and cracked and dangerously opaque. Through it one could see only the blurred outlines of the following cars; to distinguish make or type was impossible. Once or twice Winstone leaned out over the side of the Alvis to glance back, holding tightly on to his cap and gripping his raincoat at the neck. David suspected that this was more in the nature of a formality, a polite concession rather than a serious attempt to identify a possible pursuer.

Despite the rain and the poor visibility they made reasonable time at first. Obsessed by urgency, David drove faster than the conditions warranted, cutting his corners and braking late, with the Alvis responding nobly. Then, approaching Virginia Water, the car ahead of them braked suddenly, and David had to do the same. With a sinking stomach he felt the rear of the Alvis slide away from him into the kerb. While Winstone gripped the side and slid lower in an instinctive act of self-preservation, David took his feet off the controls and steered into the skid, his eyes on the gap ahead. He felt the rear wheels hit the granite sets, saw the gap narrow alarmingly. Then the Alvis straightened out and came under control, the car in front accelerated away, and David knew that the danger was past.

After that their speed dropped.

Before leaving London David had reckoned that by keeping to the A30 he would be in the Exeter area early in the afternoon; even with their reduced speed they should be there between three and four o'clock. Although May was not a peak holiday month, he had heard and read so much about the crowded Exeter bypass that he had decided to avoid it by heading farther north. The Alvis had been designed for an age when traffic flowed more freely; the gear change was stiff, the power unit willing but rough. To keep out of trouble he had intended to fork right after Basingstoke and make for Andover and Wincanton. But somehow he missed the turning. A few miles farther on they drove through Sutton Scotney, and he realized he was still on the A30 and heading for Salisbury.

Annoyed at his mistake, he braked abruptly and pulled in to the side of the road. But he had failed to appreciate how fast the car behind was coming up to him. A green Austin Princess, it swung out with squealing tyres, narrowly missing an oncoming lorry and showering the Alvis and its occupants with spray.

It disappeared round a bend without slackening speed. David said, 'Sorry about that. I should have signalled sooner. But that chap is certainly in a hurry. Now, let's take a look at the map.'

He had hoped earlier that route-finding might be left to his companion. But he had soon found that Winstone was no map-reader; nor, when David tried to explain its complexities to him, had he shown any sign of interest or recognition. Once they were out of London he had slid down in his seat as far as he could, collar up and cap well forward, leaning inward to escape the penetrating rain. It seemed that the English countryside in wet weather was not for him. Had it not been for his occasional comment David would have thought he was asleep.

As David opened the map Winstone slowly pushed himself into a more upright position. Fumbling in a pocket for cigarettes and matches, he said, in his high-pitched voice, 'Man, don't you take no more chances. They say bad luck coming in threes. Maybe we not going to escape so easy from the next one, huh?'

David acknowledged the reproof with a grunt of disdain. He resented the implied criticism of his driving (although recognizing that to some extent it was justified), and he objected to the West Indian's new-found familiarity. If he's going to come the acid with me, he thought angrily, out he goes. I don't have to keep him. He's no help as a navigator, and a dead loss as a companion.

Studying the map, he saw that he had no alternative but to make for Salisbury. A few miles past Wilton a minor road linked the A30 with the Wincanton road. He would branch off there. Traffic was lighter than he had expected, but he was taking no chances with that bypass.

They were in Salisbury by half-past eleven. The Alvis was running well, its exhaust crackling merrily, and David felt more relaxed. There was no sign of pursuit, and he had already forgotten his resentment against his companion. As they pulled up in a stream of traffic at a crossing and waited for the lights to turn to green he said cheerfully, 'We haven't done so badly. Feeling peckish?'

'Man, I'm always that,' Winstone told him, grinning. The rain had eased a little, and he sat more upright now. Although the countryside apparently held no appeal for him, it was otherwise with the towns. David wondered how much he knew of England. Probably he had never been farther from London than Brighton or Southend.

'We'll give it another hour, and then stop for lunch,' David said.

As he spoke he felt the Alvis roll slowly backward. They were on a steep hill, and he tugged at the hand brake, looking anxiously into the driving mirror to see what was behind him. The Alvis stopped rolling, but David's frown did not relax. He said, 'That's funny. That big Austin — the one that nearly cannoned into us outside Sutton Scotney — it's just behind us. The rate he was going, he should be miles ahead by now.'

Winstone did not look round. He said, 'Maybe he stopped for a drink.'

'Maybe,' David agreed. He peered into the mirror again in an attempt to see the Austin's occupants more clearly, but rain blurred his vision. He thought there were two men in front, but he could not be sure. 'We'll give them a clear field if they're going our way. That car can move.'

The Austin was going their way. But the driver made no attempt to overtake.

Outside the town David slowed to a crawl; the Austin kept close behind him, while slower cars swept past. When they were through Wilton and the Austin was still there David started to worry. Was this it? Was this the pursuit he had feared? Well, there was one way to make sure. Little more than a mile ahead, at Barford St Martin, was the minor road that led through Chilmark and Hindon to the A303 and Wincanton. That was where he had planned to turn off. If the Austin followed him his fears would be confirmed.

He nearly missed the turning. It came at a left-hand bend, and he swung the Alvis into it sharply across a stream of traffic coming from the west, leaving behind him a squeal of brakes. Winstone glanced at him quickly and then away, but he said nothing. David knew what he was thinking. He was grateful for the other's restraint, but he too was silent. He was trying to watch both the road ahead and the road astern.

The improvement in the weather had been only temporary. Now the rain was almost torrential, smacking against the wind-screen so fiercely that the wiper was unable to cope. David sat leaning forward, gripping the steering-wheel hard with both hands, his foot heavy on the throttle; he knew that he was driving the car too hard, but his fear of pursuit forced him to accept the implied risk. In her day the old twelve-fifty had been renowned for lightness of handling; now the king-pins and the steering were worn, and with every bump or rut in the road's surface David felt the wheel jerk in his hands. Pottering around London and the home counties, suiting his speed to the conditions, the wear had not been so apparent. It had not bothered him on the A30. But on this twisting road with its uneven surface he began to regret his peremptory rejection of Paul's Jaguar, and the M.O.T. certificate granted by some misguided if well-meaning mechanic to the Alvis's former owner.

Two miles down the minor road, and still no sign of the Austin. David eased his foot on the throttle and his grip on the steering-wheel; with nearly two hundred miles to go he must not put unnecessary strain on the old bus, and he began to take the corners more gently, to watch for the occasional bad patches on the road. Seeking to relax, he stretched his arms and leaned back, but the rain soon forced him forward into the protection of the wind-screen; it beat in at him from the side, and the narrow sloping wings did not entirely ward off the spray thrown up by the front wheels. He wondered how his passenger was enjoying the conditions. Winstone had voiced no complaint, but he looked the picture of misery as he sat huddled low down in his seat, his face almost hidden by collar and cap.

They came to a long, straight stretch with a gentle downhill slope. To the right high grassland cut off the view; to the left, beyond a low blackthorn hedge, the ground fell sharply to a deep valley. Far down the valley David could see a village crouching at the foot of a narrow band of trees that marched in regular procession up to the road. Intent on his driving, he had lost track of distance. Was the village Chilmark? Or would it be Hindon?

And then, abruptly, he lost interest in topography also. Coming up fast behind him was the green Austin Princess.

David put his foot down sharply, and after a momentary pause the engine responded and the car bounced ahead down the incline, the crisp note of the exhaust rising. His action had been instinctive, inspired both by anger and fear. There was no doubt now that he was the quarry. It could be the police who were tailing him, of course, but the odds were on Bandy. Whoever it was, he wanted to be rid of them.

The steering-wheel began to jerk frantically in his grip. A little over a quarter of a mile ahead the road wound to the right, and David knew that he could never take the bend at that speed, that either he must ease his foot from the throttle now or brake hard later. He glanced at the speedometer. The needle was swinging wildly between the fifty and sixty marks, but to David the speed seemed greater. Vaguely he saw the figure beside him slide lower, but he had no attention to spare for Winstone.

He needed it all for the road and the car.

And then, out of the corner of his eye, he saw the long bonnet of the Austin appear beside him. David's heart leapt; was the fellow crazy? Going into the bend together at that speed they wouldn't stand a chance. If something should be coming the other way . . .

He eased his foot from the throttle. Momentum took the Alvis on, and very gently he applied the foot brake; if the madman to his right wanted to overtake, then let him get on with it. Slowly, much too slowly for David, the Austin drew level and began to forge ahead. Through its misted side window David could see the two figures in the front; they sat bolt upright, seemingly completely impassive, unaware of or unmoved by the danger that threatened. He braked harder, felt the vibration on the front wheels, and instantly released the brake. As the vibration diminished he tried again, more gently this time. The Alvis responded evenly to the pressure, and he breathed a sigh of relief.

But relief was short-lived. The speedo-meter needle was dropping — forty, thirty-five, thirty — but the Austin's back wheels were still level with the bonnet of the Alvis. The car was not drawing away as he had anticipated it would. The madman of a driver was braking too!

David's heart leapt, and fear swamped his anger. For the gap between Austin and hedge was narrowing, the driver ahead was cutting in before the cars were clear. It was not a madman with whom he had to contend, but a deliberate killer. This was Bandy or his men, and they were driving him off the road.

As he stamped hard on the foot brake, regardless of consequences, he felt the cars touch. It was only a slight bump, but the result was disastrous. Vaguely he saw the Austin slide towards the right-hand bank and straighten out; then everything was lost save the need to hang on to the steering-wheel and try to bring the Alvis under control. But control was impossible now. With the wheel jerking madly in his hands he felt the near-side front wheel hit the verge to his left. For a moment he thought they were going over. There was a cry from Winstone, and then the Alvis went into a crazy skid. The pointed tail swung round and went on swinging, so that now they were no longer broadside to the road, but were heading diagonally backward down the incline. Briefly the car seemed to straighten out. Then the rear wheels hit the verge with a jarring thud. There came another cry from Winstone as the back of the car reared up, crashed through the hedge, and dropped sickeningly. David had a brief vision of a rain-filled sky and the long bonnet of the Alvis falling back towards him. Then something hit him on the head, and he lost consciousness.

13

Although David thought of his godfather as a confirmed bachelor, the superintendent would not have agreed with him. A disastrous love affair in early manhood had soured him towards matrimony, and to forget it he had flung himself resolutely into his career. But at heart Rees Morgan was a romantic. Although the bitterness had been diuturnal, it had not been endless, and for some years now he had been contemplating marriage with ever-increasing enthusiasm. His problem lay in finding the right mate. Partly because he felt more alert, more youthful, in their company, and partly from a subconscious desire to pick up romance where he had dropped it, he looked for a wife only among the younger women. So far he had found them unresponsive; he had proposed twice in the last five years, and on each occasion the recipient of his proposal had been flattered but reluctant.

He found this disheartening. There were only two more years to his fiftieth birthday, and then even he must begin to regard himself as middle-aged. But he had not abandoned hope. He had merely intensified the search.

He went to see Susan himself. He had met her once or twice with David, and on each occasion had been afflicted by a twinge of envy. She was a little on the young side, perhaps, but mature in many ways. And definitely attractive; plenty of flesh on her bones, the way he liked a woman to be. He had no intention, of course, of competing in love with his own godson, but there was no reason why he should not enjoy the girl's company when duty so dictated.

Susan was in pyjamas and a flowered kimono when she opened the door to him. It was only nine-thirty, and she had been in bed when the bell rang; there had been time to manage little more than a hasty comb through her auburn hair and a mere pretence of decorating her face. But Morgan thought she looked charming. He said so when she apologized.

While she brewed coffee in the tiny kitchen he stood in the doorway and explained the reason for his visit; he preferred to stand, it concealed his bald patch and made his paunch less obvious. Early that morning he had called at David's flat, to find a note for the milkman indicating that the occupier would be away for a couple of days. Where, Morgan asked Susan, had David gone?

Susan glanced up at him quickly, and then down at the simmering milk. He had a charming smile, and he was smiling now. He looked clean and immaculate and strong, and she could not understand why David should dislike him. Nevertheless, he was a policeman, and he was inquiring about David. Despite his physical attraction it behoved her to be wary.

'He was here last night,' she said. 'I had a rather unpleasant telephone call. Didn't he tell you?'

Yes, Morgan said, David had told him. 'We'll go into that later, shall we? Right now I'd like you to answer my question.

Where is David?'

She could not bring herself to lie to him. He was such a nice man. And he was David's godfather; he must have David's best interests at heart, despite David's opinion to the contrary. Pouring the milk into the jug, she said, 'Is that important? It's supposed to be a secret.'

'Very important,' he told her gravely. 'Don't confuse the loyalties, Susan. David is being secretive out of loyalty to his employer; but your loyalty is to David, isn't it? Well, so is mine.' That's a trifle hypocritical, he thought, and yet true in a way. 'Right now I fancy he's in trouble up to his neck. I'd like to be there to pull the young devil out, but I'm stymied unless I know where he is.'

Susan did not think him a hypocrite. His low, musical voice had held just the right touch of embarrassed jocularity overlying the emotion beneath. As he bent to pick up the tray he seemed to tower above her; following him into the living-room she admired his broad back and upright carriage, the smartly cut suit and highly polished shoes. For such a big man his feet were small.

'What makes you say he's in trouble?' she asked, playing for time. She needed to think. David had not asked her to conceal his destination from his godfather, but she suspected that was because he had forgotten; he had been in a great hurry to be gone. Or perhaps it had not occurred to him that Morgan might question her. But that he had not told Morgan himself was proof enough that he did not want him to know, and he would never forgive her if she were to betray him now.

The superintendent watched her pour out the coffee. She made a charming picture, he thought. The kimono did not show off her figure, but he knew that it was well-rounded. Those large, grey-green eyes could play the devil with a man, and he had always been partial to red-heads. How pleasant it would be if . . .

He pulled himself together. Charming picture or no, he had to shock her into talking. She had to believe in David's peril, in his need for police protection, before she would be persuaded into telling what she knew.

He took the proffered cup, helping himself liberally to sugar. 'Had you heard they killed Nora Winstone?' he asked. The quick, horrified look she gave him told him she had not. 'We found her body yesterday. I thought you might have seen it in the late editions.'

She drew the kimono closer about her throat, holding it there. 'Poor thing! How dreadful! The man must be a fiend.'

'He's certainly that.' He stirred the coffee and drank, taking his time. 'And if I know that godson of mine there's something else you haven't heard. One of Bandy's men tried to knife David last night.'

'Oh, no!'

He put the cup back on its saucer and looked down at her pale face. She had a small mobile mouth and a mere button of a nose, but her eyes were troubled and dilated. He could not avoid them; compelling in their intensity, they brought home to him more than any words could have done how sincere and deep was her affection for his godson. It was what he had banked on, and yet the knowledge made him a little sad.

'I'm sorry,' he said. 'But you see now what I mean by trouble. David's stubborn, he thinks he can handle these thugs on his own. Last night's attempt on his life may have hardened that conviction; he got away with it once, and he expects to get away with it again.' He shook his head; not too forcibly, for fear that his jowls might quiver. 'I don't know what he's up to, but obviously this mob doesn't approve. And if they want to rub him out they'll rub him out.' He took a deep breath, expanding his chest. 'So — where is he?'

'In Cornwall,' Susan said, without hesitation. Her doubts had vanished. David might be angry, but his life was more important than his mission. 'He thinks he knows where your missing witnesses have gone.'

'I guessed that much.' Morgan was too good a policeman to betray his satisfaction. 'But Cornwall's a big county. Can you be more specific?'

Susan had been squatting on a cushion.

David had diagnosed oriental ancestry; she was more at ease on the floor than on a chair. Now she got up, the coffee forgotten. Where was it David had said? She had been upset and frightened at the time; Cornwall had stuck in her mind, but the town . . .

'I don't remember,' she said unhappily. 'He told me, but I don't remember.'

She was standing close to him. He put down the empty cup and placed a comforting arm around her shoulders. It was intended as an avuncular gesture, but the feel of her warm soft skin under the silken kimono made him feel suddenly hot around the collar. He could feel the warmth mounting to his cheeks and, not too hastily, he let the arm drop to his side.

'Let's try to jog your memory, then.' He named such Cornish towns as he could recollect. To his chagrin he found they were surprisingly few, and to each of them she shook her head. 'There's an A.A. handbook in the car,' he said, when recollection failed him completely. 'I'll get it. Maybe that'll help.'

She was waiting at the flat door when

he returned. 'I've remembered,' she said excitedly. 'It was Helston. The Helston area, he said.'

Forgetful of his paunch, Morgan perched himself on the edge of a chair and studied the service map, with Susan peering over his shoulder. David had an uncle living in Cornwall, he remembered. Mary's brother — ex-naval type. What the devil was the fellow's name? Not that it mattered. David could hardly have arranged that the missing couple should choose his particular district for a hideout.

Susan drifted over to the coffee-table and began to tell him about the threatening telephone call. Morgan gave her only half his attention; he was busy planning. Surreptitiously he looked up Helston in the handbook. Two hundred and seventy-three miles from London: with everything in its favour the Alvis could hardly take less than eight hours. Even if David had left at dawn (a most unnatural procedure for David) and did the journey nonstop, he could not make Helston before the early afternoon. There was still time in which to act.

'What's the number of David's car?' he asked abruptly. 'Something three seven two five, isn't it? What are the letters?'

She told him. But his question indicated that she had not held his attention, and she said accusingly, 'You haven't been listening.'

He assured her that he had. And it was true; his trained mind had retained the essential while rejecting the inessential. 'I'll have the flat watched for a day or two, although I fancy you're in no danger,' he told her. 'If David really is on the right track they'll be concentrating on him. However, we'll do our best to keep him out of trouble.' He stood up, took one of her plump little hands in both of his, and gave it a friendly squeeze. 'Thanks for the coffee, my dear. And don't worry.'

He did not return to the Yard, but made for the Borough High Street to confer with Nightingale. He had his plan ready by the time he got there. There were only two routes by which David could approach Helston; the A30 to

Redruth, or the A390 to Truro. If the Cornish police could lay on cars at those two points, pick up the Alvis (praise be to Themis that David's choice in cars was so distinctive) and follow it unobtrusively to its destination, the rest should not be too difficult. But it was essential that David should not know he was being followed. It would be completely in character for him to translate his anger into stubborn silence.

Nightingale endorsed the plan. 'You think Wight really is on to something?' he asked.

Morgan shrugged, and helped himself to an acid-drop.

'Could be. I wouldn't bet on it. Between you and me, Warbler, that godson of mine isn't overburdened with brains. He tends to jump to conclusions. That's why we're not tearing down to Cornwall ourselves. Not yet.' He looked at his watch. 'Eleven-thirty. In three or four hours time we might hear something.'

'What if we're needed in a hurry?'

'I'm fixing that. There's a Royal Naval

helicopter station at Helston. That's the way we'll go. Have an acid-drop?'

The inspector declined the offer. He said, 'This may or may not be relevant, but do you remember that big stiff the river boys dug up for us on Wednesday?' Morgan nodded. 'Well, he's been identified. Name of Chapman. Wilfred Chapman. Paint salesman from Birmingham.'

'Chapman.' Morgan frowned. 'That rings a bell. Wasn't he the drunk who caused the schemozzle at the Centipede the night Nora Winstone was kidnapped?'

'The very same. The barman has identified him.' The lines in the inspector's long, egg-shaped face temporarily vanished as he pulled hard at his cheeks with finger and thumb. 'Winstone left first that evening. One would suppose he waited outside for Chapman, and got his revenge by digging a knife into him.'

The superintendent agreed one would suppose just that. 'We'd have had Winstone in the bag by now if that young fool David had played ball,' he said, with some heat.

'There's just one snag,' Nightingale

said. 'According to the barman, Winstone and his pseudo missus arrived by taxi. If Winstone killed Chapman, how did he contrive to transport his corpse nearly four miles to the river?'

14

David was not unconscious for long. He regained his senses to find himself slung across the two bucket seats, with their inside edges pressing hard on the base of his spine and his head jammed against the near side of the car. One foot was caught in the steering-wheel, the other was under the dashboard.

Winstone had disappeared.

It was the hedge that had saved him, David decided. The blackthorn was thickset and sturdy, and laced with wild bramble. It had stoutly resented the Alvis's onslaught, clawing at it to reduce its momentum as it burst through, and finally grabbing and holding the front axle and hubs as an arrester wire catches a plane on a flight-deck. Nevertheless, the car's position was precarious. If the hedge should loose its hold it would plunge backward down the steeply sloping field to the bottom of the valley. There would be nothing to bar its progress.

A wave of pain swept through him. He screwed up his eyes in agony and arched his back, slipping a hand behind him to relieve the pressure, and then breaking into a sweat as he felt the car move. Hardly daring to breathe, he held his body rigid until the movement ceased. The engine had stalled, but a cloud of steam obscured his vision as water from the holed radiator trickled on to the hot metal. There was a strong smell of petrol.

Cautiously he raised his left hand to grip the windscreen support; dangerous as movement might be, he could not remain indefinitely in his present position. He shifted his foot from under the steering-wheel and placed it against the off side of the car, hoping that by keeping an even pressure on both sides he could save himself from sliding over the backs of the bucket seats. But there was nothing more he could do. Each time he tried to lift himself he felt the car rock dangerously, and immediately desisted. He must stay suspended until help arrived.

Drops of moisture rolled down his cheeks, missing his mouth so that he had no way of knowing whether they were rain or blood. The back of his head was sore and there were pains in most of his body, but he decided that no bones were broken. He wondered about Winstone. Winstone must have been flung from the car as it hit the bank. He would be lying out in the field, unconscious or badly injured, perhaps even dead.

Help was not long in arriving, but to David it seemed like an age. A car pulled up on the road, and then another. He could hear excited, agitated voices, a woman's among them. There was the sound of tearing cloth as someone pushed too impetuously through the hedge, and David felt the Alvis slip a little. He braced himself, expecting it to escape from the tenuous clutch of the hedge and slide farther. But his nerves had played him false. The Alvis stayed put. The voices came from his left now, and he called out shakily, 'Over here! I'm stuck!'

Almost immediately faces were peering

down at him; one bearded, one bespec-tacled, one smooth and round and shining. The Beard said heartily, 'Hang on, old man. We'll soon have you out of this,' and insinuated a pair of large, capable hands behind his shoulders. As the hands pressed down into his armpits David said desperately, 'Take it easy, for God's sake! Don't rock the boat. She'll slip.'

'We'll watch it.'

The hands gripped his arms. There were other hands at his ankles. The Beard said cheerfully, 'We've got a rope round the axle. She may wriggle a bit, but she can't slip. Firm as the Rock of Gibraltar.'

David went limp with relief. Gently they lifted him from the Alvis and laid him on a rug on the wet grass, and then stood gazing anxiously down at him. He closed his eyes, allowing new life to flow through him. Then a girl's voice said, 'You shouldn't have moved him. There may be broken bones, internal injuries.' She sounded nearer than the others, and he opened his eyes to find her kneeling beside him, a handkerchief held in readiness above his head.

He smiled at her. She was a pretty girl; dark-haired, with sad oriental eyes in an olive, pear-shaped face. He said weakly, 'I'm all right, thanks,' and started to raise himself on his elbows. The bespectacled young man knelt quickly to support him. 'Thanks,' David said again, and sat up. A few yards to his right a man and a woman were kneeling; another man stood behind them. They had their backs to him, obscuring the object of their attention. All he could see was the top of the dark woolly head. 'Winstone!' he exclaimed. 'How is he?'

'The darkie?' The bearded man grinned reassuringly. 'Sore, I guess. The hedge did its worst, but it wasn't lethal. No serious damage. He could do with a few stitches and some plaster, though. We ought to get him to a doctor.'

It was still raining. David wiped the drops from his face and struggled to his feet. They held him while he tested his legs and felt them firm under him; then they let him go. He walked unsteadily across the sodden, uneven ground to the group on his right, the girl hovering anxiously beside him, her hand at his elbow. She seemed reluctant to leave him.

Winstone was sitting up. His face was a mass of cuts and scratches, from which the blood seeped steadily, despite the gentle staunching from the kneeling woman. There was blood on his hands, a long slit in the black raincoat. One of his sandals was missing, the big toe protruding aggressively from a large hole in his sock. With the scars of his previous injuries still fresh on him he looked a sorry mess.

When he saw David he grinned. He said jerkily, his voice high pitched, 'Man, you sure made the third one a real beaut!'

David grinned back. For the first time since they had met he experienced a feeling akin to amity towards his companion.

'Sorry,' he said. 'But it wasn't my fault.'

'What happened?' the bearded man asked.

David hesitated. He looked at the dark, blood-stained face of the man on the ground. Did Winstone realize what had happened? Perhaps. But for the present it must remain their secret. He did not want to be delayed by questions, by police investigation. He and Winstone had a job to do, and the sooner they got on with it the better.

'A car overtook us. It crowded me a bit, and I got into a skid. Then we hit the bank, and over we went.' He shrugged. 'We could both have been going too fast.'

'Didn't the other chap stop?'

'No. I don't think he realized what had happened.'

There were other cars pulling up on the road, more people pouring through the hedge and crowding round and asking questions. David looked at his watch. It indicated twenty minutes past twelve, and he held it to his ear, thinking that it had stopped. No, it was still ticking evenly. Was it only fifty minutes since they had halted at the traffic lights in Salisbury and he had seen the green Austin behind him? Had so much happened in so short a time?

He tried to plan constructively. Unless they were lucky enough to obtain a lift they could not continue their journey by road. The Alvis had had it; they must go on by train. It was unlikely that they would make Helston that night, but provided they could reach a main line station quickly they should be able to get within striking distance. Salisbury was the obvious choice, and he said to the bearded man, 'How about that doctor? Can you give us a lift back to Salisbury?'

'Well, I could. I was making for Wincanton. But if no one else — '

'We'll take you,' the bespectacled young man broke in. 'My father's a doctor there; we're on our way to have lunch with him. He'll fix your friend up.'

David thanked him. He presumed that the almond-eyed girl was his wife. He said, 'We have to get to Cornwall to-night. I suppose there's a train?'

'Should be. We'll sort that one out later, shall we?'

They retrieved Winstone's missing sandal and helped him to his feet. David was worried about the man. He was shaky on his legs and his eyes looked dazed; it was possible that he was suffering from shock or concussion. I may have to leave him in Salisbury, he thought, and go on without him. He doesn't look as though he could take a long train journey.

While willing hands helped Winstone to the road, David collected his gear from the Alvis. He felt sad at leaving her. The obvious damage was bad enough; buckled wings and battered coachwork, torn hood, petrol tank and radiator holed and leaking, lamps smashed. But there was probably unseen damage that was far more serious; bent axles, perhaps, or a twisted chassis. The rope that held the front axle to a shattered stump of the hedge did not look very secure, but he supposed the anchorage was the best available.

Winstone was already in the car when David reached the road. Others were about to leave, including the bearded man and the woman who had attended to Winstone's injuries. David thanked them both. As he climbed in beside the West Indian he gave a last look at what was visible of the stricken Alvis. It was like deserting a wounded friend. He wondered if they would ever be together again. If so it would probably be an expensive reunion.

The bespectacled young man introduced himself as Cyril Kingsley. He drove fast, hunched behind the wheel, his body swaying backward and forward. On the seat beside him his wife Olive, her dark eyes full of solicitude, kept turning to look at the two men in the back. Winstone had his eyes closed, his dark head resting against the grey upholstery; he had lost his cap, and no one had thought to look for it. There were dark stains on his raincoat, and he dabbed incessantly at his face with a blood-soaked handkerchief, occasionally opening his eyes to find a dry spot in the handkerchief before applying it again to his face.

David had a bump on the back of his head, and his body ached. But he felt surprisingly alert. He said, 'We were lucky to come out of that alive, let alone without serious injury. Particularly Winstone here; his skull must be made of teak. As for me — well, it was just a toss up how long that hedge would hold. It felt pretty dicey.'

'It wasn't,' Kingsley told him. 'She might waggle a bit, but it would have taken a hell of a tug to shift her. You could have climbed out any time you felt like it.'

David felt deflated. The girl said quickly, 'You weren't to know that, of course. It must have been ghastly.'

They were in Salisbury before one o'clock. Dr Kingsley was a kindly little man who oozed energy and efficiency, and he set to work on Winstone immediately. David was relieved to learn that the cuts were superficial, and that no stitches were necessary. But the man had had a nasty shock, the doctor told him, and was suffering from slight concussion. Bed was the place for him.

Winstone at once vetoed the suggestion. Fingering the plaster on his face, he said, 'If Mr Wight going on, then I going with him. No bed for me, Doc. I feeling fine.'

He looks better, David thought. His eyes are more lively, the grey tinge has gone from his skin. Dr Kingsley shrugged. 'It's your body, son. But you won't feel so chirpy in a few hours from now. That I promise.'

While Olive Kingsley made what repairs she could to Winstone's raincoat, David telephoned a garage and the police; impatient of delay, he was relieved to find the latter sympathetic to his desire for haste, a visit to the police-station being obviated by their offer to send an officer to the house. Despite David's professed reluctance to impose on the little man's hospitality, Dr Kingsley insisted on giving them lunch. He was a widower, and his sister was also his housekeeper. Unlike the rest of the family, she did not hide her dislike of sitting down to the same table as a coloured man, and studiously avoided addressing Winstone. David did not entirely blame her. Apart from his colour, the West Indian was an unprepossessing sight. With that jagged scar across his forehead, the still evident wounds inflicted by Bandy and his men, and the injuries he had sustained in the accident, Winstone's face looked like a battlefield that had been fought over many times. Perhaps because he was aware of her disapproval, for most of the meal Winstone was silent. He also ate little. David wondered whether the doctor's promise was already being fulfilled.

It was the doctor who sorted out the timetable for them. The two forty-three from Salisbury would take them direct to Okehampton, arriving there at five thirty-nine. 'There's a stopping train leaves Okehampton for Wadebridge at five fifty-one,' he told David. 'But it's a damned slow journey. Close on two hours. And I don't know how you go from there. You'll probably be stuck at Wadebridge for the night. It's about forty miles from Helston.'

Forty miles was not far, thought David. Paul had expected to be in Pendwara by late afternoon; he might be persuaded to send the Jaguar over to Wadebridge to collect them.

To the police-officer who called after lunch David gave the same account of the accident as he had given to his rescuers. When he mentioned the green Austin the man looked up sharply from his note-book.

'Did you get the number, sir?'

'No. It all happened too quickly.' The policeman's obvious interest told David that the question had been more than purely formal. 'Why?'

'We've been notified that a similar car was stolen from a garage in West Kensington early this morning. I suppose you didn't happen to notice the occupants?'

'Only vaguely. It was pelting with rain, and they had the windows closed. There were two men in front. I think they both wore trilbies, but that's about as far as I can go.'

Cyril Kingsley drove them to the station. His wife came with them. For her own peace of mind, she said; she was worried about Winstone. David thought her all a ministering angel should be; gentle, sympathetic, efficient, and beautiful. And he shared her concern over Winstone. The man looked all in. But when, just before leaving the house, the doctor had insisted that he should retire to bed, Winstone had again refused.

As the train drew out of the station

David closed the window and sank into a corner seat. Winstone had already stretched himself out on the cushions opposite, closing his eyes and completely ignoring the only other occupant of the carriage. To the latter, a middle-aged man in a check suit, David offered apology and an explanation.

The man grunted. 'Speed!' he snapped. 'It's the cause of most accidents. Every one trying to reach their destination before every one else.'

David leaned back in his corner and closed his eyes. The journey to Okehampton was for him a mixture of fantasy and reality. For much of the time he slept, and his dreams were not pleasant; but the waking moments were the more uncomfortable. He was obsessed with guilt. He had had twinges of it ever since he had denied his godfather the diary, but for the most part it had remained dormant. Now, with time on his hands and little to do but think, it reared up like a spectre to confront him. He had boasted to Susan that he was way out in front of the Bandy mob, and at the time he had believed that to be true. He had persuaded himself into believing that only he could know where Lumsden and the girl had gone. Now, very forcibly, he had been shown his mistake. As Morgan had suggested, the gang had not only caught up with him, they were ahead of him. They no longer needed him as a guide, or they would have been content to follow. Now he was just an interfering nuisance, to be eliminated as expeditiously as possible. They had tried to knife him, and, when that had failed, they had ruthlessly run him off the road. One slight consolation remained. Since they had not stopped to inspect the result of their manoeuvre, they would assume that he was either dead or incapacitated, and that whatever it was they intended to do with the Lumsdens when they caught up with them could be done in their own time. They would no longer fear pursuit or interference. Not from him.

The thought did not greatly comfort him. It was no sop to his conscience. As Susan had said, this was not a game he was playing; he was gambling with people's lives. He should have confided in Morgan last night, when it had been made clear to him that he was no longer leading the field. He might even have telephoned him from Salisbury. Instead, he had allowed a selfish desire to be first to outbid his conscience.

Between these moments of truth and self-obloquy he dozed, or gazed out of the window, or read his newspaper. For the first hour Winstone stayed flat on his back, apparently asleep. When they stopped at Yeovil, however, he sat up and announced that he felt better — an announcement which was greeted by a scowl from the check-suited gentleman, as though it were reprehensible. Once, when David awoke from a bout of uneasy slumber, it was to hear Winstone muttering a string of imprecations; he was staring out of the window, a deep scowl on his dark, battered face, his fist thumping up and down on his knee. David supposed he was cursing Bandy and all his works — a sentiment with which he wholeheartedly concurred.

They were ten minutes late at Okehampton, but in time to catch the Wadebridge train. It was, as Dr Kingsley had predicted, a seemingly interminable journey. They shared a carriage with a married couple and their progeny of four, the two youngest of whom were never still, and comparatively silent only when they were sucking sweets. By the time they reached Wadebridge David was tired and depressed; reaction from the accident had begun to set in, and without bothering to inquire if there were a train to take them further he made for a telephone kiosk. If Paul could not arrange to collect them they would stay put for the night. He had had enough of trains.

He had no luck with Paul. He spent some time trying to raise the inn, only to learn from the supervisor that there had been a violent storm in south Cornwall and that many of the lines were down.

'Well, that's that,' he told Winstone. 'Let's go find ourselves a bed for the night.'

He had been through Wadebridge

several times, and it had never aroused enthusiasm in him. It did not arouse it now. As they trudged down Molesworth Street looking for an hotel it occurred to him that he was about to be confronted by yet another obstacle; the colour bar. Winstone thought so too. He said, 'Man, this not going to be easy. They not liking coloured men in hotels. I know.'

Their pessimism was unjustified. At the first hotel they tried there were vacant rooms and no firm colour bar; the receptionist was startled more by the West Indian's obvious injuries than by his dark skin. When David told her of the accident she was even sympathetic. They were a little late for dinner, she said, but there was soup and cold ham and salad if they were hungry.

They went to bed immediately after the meal. As he lay waiting for sleep to come David had the comforting thought that, if he were beset by enemies, at least there were friendly people around. The Kingsleys, the receptionist, Paul waiting for him at Pendwara — even Winstone. He knew that he could never learn to like the West

Indian, but at least he could trust him. The accident had dispelled the last vestige of doubt. If Winstone had been one of Bandy's men there would have been no accident. Not with Winstone in the car. They would have managed it some other way.

There was also Morgan. Despite the attack of conscience in the train he still had not telephoned Morgan. And he would not telephone him on the morrow; he knew that. He had accepted a challenge, and each fresh obstacle merely stiffened his determination to succeed. Irrespective of right or wrong, this was something he had to do.

I suppose Susan is right, he thought wryly, with unusual insight. I *am* selfish and stubborn. But at least I'm honest about it.

★ ★ ★

Fingers drumming impatiently on the desk, the inevitable acid-drop on his tongue, Morgan's eyes were unblinking as he stared fixedly at the inspector's face. It was as though he were willing his luck to change.

'Well?' he demanded, as Nightingale removed the telephone receiver from his ear. 'Any news?'

Nightingale shook his head. 'They want to know if the cars can come off watch.'

'Still no sign of him?'

'None. They're positive he hasn't passed through Redruth or Truro.'

The superintendent looked at his watch. 'Ten o'clock. Either that rattler of his has broken down or he's met with an accident. Or . . . ' He frowned. 'Ask them to hang on for another hour and then give us a buzz.'

'Or what?' asked Nightingale, when he had transmitted the message.

'It's just possible that the young devil has more nous that I gave him credit for. He knew I'd be getting in touch with his girlfriend about that telephone call. What if he deliberately misled me through her?'

'You mean Cornwall could be a blind?'

'I mean just that. The girl asks where he's off to, and he tells her the first place that comes into his head; he has an uncle lives there. Or maybe he says Cornwall because it's a long way off. And he doesn't tell her to keep her trap shut, because it would suit his purpose should she decide to pass the information on to me.' Morgan's teeth snapped together, cracking what remained of the acid-drop. He banged his fist on the desk in mounting anger. 'By Themis! If he's deliberately laid us a false trail, Warbler, I'll crack down so hard on the young devil he'll wonder what hit him.'

Inspector Nightingale's face was impassive, but inwardly he was amused. As a policeman he was no stranger to false trails; neither, he knew, was Rees Morgan. It was the suspicion that his own incursion into guile had been inferior to his young godson's that had infuriated the superintendent.

'So where do we go from here?' he asked.

Morgan stretched, flexing the muscles of his arms.

'Back to routine. What else have we?' His voice was calm again. 'But check on any accident involving an Alvis between here and the West. Are your chaps still flogging the Rotherhithe area?' Nightingale nodded. 'How's the night watchman?'

'I saw him on Saturday. Still weak, but he'll make it.'

'Have another go at him in the morning. Maybe his memory will increase with his strength.' Morgan fumbled for an acid-drop, found the bag empty, and crumpled it into a ball. 'Have you ever felt murderously inclined yourself, Warbler?'

'Occasionally. I've always managed to resist the inclination.'

'So have I. But when I think of that godson of mine . . . ' He hurled the paper ball into the waste basket and stood up. 'Well, I just hope I can continue to resist it.'

15

The line to Pendwara was still out of
order the next morning, and David was
confronted with yet another worry — lack
of money. He had not budgeted for train
fares and hotel bills; by the time he had
settled the latter he and Winstone had less
than two pounds between them. Winstone
had been no help at all; David had had to
pay for both. It surprised him that
anyone, even an uneducated West Indian,
should set out on a long journey with an
empty note-case; but to Winstone it
apparently seemed perfectly natural. He
had spent the previous night at Barney's,
he said; and since he had known David
was to make an early start he had not
bothered to return home first to collect
his money.

There was more than enough in the
kitty to pay their fares to Helston, but
David was through with trains. Snowball
had told him he lacked initiative; now was

the time to prove him wrong, and at the old man's expense. The cross-country journey to Pendwara would be considerably quicker by car than by rail and bus, and time was important. And he would need to be mobile when he got there. There was no guarantee that Paul had not changed his mind or been delayed, and he could not borrow his uncle's ancient Wolseley. That was insured for one driver only.

The first garage he tried did not loan out cars on hire, but the second was more accommodating. The proprietor, a middle-aged Cornishman with a lined face and a greasy cap stuck flatly on top of his grizzled hair, said richly, 'Up to Helston, eh? And how long would you be wanting she for?' Two or three days, David told him. Whereupon the man led the way to a black Morris Traveller of recent vintage, slapped a heavy, grimy hand on the bonnet, and informed him that for a deposit of ten pounds and a daily charge of forty shillings the car was his.

Now for it, thought David. Trying to

sound casual, he said, 'There's just one snag. I don't happen to have the money on me, and I've left my cheque-book at home. Can you waive the deposit? I can just about manage the first day's hire in advance, if that will help.'

The man took it more calmly than David had expected, but the answer was a firm no. 'I don't like for to be awkward,' he said, removing his hand from the bonnet to leave a hazy imprint on the cellulose, 'but 'tisn't possible, m'dear.'

David had not expected that it would be; not on the bald facts he had given. He launched into his story — that he was a reporter on an urgent assignment, that his car had been wrecked in an accident, and that unexpected fares and hotel bills had left him short of cash. 'You don't have to take my word for it,' he said, producing the copy of *Topical Truths* he had bought on the way from the hotel. 'Ring my editor — I'll pay for the call — and check with him. He'll guarantee the money.' He grinned knowingly. 'Add a few bob to the daily rate for your trouble. The magazine can stand it.'

The man was impressed; it was the sight of the printed word that convinced him, David thought. Without further ado he went into the office, checked the number David had given him with the number printed in the magazine, and put through the call. Then he handed the receiver to David.

''Tis best you speak to he first, m'dear,' he said, lifting the cap to scratch his head and then replacing it. 'I'll have a word with him when you're done.'

Snowball was in his irritable mood. 'Wadebridge?' he bellowed. (Snowball always bellowed on a long-distance call. It was odd, thought David, that a man reared on the telephone system should so misuse it.) 'Where the hell's that? I thought you were making for Cornwall.'

Patiently David explained that Wadebridge was in the right county but on the wrong side of it. He also explained how he came to be there. The snort that greeted this almost shattered his eardrum.

'Accident? You feckless, incompetent young — '

'I'm calling it an accident,' David said,

keeping his temper. 'In fact it was a deliberate attempt to run me off the road.' He saw interest quicken on the garage proprietor's face. 'You can guess who was responsible. But now I'm stuck for cash. I need a car for a few days, and I need it quick. There's a chap here ready to oblige provided you guarantee me. How about it?'

'Put him on.'

David handed over the receiver, reflecting that for all his faults Snowball was no procrastinator; he might not like the situation, but he would not avoid it. He grinned back at the man as the latter winked at him and raised his price to fifty shillings a day. The grin broadened as the man hastily removed the receiver an inch or two from his ear.

But it worked. ''Tis all right,' the man told him, replacing the receiver on its cradle and massaging his ear. He jerked a thumb at the Morris. 'Shall I fill she up with petrol? He said for to put it on the bill.'

As he drove out of the garage to pick up Winstone David decided that the day had made an auspicious start. He hoped the rest of it would go as well.

*   *   *

Pendwara is a small hamlet on the Lizard peninsula, tucked away on the western slope of the moor, with the main Helston road to the east and the secondary road through Cory, Poldhu, and Mullion to the west. The Falcon is its only inn; two storeyed and low ceilinged, and with a pleasant garden at the back, it is a long rambling building of local stone abutting directly on to the lane that leads down to Poldhu. Rupert Ellington, its proprietor, a retired Lieutenant-Commander in the Royal Navy and David's uncle, will tell you that it dates from the sixteenth century, but in fact the present building is less than a hundred years old; the original building was destroyed by fire. Ellington is a pale-faced man of forty-four, with deep-set eyes and a flat nose, and a thick crop of black hair that flows down the sides of his face to the magnificent beard adorning the jutting jaw and chin. Some of his tastes, such as his preference for Gauloise cigarettes and home-made punch, are not approved of by his wife Angela. But she is a timid little woman, indefatigable but content to remain in the background, and she keeps most of her opinions to herself.

David and Winstone arrived at the Falcon at midday, to be greeted by the Ellingtons with relief and some surprise. 'You didn't mention there'd be two of you,' the Commander said, drawing David aside. 'Who's your coloured friend?'

'He isn't a friend. He just tagged along. You can fix him up, can't you? No colour bar here?'

'We can fix him,' his uncle said, with no great show of enthusiasm. 'What kept you, David? We expected you yesterday. Your friend Brenn-Taylor has been doing his nut.'

Before David could reply Paul came out of the saloon bar. He stopped short in surprise when he saw them, then walked slowly forward to thump his friend on the back.

'So you made it, dear boy. A trifle off schedule, perhaps, but never mind. Punctuality can be such a dreary virtue.' For the first time he caught sight of Winstone, who stood apart from the others regarding them with uneasy suspicion. 'Merciful heavens! Where did he come from?'

'I brought him,' David said, nettled. 'He's Nora Winstone's husband.'

He did not think it necessary to explain the exact relationship.

Paul continued to stare at the man. He was clearly startled. 'In need of repair, isn't he?' He frowned. 'I've seen him somewhere before. Sure of it. In better condition, too.'

'Probably. He plays the trumpet at the Seventy-Seven.'

In accounting for his late arrival David again implied that the accident had been fortuitous. He knew that his uncle would have to be told at least something of his mission, and the little knowledge Paul already had would undoubtedly have whetted his appetite for more. But their curiosity must wait. Right now he needed a drink.

The bar was long and narrow. Some half-dozen men, all obviously locals, sat on wooden benches against the wall; they eyed the newcomers with casual interest. But David was not concerned with them. His attention was immediately arrested by the two men who stood at the far end of the bar. Both wore light-coloured sweaters above dark, narrow trousers and rope-soled plimsolls; both had close-cropped hair and white, untanned faces. They were so clearly alien to the district that inevitably David was suspicious. He stopped Paul with a hand on his arm.

'When did those two arrive?' he asked, in a low voice.

Paul nodded to the two men, who returned his greeting with a casual wave of the hand.

'Saturday, according to your uncle. Why? Think they mean trouble? They seem harmless enough to me. Come and meet them.'

Their voices proclaimed them cockneys, but they greeted David with reserve unusual in a cockney. Dunn, the shorter of the two, asked him to have a drink. He had a long, pointed chin, on which the bristles suggested that he had not shaved recently. Grey eyes protruded from under almost lashless lids, his nose was clean-cut and narrow; he had a small mouth, thin lipped and with white, even teeth. But it was his hands that caught the eye. They were long and slender and restless; he used them in the Italian fashion, as a substitute for words as well as a complement to them. The nails were well-manicured, their polish suggesting that he used varnish.

David declined the drink; his uncle had already attended to his need. But his suspicions were lulled; these could not be Bandy's men. The Lumsdens, if they were here, would have arrived on the Sunday. These men had come the day before.

'Staying long?' he asked.

'Just a week,' Dunn told him. He had a sharp, incisive voice. 'And you?'

'Two or three days. Can't get away for more.'

The other man, Baker, wore thick-rimmed spectacles. He was bigger and looked tougher than Dunn, and his pale skin was coarser, with mottled patches on the cheeks. His nose was flat and spread, and the drooping mouth gave him a morose expression.

'Know this part well?' he asked.

David told him he knew it extremely well.

Paul finished his pink gin and ordered another, with a beer for David and the two visitors. 'Where's your coloured friend?' he asked. 'Doesn't he drink?' David shrugged; he was a little tired of Winstone; the man had become an encumbrance. Paul said, 'I'll get him. He looked as though he needed a bracer, poor devil.'

David walked to the other end of the bar and began to drop pennies into an ancient mechanical device whereby a rampant, moth-eaten bear was induced to clash a pair of cymbals. Interpreting the signal, his uncle joined him.

'I'm looking for a camping and caravan site run by a woman,' David said. 'Her name could be Lumsden. Know it?'

His uncle nodded. 'Other side of the

Poldhu road. Small place, not very successful. But Miss Lumsden's a nice person.'

'Have you met Robert, her nephew?'

The Commander shook his head. He had a habit of stroking his beard upward from under his chin with the back of his hand, so that it projected fiercely. He did it now. 'What's afoot, David?' he asked. 'This isn't just a social call, is it? What's the game?'

'No game,' David said. 'Just a spot of thuggery.'

Very briefly he gave his uncle the facts. They were apart from the others, but even if he were overheard it would not greatly matter. The need for secrecy was almost gone; with luck his mission should be accomplished before the afternoon was out. The Commander listened calmly to what he had to say. When David had finished he said, 'There's been no trouble here so far. If the Lumsdens are around they're still breathing. What do you do with them when you find them?'

'Get their story and hand them over to the police.'

His uncle lit another Gauloise. 'Why not take the police to them?'

The faint chatter in the room died. David turned. Paul had come into the room with Winstone, and all eyes were focused on the West Indian. Baker and Dunn seemed particularly startled. That surprised David. A coloured man should be no novelty to a cockney. But then right now colour was not Winstone's primary claim to unconformity. Because of the damage to his face he had temporarily discontinued shaving. Even his chevron of a moustache was untrimmed, so that his full lips, still slightly swollen, were framed by an irregular oval of hair and bristle. The jagged scar on the high domed forehead was intersected by smaller, fresher scars, and above the right temple a large piece of sticking plaster had invaded the black mass of his hair. He still wore the tight jeans and the black sweater and rope sandals in which he had started the journey. One of the sandals, the one that had been torn off in the accident, had lost a strap and was tied with string.

He stood by the door, not following

Paul to the bar, non-plussed by their stares. David stared too. He had become so accustomed to the man's colour and battered face that, alone with him, they had seemed in no way remarkable. Now, with the others regarding him as though he were a curiosity, he found himself doing the same.

Annoyed that he could be so easily influenced, he said heartily, 'Hello, there! Come and have a drink.'

The three of them — David, Paul, and Winstone — lunched at the same table. Over the meal David explained more fully why they were there and what he intended to do. It was simple enough. So simple that Paul's dark eyebrows lifted in surprise, and he said drily, 'Is that all that happens? You drift over to the camp, politely ask the Lumsdens for their story, and then the three of you pile into the car and away to a *tête-à-tête* with the police at Helston? Because if so I fail to see where Winstone and I come in. Winstone at least has had his share of excitement. Where is mine?'

David suspected the complaint had not

been made seriously; but, as he explained, excitement of the kind Paul envisaged was the last thing he wanted. Winstone was there under sufferance, Paul as an insurance. If everything went smoothly, if Bandy did not interfere, Paul would not be needed. But if things went wrong . . .

'Where are Dunn and Baker?' he asked.

Paul looked round the room and shrugged; they had it to themselves. Winstone said, 'I hear them say they going for a walk before lunch. They tell your uncle they may be late.'

David would have accepted the explanation had it not seemed so improbable. The two men had had the whole morning for their walk, they had apparently been comfortably settled in the bar when he arrived. Why should they suddenly decide to go out less than half an hour before lunch?

'Why not?' asked Paul, when David put the question. 'On holiday one obeys one's impulses, not the clock. That's what makes it a holiday. Come off it, dear boy. You're not still suspicious of those two characters, are you?'

'I don't know.'

It was true. He did not know. There was no reason to suspect Dunn and Baker, since they could not have followed the Lumsdens to Pendwara. Yet the sudden calm after the excitement and dangers of the previous day made him uneasy. It was all wrong. That he himself was no longer being hounded was understandable; Bandy and his gang believed that his corpse or his mangled body was still in Wiltshire. But if his uncle was right they had made no move towards the Lumsdens. Why? What were they waiting for?

'Search me, dear boy,' Paul said. 'You know the gentleman better than I do. I suppose you are quite sure you have come to the right place?'

Was he sure? Lumsden had an aunt in Pendwara, had spent his holidays there; but wasn't it possible that he had chosen to take his new wife somewhere else, somewhere where he was unknown and could be traced less easily? The accident to the Alvis had indicated to David that he had guessed correctly; why else should

Bandy try to stop him? But he realized now that that had been a false assumption. It indicated only that he had been headed in the right direction. It did not confirm Pendwara as the right destination.

Half-way through the sweet he could stand the suspense no longer. Pushing his plate away, he stood up.

'I'm going down to the camp,' he announced brusquely.

'Now?' Paul's spoon paused half-way to his mouth. 'But you haven't finished. First things first, dear boy. This is excellent apple pie.'

Paul could be irritating at times, thought David; he overdid the badinage. At school, and in their meetings since, life had not been sufficiently serious for that to grate. Now it was.

'I didn't come here to eat apple pie,' he said stiffly.

The spoon completed its journey. Swallowing hastily, Paul said, 'Your aunt will be disappointed. It's a reflection on her cooking.' And then, in a more serious tone, 'Like me to come with you?'

David declined the offer. Lumsden might be more willing to talk if he went alone and there were no witnesses. But Paul followed him into the hall. As they stood talking Dunn and Baker came in from their walk and went into the dining-room after a casual greeting. David said, 'Keep an eye on those two. I don't trust them. They don't look right here.'

Paul said drily, 'If I may say so, neither does your friend Winstone.'

The track to the camp site was primitive. An attempt had been made to fill the ruts and hollows with rubble, but it was impossible to drive at much more than walking speed. David imagined Snowball's rage should the cost of a broken axle be added to the hire charge, and when he came to a comparatively level clearing at the side of the track he abandoned the Morris and proceeded on foot.

The camp lay on a slope that stretched upward to the cliffs some four hundred yards away. A long, rectangular field, fenced with cattle wire, it had a small, tin-roofed building of concrete in one of the seaward corners and crudely constructed latrines in the other. Most of the caravans spaced evenly round the perimeter had cars parked beside them and were obviously migratory, but one had an appearance of greater permanence. Metal supports on a hard standing had replaced the wheels, there was a small fenced garden. This, David decided, would be Miss Lumsden's home.

He picked his way across the rutted quagmire that the previous day's rain had made of the entrance, and rapped on the pale-blue door. But no one answered his knock, and he went on to the next caravan, where three children were playing tag and a man and a woman lazed in gaily striped deck-chairs, the sun glinting on the man's bald head.

Then he saw Lumsden; there was no mistaking that curly, carroty hair. Dressed only in a pair of shorts and plimsolls and carrying a pail, Lumsden came down the steps of a small yellow caravan on the far side of the field and half-walked, half-trotted towards a standpipe near the tin-roofed building. David, relieved that his premonitions of disaster or mistake had been wrong, strolled to join him. There was no hurry now.

Lumsden was bending over the pail, his hand on the tap. His back was white and dotted with pimples, his body flabby. When David spoke his name he half turned, then screwed up the tap before straightening.

'So you finally got the message, did you?' Lumsden said. David stared at him, uncomprehending. 'I mean, you guessed I'd be here. Didn't you say your uncle kept a pub in Pendwara?' David nodded. 'All right. Now what?'

It was not quite the greeting David had anticipated. Surprise, anger, fear — yes. But not this somewhat petulant toleration. Had Lumsden actually been expecting him?

'Did you get my note?' he asked.

'All that baloney about my being in danger? That I did.' He gave a little grunt that was almost, but not quite, a laugh. 'You've been reading too many of your own stories, Mr Wight. I'm in no danger.'

'And your wife?' David asked quietly. 'Is she of the same opinion?'

Lumsden had stooped to lift the pail. He straightened at the question.

'You know I'm married, eh?' A scowl spoilt the engagingly freckled face. 'Get around, don't you? Well, you've made your point. But it's up to me to take it or leave it, and I choose to leave it. So how about laying off me and my affairs and going some place else? I'd like to enjoy my honeymoon.'

David struggled to control his temper.

'I'm trying to see that you do. Only that doesn't happen to be my main purpose. I dislike to see anyone get away with murder.'

'Speaking figuratively, of course.'

'Speaking literally. You should know that. You and your wife were there.'

Lumsden blinked furiously, wetting his lips with his tongue. David noticed how red were his lips and how pale his eyebrows. The scowl was still there, but he sounded more resigned than angry when he spoke.

'So that's it. Well, what is it you want? I

suppose I'll have to listen.'

It was something that he had not denied his presence in Rotherhithe Street that Saturday night. But the conditions were not ideal for persuasion. David would have preferred the sitting-room of the Falcon rather than a damp field with a pail of water between them. But he did his best. He wasted few words on the initial tragedy; Lumsden would know more than he of the murder of Constable Dyerson. He told him about Bandy, and how Winstone had been beaten up and Nora murdered. He told him of his own part in the affair and of the two attempts on his life, stressing his conviction that Bandy knew where the couple were in hiding and was determined to get them. As he talked he watched Lumsden's face, trying to gauge the effect his words were having. There was little evidence of fear; just a twitch of the lips and a narrowing of the eyes at the mention of Nora Winstone's death. For the most part he looked incredulous or bewildered. He did not interrupt, but he was never completely still; his hands were fiddling with the tap or hitching up his shorts or jingling the coins in his pocket. When David offered him a cigarette he took it and accepted a light without thanks; he drew on it continuously without inhaling, which seemed to indicate that he was not completely at ease. Yet David was sure he did not realize his danger. Perhaps he suspected that here was just an eager beaver of a reporter, out to get a story and willing to distort the truth to get it. He would have no confirmation of David's claims. If he had been out of touch with the news since leaving Rotherhithe he might even doubt that Nora was dead.

There was a short silence while the two men stared at each other. David said desperately, 'Damn it, man, don't you believe me?'

Lumsden shrugged. 'Why should I? It's more than a week since that copper was shot. If they were going to kill us they'd have done it days ago.'

'They didn't know who you were.'

'Then how do they know now? Who told them?'

There was no positive answer to that. Only theory. And theory would stand no chance with Lumsden in his present mood. Yet it seemed incredible that any man could receive such information so calmly. Even though he doubted its accuracy, surely he would not dismiss it out of hand? Particularly when he had actually seen murder committed.

There was something strange here. David said, 'If you doubt my word why did you scuttle down here as soon as you got my note?'

Lumsden frowned. 'I didn't scuttle. I told you, we're on our honeymoon. Your note had nothing to do with it.'

'Why didn't you tell the Einsdorps?' David persisted. 'Why all the secrecy?'

'Because I didn't want trouble with Wilhelmina's old man. He doesn't like me.'

David reflected that Mr Einsdorp was in no condition or place to cause trouble. But he was getting nowhere; a new approach was needed. He wished he could talk to the girl; she might be more awake to the danger, more easily frightened. No doubt Lumsden appreciated that — which was why they were still standing by the standpipe instead of sitting in the comfort of the caravan.

'All right,' he said. 'Ignore the danger to yourself and your wife if you wish. But you can't escape from facts. That copper was murdered, and you saw it happen. You can kid yourself that the murderers aren't interested in you, but you know damn well the police are. You're a vital witness.'

'But I'm not.' For the first time he was vehement. 'I was there, but I didn't see the actual shooting. I was looking the other way.' There was a slight smirk on his freckled face as he added, 'We had something else to think about.'

David stared at him, incredulous. That most certainly was a lie. According to Nora there had been the noisy clanging of the yard doors, the sound of the van's engine, the policeman's pounding feet, the sharp interchange of words between him and Bandy before the shot was fired. It was impossible that the couple could have stood only a few yards away from so much noise and drama and have seen nothing, no matter how ardent their love-making. Yet why should Lumsden lie now? To Bandy, yes — but why now? There was only one answer to that, and he said, 'Is that why you did not offer yourself as a witness?'

'That's right,' Lumsden agreed eagerly. 'What was the use? I could identify no one. Why stick my neck out?'

So he had recognized the possible danger once. What had happened to blind him to it now? 'And your wife? Did she see the shooting?'

'I don't know,' Lumsden said.

That was as obvious a lie as the other. Puzzled, David said, 'May I talk to her? It's a question that has to be answered.'

'No.' For the first time there was a hint of fear on the man's face. His grey eyes were wide, his mouth open. But he recovered quickly. He said, 'I'll not have you messing up our honeymoon.'

David decided it was time to get tough. Persuasion and argument were getting him nowhere.

'You've no choice, Lumsden. No

choice at all. If I don't question her the police will. Come to that, they'll question her anyway. You too.'

There was a little bunch of gingery hair on Lumsden's pale chest, damp with his sweat. He took a hand from his pocket and began to twirl the hairs mechanically between his fingers into a thicker and darker spike, his eyes fixed on the yellow caravan. He said slowly, 'The police know nothing about us.'

'I'm making it my business to see that they do,' David told him, delighting in the other's discomfiture.

A round ball of a woman came down the steps of the nearest caravan and waddled over to them with a canvas bucket. Lumsden moved his pail from under the tap, and the two men stood silent while the woman filled hers. She seemed to sense the tension between them, for after a cheery greeting and a gay comment on the weather she gave a quick look at their faces and said no more.

Lumsden lit a cigarette without offering one to David and watched the woman until she was half-way back to the caravan. Still watching her, he said tonelessly, 'What do you want me to do?'

David took a deep breath.

'First, I'd like a few words with your wife. Then I want you both to come with me to Helston Police Station. They'll want statements, I expect, and they may ask you to wait while the officer in charge of the case can get down from London to see you. And lastly, I want your signature to a contract giving my magazine the exclusive rights to your story. Your wife's, too, of course.'

'For free?'

'Let's say a hundred quid as an option. We'll bump it up if you can impress us.'

A cloud crept across the sky, obscuring the sun. As its shadow swept over the two men Lumsden shivered and crossed his arms over his bare chest. It was a pity, thought David, that the story should end so tamely after such a dramatic opening. He wished neither Wilhelmina nor her husband harm. Nevertheless . . .

Lumsden said nervously, 'I don't seem to have much choice, do I? All right. But on one condition. We came down here Sunday and it rained all yesterday. This is our first drop of fine weather, and we're all set to go on a picnic this afternoon. My wife's preparing for it now; she's been looking forward to it all morning, and I'm damned if I'm going to disappoint her. It may be our last chance once the cops take over.' David frowned, shaking his head. 'You've met my wife; you know it won't be easy for her. I've got to prepare her, and the picnic would give me the opportunity to do that.'

It was difficult to refuse. Lumsden was right in saying it would not be easy for the girl. And since Bandy seemed either to have lost the scent or abandoned the chase what harm could result?

'Where's the picnic to be?' David asked.

'In one of the coves. Poldhu, I expect.' The pale eyes narrowed. 'You weren't thinking of following us, were you?'

'You can have your afternoon,' David told him. He felt good. Power such as this was a tonic. 'I won't intrude. What time will you be back?'

Lumsden looked at his wrist-watch. 'We shan't get away before two-thirty. Some time after six, I imagine.'

'I'll be waiting,' David told him.

His step was light as he walked back to the car. The scoop might not have the dramatic quality he had expected, but it was certainly a scoop. He had unearthed and would be handing over to the police the vital witnesses for whom they had searched in vain; and although Lumsden might protest that he and his wife were merely on their honeymoon and had not fled in terror, no doubt a more sensational interpretation could be made. Wilhelmina herself, with her dramatic and tragic little life, would make excellent material. So too would her marriage. It would be just the stuff for the readers of *Topical Truths*.

He had almost reached the Morris when a motor cycle came bumping slowly up the track from the road. Two men sat astride it; in shorts and brightly coloured T-shirts, they looked typical campers on holiday. David, exuberant with success, hailed them cheerfully. The driver kept his eyes on the track, his hands firm on the controls, his bare knees pressed into the tank; but the pillion rider acknowledged the greeting with a brief grin. He sat close behind the driver, his hands on the other's waist.

It was the sight of his right hand that chilled David's exuberance. The top of one of the fingers was missing.

16

Paul drew on his cigarette and flicked it with his fingers; the carpet to his right was grey with ash. Then he lay back and gazed at the ceiling through half-closed lids, one leg cocked indolently over the arm of his chair.

'You're too jumpy, dear boy,' he drawled. 'There must be scores of johnnies who have lost a finger. Besides, you say this one was minus on the right; according to Winstone it should have been the left. If he's one of the mob, that is — which he obviously isn't.'

'Winstone could be wrong. It's not easy to tell right from left when you're having the daylights knocked out of you.' David glanced round the sunlit lounge and out at the garden. Despite the breeze that had sprung up it looked peaceful and pleasantly warm outside. 'Where the hell has he got to?'

Paul sighed resignedly. 'You may

remember that when you left so abruptly during lunch Dunn and Baker were the current suspects. You said to keep an eye on them, and that's what he's doing.' He blew a perfect smoke ring and watched it soar and hover and gradually vanish. 'If they're off on a long hike he may be cursing you roundly. Winstone didn't strike me as the athletic type.' Another ring drifted slowly upward. 'I feel for the poor devil.'

David looked at his watch. A quarter to three. The Lumsdens were unlikely to come to much harm in the camp or on the beach; it was only if they hid themselves away among the rocks or on the cliffs, as honeymooners were wont to do, that Bandy would be able to strike. When he had seen that mutilated right hand he had wanted to return to the camp and warn Lumsden; only the knowledge that his warning would be disregarded had stopped him. So he had hurried back to the inn to check with Winstone, to find that the West Indian had gone out on the heels of Dunn and Baker.

It was typical of Paul to send Winstone instead of going himself, David reflected. The true prefect reaction. He stopped biting his nails and heaved himself out of the chair.

'We can't just sit,' he said. 'We've got to do something.'

'Such as what? I thought you promised Lumsden not to interfere in his post-prandial marital pleasures.'

David turned from the window. 'You don't know this mob as I do, Paul. They're thorough and they're ruthless; if they want the Lumsdens they'll get them. And they must want them. Sooner or later the police will uncover a working lead, but they'll need the Lumsdens' evidence for a conviction. Bandy must know that.' He passed an impatient hand through the unruly thickness of his hair. 'I'm only surprised that they haven't acted already. They're not the waiting kind.'

Paul stretched his one arm, unhooked his leg, and slowly eased himself from the chair. He stood moving his feet up and down, as though trying to obtain a proper balance.

'Neither are you, dear boy. All right, let's have some action. I'm not given to brilliant ideas at this time of day, but we could drive down to Mullion or Poldhu or wherever it is they've gone, and indulge in a little discreet snooping. No need to interfere unless circumstances demand. Will that satisfy your restless spirit?'

David welcomed the suggestion. They might not find the Lumsdens, but any action was better than none.

'We'll try Poldhu,' he said.

They parked the car among the sand dunes at the head of the cove. The tide was coming in and the wind had freshened. There were few bathers, but small groups of holidaymakers sat against the rocks while children paddled or dug castles in the sand. The huge masses of boulders that struck out to sea on either side of the cove were dotted with people, and at David's suggestion they split up, Paul taking the southern side, and David climbing the track that led to the northern point; it was from the north that the Lumsdens would have come had they walked over from the camp. Paul was sure he would have no difficulty in recognizing their quarry from David's description. 'Male carrots and a twitching female face,' he said. 'I can't miss.'

They had intended only a cursory search, but David was back at the car even sooner than he had anticipated. The cliff-top would have been too breezy for a picnic; if the Lumsdens were at Poldhu they would be somewhere among the rocks that spilled out to sea in riotous confusion, and he was not going to look for them there. He would be too conspicuous. Paul had had the same thought, although he took longer to return. 'I'm not clambering over that lot,' he told David. 'It wouldn't be good for my health. Let's press on to Mullion.'

'No,' David said. It would be no easier at Mullion than at Poldhu. 'I'm going back to the camp.'

'Why? They won't be there.'

'Maybe not. But that's where I'm going.'

He took the car right up to the camp entrance, bumping over the rough track regardless of possible damage. He was suddenly possessed by a tremendous sense of urgency. Yet the camp itself was placid enough. A few adults lazed in the sun in deck-chairs or on lilos, screened from the wind by their caravans; two youths were playing a desultory game of French cricket. There was no sign of the motor cycle or its owners.

'Now what?' asked Paul.

They were standing by the yellow caravan. Some yards away the fat woman David had seen earlier that afternoon stood regarding them. Rightly assessing their uncertainty, she called out, 'Your friends have gone out, young man.'

David walked over to her, with Paul in his wake.

'Thank you,' he said. 'How long ago did they leave?'

'Oh, about half an hour. I think they were going on a picnic; they took a basket with them.' She looked from one to the other, and then turned and pointed over to the concrete hut in the far corner of the field. 'They went that way. Through the wire.'

David stared at her. 'You're sure?'

'Certain sure. I saw them walking up the slope towards the cliff.'

He set off briskly in the direction the woman had indicated. Paul followed, but more slowly. David had almost reached the fence when he caught up with him.

'Where's the fire, dear boy?' he drawled. 'Do we really have to run for it?'

'I don't know.' David ducked under the wire and turned to face him. 'I don't like it, Paul. There's something wrong. Why should they go this way? It would be too windy up on the cliff for a picnic. There's Tremmaes, of course, but they wouldn't be there.'

'Why not?'

'Well, for one thing, only a few people know the way down; there's no proper path. Nor is it particularly attractive when you get there. Practically no sand, even at low tide.'

David turned to gaze at the not so distant cliffs. Paul said, 'Let's conserve our energy and retire to the pub.'

David was not listening. As though thinking aloud he said, 'Lumsden would know the way down to Tremmaes, of course. This is his country. It would be tricky going for the girl, but once there they'd have the cove to themselves.'

'One doesn't risk a new wife quite so soon,' Paul objected. 'Forget it, dear boy.'

But David could not forget it. Lumsden had mentioned Poldhu, but he might have switched to Tremmaes because he doubted David's promise not to follow. He said, 'I think I'll just take a look. You wait in the car. I shan't be long.'

Paul sighed and bent his long body to duck under the wire. 'Whither thou goest I go also,' he murmured. 'Such is friendship.'

The lip of the cliff was indented where the ground had broken away, and some ten yards from the edge progress was barred by a wire safety fence. David did not pause. He followed the fence southward, then climbed over and, rounding a clump of bushes, confidently approached the edge. The ground shelved steeply under the overhang, but a narrow ledge of shale and gravel, and later of smooth rock, hugged the cliff-face at an

acute angle to form an almost impercep-
tible path down it.

David started to slither gingerly along
the ledge. As his chin reached the level of
the cliff-top he looked back to see his
friend watching him. Silhouetted against
the sky, the veins in Paul's large,
transparent ears showed clearly.

'Don't try it, Paul,' David shouted.
'Not worth the risk. Not with one arm.'

Paul did not answer, but there was a
scowl on his face and his lower lip
protruded aggressively. I suppose I
shouldn't have said that, David thought
ruefully. He's touchy about his missing
member.

He went on down. The slope became
less abrupt, the outward angle less acute.
As the ledge started to curve inward
under the cliff wall he paused to look
down. The cove formed a deep V, with a
few square yards of grey sand at its
vertex. The weedcovered rocks projecting
out to sea to the north were inaccessible;
if the Lumsdens had come this way they
would be somewhere on the massive pile
of boulders which formed a continuation

of Tremmaes Head.

Above the sound of breaking waves and chattering gulls came the sharp rattle of falling stones. David looked to his left and smiled. His back propped against the cliff wall, Paul was coming after him. If he saw the thumbs up sign that David gave him he did not acknowledge it. As he turned to go on David wondered idly if Paul's big feet would be an advantage or a disadvantage on such a descent.

A few yards farther, and he paused again. He was round the curve. Immediately below him was the vertex of the cove, and to the south he could now see the rocky promontory of Tremmaes, with its green-topped overhang and the black line of boulders cascading raggedly down to the white-capped sea. And half-way down the cascade, clearly silhouetted against the grey-blue of the sky, stood Robert Lumsden.

David did not immediately see Wilhelmina. Dressed in a brown windcheater and dark-grey slacks, a gay scarf covering her hair, she stood several feet below her husband on the near side of the promontory, with the rocks for background and the sea foaming and spouting below her. She was too far off for David to see her face, but he guessed that she was happy — happier, perhaps, than she had ever been. While he watched, a column of spray reared and fell, catching her in its fringe as she retreated. She did not appear to care. The water swirled and slid away, and she came back to the edge to peer down at it, arms outstretched behind her as though she were about to take off in flight.

Neither of them had noticed David. Lumsden, in dark sweater and khaki shorts, was gazing in the opposite direction at something beyond David's vision. David, mentally at ease now that he had found them, wondered how the girl had managed the tricky descent. The couple must have been most anxious to be alone to have attempted it, and they would resent his intrusion on their privacy now. He would be wise to return before they discovered him.

He turned to signal to Paul, still slowly making his way down the ledge. But Paul was concentrating on his feet. With a final glance at the couple, David started on the climb back — to stop abruptly as he saw what had been engaging Lumsden's attention. From behind the far cliff-face came two men, and at the sight of them David's contentment vanished. Even at that distance there was no mistaking those light sweaters and dark trousers and close-cropped heads.

Dunn and Baker! Involuntarily David shouted. The wind carried the sound back to him, but he went on shouting and waving his arms in a vain attempt to put Lumsden on his guard. But Lumsden, it seemed, was unaware of danger. Obviously the men were not strangers to him, for as they approached he pointed away to his left, where Wilhelmina still played hide-and-seek with the breakers. The two men ignored his gesture; they continued to pick their careful way towards him across the slippery boulders. But there was nothing menacing in their approach, and David stopped shouting. He even began to feel slightly foolish at his behaviour. Dunn and Baker were unlikely to have found the way down to the cove unaided, they must have followed Lumsden and the girl and then gone exploring on their own. If murder had been their intent it would have happened already. It was the men on the motor cycle the Lumsdens had to fear.

It was as he reached this comforting thought that Paul cannoned into him. He came slithering down the precipitous slope, grabbed despairingly at the smooth cliff-face, failed to obtain a grip, and rammed David in the side. Arms flailing wildly, back arched, David fought to keep his balance. The foothold was too insecure, the angle of the ledge too abrupt. His feet slid away, and he fell.

The drop was not far, and luckily for David he had been standing immediately above the vertex of the V. He hit the rocky slope once with his back, and landed asprawl on his stomach on the soft sand. The impact jarred his body, and for a moment he lay inert, recovering his breath. Then, spitting sand from his mouth, he stood up.

Paul had managed to stay on the ledge.

His back against the cliff, he was staring down at David. But David had no time for his friend now. He shook his fist at him and started to climb the rocks that blocked his view to the south. There was no urgency, he told himself, wincing at the pain in his back. For his peace of mind he would assure himself before returning that all was well, but there was no urgency.

It was neither a difficult climb nor a long one, but as he heaved himself over the last of the slippery, shell-clad boulders that obstructed his view he was sweating profusely. One hand to his aching back, he stood up. Then his body went rigid. The three men were still on the promontory, but the scene was no longer peaceful. Locked in a trio of straining bodies and thrashing arms, they were moving jerkily towards the far edge of the rock on which they struggled.

Cursing and shouting, David started forward. The action was instinctive, for he could not hope to reach them in time. He had covered only a few yards when the trio seemed suddenly to burst apart.

David saw the red-headed figure of Robert Lumsden crouching between the other two, his back to the sea, his arms outspread. Then Dunn's foot came up and caught him in the face, and he toppled backward and disappeared.

His agonizing scream came faintly to David's ears.

David was shocked into immobility. There was nothing he could do for Lumsden now; if the fall had not killed him outright the pounding waves would finish him. The two men were peering down at the spot where their victim had vanished, their backs to David. And below him and to his right the girl, apparently unaware of tragedy, still played tag with the spray.

The tall figure of Baker straightened and turned. David was too far off to see his face clearly, but he knew he had been recognized. For a few seconds they stared at each other across the chaos of grey rock. Then Baker tapped Dunn on the shoulder. The smaller man stood up and turned to stare also, thumbs hooked into the pockets of his trousers. To David it seemed an age before, without any apparent communication between the two men, they started towards him.

David was no braver and no more of a coward than most men. He had never courted danger, never fled from it if it came. But he wanted to flee now; only the presence of Wilhelmina stopped him. A quick glance over his shoulder showed him that Paul was no longer on the ledge; he must have completed the descent. Yet even if Paul came to his aid he knew they would stand little chance against two professional thugs. Paul had guts, but he was also minus an arm.

In an agony of indecision he watched the two men pick their way towards him. There could be no doubting their purpose. Should he stand his ground, wait for Paul to join him? Or should he make a dash for the girl? There would not be time to get her back to the cliff-face before the men reached him, and the ledge on which she now stood was dangerously exposed. Yet if they should decide to deal with her first . . .

It was then he saw Winstone. Winstone

came from behind the promontory as Baker and Dunn had come; he must have been watching them, he would have witnessed Lumsden's murder. David's spirits rose. Now there were three of them. They might not be as tough or as ruthless as their enemies, but at least they would outnumber them.

The two thugs came on steadily, with Winstone keeping his distance behind them. David looked back, saw Paul's head appear above a high boulder, and made up his mind. The girl must be his first concern; moving as swiftly as he could, he scrambled and slid across the rocks towards her. As he dropped down on to the ledge she shrank back against a high boulder, gazing at him wide-eyed. The brown hair was sodden and lank where it showed beneath the gay scarf, her cheeks were damply flushed, her feet bare. Yet despite her dishevelment she looked a more vital person than the girl he had met in Rotherhithe. The twitches were there in her face, but that could be because she had been startled by his sudden and unexpected appearance.

David had no time for explanations and reassurances. On the south side the ledge was flanked by an enormous boulder which at the seaward end projected over the rocks below. If he could get the girl under that projection it would be more difficult for the men to reach her. Without a word he caught her by the arm. But she was stronger than he had expected. She struggled fiercely to release herself, her mouth working soundlessly.

'Get back!' he snapped. 'Quick! You're in great danger.'

He caught both her arms and began to force her along the ledge. Perhaps she misunderstood his meaning, may even have thought he was trying to push her over the edge. Writhing and kicking like a wild thing, she fought the harder. There was a terrible fear in her eyes, and once she managed to scream her husband's name. Then suddenly she went limp. Carried forward by his own impetus, David nearly fell over her. A large wave hit the rocks below the ledge, sending up a fountain of spray that drenched them both. As the water slid away from around his feet David saw that the girl had fainted. He propped her against the dripping boulder, and turned to discover what had become of Dunn and Baker. Only seconds had passed, but they could not be far off.

They were not. They stood on a clump of rocks above the far end of the ledge, watching him. There was a scowl on Baker's mottled face, a scowl intensified by the heavy spectacles and the drooping mouth. Dunn was stroking his long, pointed chin, a twisted grin on his thin lips but with no hint of mirth in the prominent grey eyes. Neither man made a move towards him, and David wondered why. Time was on his side. They might not know that somewhere behind them Paul and Winstone were coming to his aid, but there was always the possibility that a newcomer would stray on to the scene, or that they might be spotted from the north cliff by some chance visitor undeterred by the safety fence.

Another wave invaded the ledge, but David did not heed it; he could hardly be wetter were he to plunge into the sea. The stillness of the two watchful figures at the far end of the ledge was becoming unnerving, but he would not be the first to make a move. Let them come to him. The ledge was narrow at his end. They would hamper themselves were they to attack him together. Even when Winstone appeared he made no move, no sign. He wanted to signal to him to wait for Paul, but he knew that to do so would be to betray Winstone's presence to the two thugs. Heart pounding, he watched the lithe figure of the West Indian approach, willing him to stop. But Winstone did not stop. He came quietly down to where Dunn and Baker stood and sidled between them, to add a diffident third to the waiting pair. He gave David a nervous grin, a thin shaft of sunlight glinting on his gold teeth, and then looked away.

It was too much for David's phlegm. The two thugs' silent acceptance of Winstone's presence could mean only one thing. Morgan had been right. Winstone was one of Bandy's men.

'You filthy, despicable little rat!' A flurry of spray slapped David in the mouth, and he spat it out. Caution forgotten in his anger, which was directed as much at his own gullibility as at the West Indian's deception, he advanced a few paces along the ledge, fists clenching and unclenching. 'I'll do you for this.'

Winstone gave him a quick glance, shrugged his slim shoulders, and took a pace back. He was clearly nervous. Dunn put a hand to his waist and laughed. It was a dry, brittle sound.

'It's you what's going to be done, mister,' he snapped.

The glint of steel in his hand restored David's caution. He retreated backward to the girl, felt her hand at his back, and knew she was conscious again. He could hear her crying, sucking in air noisily as she caught her breath, and amid the fear and sickness that was in him he was able to feel a twinge of pity for her. It might have been better, poor thing, had she remained unconscious. For this was it. The waiting was over.

Where the hell was Paul?

'Get back,' he urged. 'Get as far back as you can.'

With relief he felt her obey. He needed room in which to manœuvre. For a brief moment he looked down to his left; where he stood the ledge was less than three feet wide, and below it sharp pinnacles of rock protruded from a heaving, creamy sea that even as he watched burst into a volcano of spray. The drop was not long, but it would probably be fatal.

His eyes returned to the knife in Dunn's hand. The man had moved forward to the edge of the rock. So had Baker. A cloud drifted away from the sun and the promontory was bathed in sudden light. David felt the warmth on his damp head, and shivered; sunshine was inapposite, it did not go with murder. The thought flashed through his mind that perhaps he was dreaming; could this really be happening to him, David Wight? The subdued thunder of the surf, the sobbing girl behind him, the sun glinting on Baker's spectacles and the knife in Dunn's hand, assured him that it was.

'No knives, you fool!'

The peremptory command caused David to look up quickly. Paul was there.

He stood on a rock behind the three men, seeming to tower above them, the wind ruffling his hair and an expression on his face that David had not seen there before. Lower lip thrust forward, yellow teeth bared, he gazed viciously down at David. There was no recognition in his eyes. It was as though he were seeing a stranger and detested what he saw.

David stared back, fascinated as a rabbit might be fascinated by a snake. He too saw a stranger. But he had no need to ask for an explanation. It was there on Paul's face, in his air of authority, and in the deference the others accorded him. Paul — the bon viveur, the wealthy young man-about-town, the friend he had trusted — was a thief and a murderer!

Paul was Bandy!

Something flashed in the sunlight, breaking the spell. Dunn had put away the knife. But to David, Dunn and Baker and Winstone now seemed insignificant. His anger at Winstone's duplicity had been as nothing to his rage now. It was so intense, so over-powering, that he could find no words with which to voice it.

Danger and fear and the girl forgotten, body rigid, teeth locked so that his gums ached, he sought to convey through his eyes the hatred and loathing his tongue could not express.

'No knives,' Paul repeated. No drawl now, the voice was curtly incisive. 'If the bodies are ever recovered they must appear to have been drowned. We're too conspicuous down here for there to be any hint of murder.' He drew a deep breath. 'Get on with it, Joe.'

Baker removed his spectacles, handed them to Winstone, and slid down on to the ledge. He looked a tough and menacing figure, with his large frame and spread nose and expressionless eyes. But David experienced no sensation of fear. He was almost eager for battle; it would be a relief to express physically the rage that consumed him. He would have preferred Paul or Winstone at the end of his fists, but if it was to be Baker — well, he was ready.

As a shower of spray enveloped him he shook his body free of the tenseness that had held it, spread his feet wider on the wet, slippery surface, and awaited Baker's onslaught. From behind him came the sound of the girl crying, punctuated by hiccups. But Wilhelmina had lost much of her importance for David. This was now a personal battle.

It was never joined. All except Winstone were watching Baker. Winstone, who since his arrival had shown little interest in the proceedings, had turned away, his aspect one of unhappy dejection. Now his body stiffened. In his high-pitched voice he shouted excitedly, 'Hey! Look there!'

His voice held such urgency that they all, David included, followed his pointing finger. 'There' was the cliff-face down which they had come. From where they stood they could see only the lower half of the rude track, but that was enough for David. Hope was something he had abandoned; now it surged through him anew. For there were men on the track; men in uniform, men in civilian dress. And they were coming down remarkably fast.

Winstone was the first to act. He gave a

frightened look at Paul, hesitated, then turned and ran, slipping and sliding over the greasy, uneven surfaces. Once he fell. But he picked himself up and went limping on towards the far side of the promontory, away from the men on the cliff. He did not know, as David knew, that there was no escape that way.

Baker went next. Like the others, he appeared to have lost interest in David and the girl. Agile for such a big man, he hoisted himself off the ledge and without a word to his companions set off in pursuit of the West Indian. He took a more direct course, clambering over rocks where Winstone skirted them, and moving faster.

David took a cautious step forward. Paul and Dunn had their backs to him, and he prayed that neither would look round. The knowledge that rescue was on the way had not dispelled his anger. Paul had trapped him. Now he wanted to be the one to trap Paul.

Dunn said, 'Looks like a good idea.' His voice was sharp and incisive, without a tremor. 'We can't handle a mob that big.' His eyes turned from the cliff to follow the retreating figures of Baker and Winstone. 'I reckon it's time to go, Bandit. Coming?'

Paul was watching the cliff. He stood with his feet firmly apart, legs straight, shoulders square. The empty sleeve at his left side was still tucked neatly into the pocket of his blazer.

'I've business to attend to first,' he said evenly.

As Dunn turned to look at him David froze into immobility. The man gave him a twisted grin, raised slim fingers in a mock salute, and strolled casually away, picking his path delicately. The last man on the cliff-face disappeared into the deep V of the cove. It seemed to be the cue for which Paul had waited. Hand in pocket, he turned to peer down at David.

'You're a fool,' he said. 'A fool and a meddling nuisance. Now you're going to pay for your meddling.'

David saw the small automatic in his hand as he withdrew it from his pocket, and braced himself. It was agonizing to realize that those men on the cliff, despite their nearness, could not help him now.

'You're a fool yourself, Paul.' His throat was dry and his voice hoarse. He swallowed painfully. The grim expression on the other's face told him that no appeal for mercy would succeed. Only if he were persuaded that to linger would imperil his own safety might Paul decide to forgo his murderous intention. 'It's not all that easy to kill a man; not with a toy like that. And what about the girl? You'll have to kill her too — she's the star witness against you. Only there won't be time; not for both of us. They'll get you first, Paul.' Water buffeted into his face, and he blinked furiously. His voice was shrill as he repeated, 'They'll get you, Paul. They'll get you.'

Paul took a step forward and raised the automatic. Now he was at the very edge of the rock. David felt sick. Courage was rapidly deserting him, and he had to force himself to stand his ground. He knew that his one slim chance lay in attack.

'There'll be time,' Paul said.

The automatic came up slowly. David watched it, mesmerized by its snub nose.

Summoning all his nerve, he tore his eyes away and stared across to his left.

'There won't, damn you!' he said hoarsely. 'They're here now.'

It was an old trick, but it almost worked. In the fraction of a second in which Paul started to look over his shoulder and then changed his mind, David sprang. But the tension and the wet had stiffened his limbs, and he was not quick enough. He scarcely heard the report. He felt the impact of the bullet and a stabbing, searing pain in his side, but it did not stop him. Momentum carried him forward, and he flung both arms round Paul's legs and tugged. The gun fired again, the bullet grazing his left leg. Momentarily his clasp weakened. But before Paul could free himself David had slipped his hands down and gripped him by the ankles and, exerting all his remaining strength, had tugged again. Paul's feet slid from the rock and he fell heavily on to the ledge, striking his head against it and sending David sprawling.

Slowly David got to his knees. He was too weak to stand. But weakness had not dimmed his rage. Through misted eyes he saw the prostrate figure of his enemy and, unaware that the fall had knocked the other senseless, he smashed a fist into the hated face. The effort weakened him further, and he fell across the still body. For a moment or two he lay inert. Then he thought he felt Paul stir, and again he pushed himself up and raised his fist.

Before he could use it a hand gripped him by the wrist.

'That's enough, sir,' a voice said. There was an arm round his shoulders, a peaked cap was bending over him. 'Leave him to us. We'll know how to deal with him.'

17

'Bandy or Bandit, I hate his guts,' David said. He eased his body into a more upright position, felt a stab of pain in his side, and sank back on to the banked pillows. 'Which was it, by the way? I'm sure Dunn addressed him as Bandit.'

On the tiny square of grass beyond the ward windows two nurses were chatting. One was young and blonde and pretty, and Rees Morgan watched her contentedly. It was at his request that David had been brought to London by ambulance as soon as the Helston doctors had pronounced him fit to travel, and it was at his insistence that David had been given a room to himself in the hospital here. David was an important police witness, he had told the protesting authorities; he had to be readily available for questioning. The protests had continued, but with the support of his superiors he had overcome them.

'Bandit,' he said. 'The One-arm Bandit — that's what the gang called him.'

A fresh wave of anger engulfed David. Even now he could not reconcile himself to the recollection of how easily he had been duped. Would he have been suspicious of Paul, he wondered, if Nora and Morgan between them had not started him off on the wrong foot, if he had been given 'Bandit' instead of 'Bandy'? It was such an obvious nickname for a crook with one arm. He knew that Paul had been at the Crocodile when Elsie Sheel had broadcast that her room-mate had witnessed the murder; it was Paul who had hastened to get in touch with him, not he with Paul. That last should certainly have made him wonder; they had had nothing in common at school, could expect to have little or nothing in common now. Instead he had felt flattered, had allowed Paul to hoodwink him completely. And with chagrin he remembered that Paul himself had used the word 'Bandit' when they had lunched together at their first meeting.

'Why did he do it?' he asked wearily. 'What makes a man like Paul become a thief and a killer?'

Morgan shrugged. 'I dare say he got a kick out of it. He also seems to have had a grudge against society and against policemen in particular. But principally for the lolly, I imagine. He had expensive tastes.'

'Lolly?' David sat up sharply, winced, and fell back. 'But he was loaded! An aunt in America left him a fortune. He told me so.'

'He told you a lot of things. I'm surprised you bought that one. He hasn't got an aunt; never did have. Susan knew that. What's more, she says she told you so.'

Had Susan told him? He could not remember. They had discussed Paul and his parents after they had met him at the Seventy-Seven, but had there been anything about an aunt? Not that it mattered. It was just another instance of his own magnificent credulity.

'And the chip on his shoulder? Was that because of his injury?'

'Against the police, yes. The driver of

the other car involved in the accident was a constable off duty, and he happened to be drunk.' Morgan sighed. 'We have our sinners, unfortunately. And it robbed your friend of an England cap. I gather that was something he'd set his heart on.'

'He hasn't got a heart. And don't call him my friend. I told you, I hate his guts.'

'It's a pity you didn't get to hating them earlier.'

The superintendent was looking particularly smart that afternoon. David had not seen the suit before — a discreet mixture of yellows and browns and reds, perfectly cut and immaculately pressed — and guessed it to be new. The familiar bow tie had been discarded for a Jacques Fath, square cut and admirably knotted, and the cream shirt had just the suspicion of a check to relieve the monotony. From where he lay David could not see his feet, but he had no doubt that the socks blended perfectly and that the shoes had a high gloss polish.

The picture irritated him. To his mind policemen should look like policemen and not like tailors' dummies. And the old buzzard hadn't the right figure; too much paunch and too much neck. David suspected he had a girl lined up for the evening. Probably been dating one of the nurses. Certainly he had been a more frequent visitor to the hospital than official business would seem to warrant.

'How about handing out some information for a change?' His tone was peevish. 'Unsatisfied curiosity can't be good for an invalid; it increases the blood pressure. And you must know all the answers by now.'

'You're no invalid,' his godfather told him. The blonde had moved from his line of vision, and he shifted his gaze to the flowers. The yellow tulips were his, the red ones probably Susan's. The rather ragged wallflowers had no doubt come from David's editor, if the rascally old blood-sucker had thought to send flowers at all. 'You've got a hole in your side through being a damned sight too impetuous, but you're as healthy as I am. Healthier.' He put a hand in his pocket and rustled the inevitable paper-bag. 'However, you're right about the answers.

Properly scared, Winstone is a great talker — though neither he nor the others would say a word about Dyerson's murder. Killing a copper is something no crook will confess to. However, I'm not worrying. We have our eye-witness. She'll do the trick for us.'

David glowed with smug complacency. The police might say what they liked about his handling of the affair — and Morgan for one had said plenty — but they owed their witness to him. It was he who had saved Wilhelmina.

When, with a proper show of modesty, he pointed this out to his godfather, he was answered by a non-committal grunt. Aggrieved at this refusal to give praise where praise was undoubtedly due, he said sharply, 'Well? Do I get the story, or don't I?'

'You do.' Morgan put an acid-drop into his mouth and delicately licked the tips of his fingers. 'Where shall I start?'

'For crying out loud! What's wrong with the beginning?' The frown on the superintendent's face warned David that he had overstepped the bounds of permissible familiarity. 'I'm sorry, sir. I've been in this blasted bed too long; it's getting me down. All right, then — let's start with the Rotherhithe job. Surely it wasn't a coincidence that the gang picked on a warehouse almost next door to Nora's parents?'

'Not entirely. On one of the rare occasions she spoke about her family she mentioned to Winstone that her father was night watchman there, and how her mother was worried about him. That was while she and Winstone were living together; she knew nothing of his criminal activities, of course. Winstone passed the information on to Brenn-Taylor, who saw its possibilities. His first idea was that Nora should try to fix the old man. Winstone squashed that flat. He knew Nora wouldn't play. Incidentally, did you know Brenn-Taylor owned the Seventy-Seven Club? That was the gang's headquarters.'

David shook his head. 'So it was entirely a coincidence that Nora chose that particular night to visit her daughter?'

'Must have been.'

According to Mrs Einsdorp, Nora had left without seeing Wilhelmina. Perhaps she had spotted the couple on her way to the bus, and had followed them to Rotherhithe Street. She had mistrusted Lumsden's intentions, the old woman had said.

'O.K. So they raided the warehouse and coshed old Einsdorp, and Nora and Lumsden and Wilhelmina saw them shoot the constable. I know that bit. Can we take it from there?'

Morgan smiled his attractive smile and looked sly.

'You never learn, do you?'

'What do you mean by that?'

'Skip it. Well, taking it from there brings us to Brenn-Taylor reading the newspapers, and learning of the existence of witnesses.'

'Thanks to you.' Crack for crack, thought David, still mystified by his godfather's comment.

'If you care to put it that way.' Morgan was unperturbed. In his low, musical voice he went on equably, 'Elsie Sheel was a slice of luck for them. That one of the witnesses should turn out to be not only Elsie's room-mate but also Winstone's ex girl-friend was an even larger slice. Winstone was detailed to discover how much she had seen and heard. Unfortunately for Nora she knew how to keep a secret.'

'Why unfortunately?'

'If she had told Winstone then why she could not identify the killer they might have believed her. Not later, of course; not when the heat was on. But she didn't. Not because she mistrusted him, but because we had told her to mention it to no one. Winstone couldn't put direct questions without revealing his connexion with the crime, so he got no direct answers. No answers at all, in fact.'

'Was Winstone also in on the kidnapping?'

'He was. He couldn't care less what happened to her so long as any violence done was not done by him. He was squeamish that way. The plan was for Baker and Dunn to pick her up as she left the Centipede. Winstone was to arrange that he and she did not leave the building together; he could be of more use to the gang if she remained unaware of his complicity.' Morgan cracked the thin remnant of the acid-drop between his teeth and sucked the fragments avidly before swallowing. 'Chapman made that easy.'

'Suppose Nora had insisted on leaving with Winstone?'

'They would probably have pretended to knock him out, and carried on as planned.'

David shifted his position in the bed. With each day the mattress seemed to grow harder. 'What went wrong?' he asked. 'Me?'

'Chapman. Winstone's job finished when he left the club. He should have gone back to the Seventy-Seven, but he stopped to look at your Alvis. To him it was something of an oddity.' The fleeting smile that invaded the superintendent's round face aroused David's resentment, but he let it pass. 'And then Chapman came out, spotted Winstone, and decided to finish what he'd started. Beat him up good and proper. Winstone's as crooked as they come, but physically he's a coward; Chapman would have eaten him had not Dunn intervened. Unfortunately for Chapman Dunn's intervention took its usual course. He stuck a knife into him.' Morgan shrugged. 'So there they were, all set for a snatch, and with a large and unexpected corpse on their hands. Tricky, eh?'

'Very,' David agreed. This was news to him. He had not supposed that Chapman, dead or alive, could have any bearing on the events subsequent to that evening. 'Was that why they delayed the snatch, as you call it?'

'Chapman had priority. Winstone went off in a taxi, and Dunn and Baker bundled the corpse into the back of their car, drove down to the river, and dumped it. We don't know exactly where, but it was fished out near Hungerford Bridge the following night. They then returned to the main business of the evening. Only now they decided to wait for Nora outside her flat. For one thing, it was nearer. For another, she might already be on her way home. I imagine they were somewhat dismayed when she arrived with a companion. Happily for them, you were not the sort of escort to go upstairs with the lady.'

David nodded absently. At that moment he was not interested in his godfather's opinion of his morals. He said, 'Winstone was speaking the truth, then, when he said Nora was alive. The blood you found in the Zodiac was Chapman's.'

'It was about the only truth he did speak.'

The door opened to admit a tea-trolley. Morgan stood up, smoothing down his jacket. The trolley was followed by a tall negress, who beamed at them out of a shining black face, her thin drain-pipe legs apparently having difficulty in supporting the heavy body.

'You want some tea?' she asked the superintendent, arranging a tray on the bed trolley. 'I brought another cup.'

He thanked her politely. David thought he looked somewhat dejected; had he been expecting the blonde? When the negress had left them he said, 'A teapot! This must be in your honour, sir; usually it's just a cup. Care to pour out? I must conserve my strength. And go easy on the milk, will you? I like mine strong.'

With a derisory grunt his godfather complied. Into his own cup he poured almost as much milk as tea, adding a generous quantity of sugar. He eyed the two pieces of bread and butter and the two small cakes, decided there was only enough for one, and sat down.

'So it was Chapman, not the gang, who messed up Winstone's face?' David said, spreading jam. 'Came in handy, didn't it? I mean, I suppose he really did have that interview with Nora.'

'I imagine so. It was the obvious tactics to employ. But whatever lies he invented to persuade her to talk, he had no success until she inadvertently mentioned the name of Robert. Then, of course, he pressed her for the man's full name and address. He says she told him she'd forgotten it; it was in her diary, she said, but she must have lost that when she dropped her handbag in your car.'

David felt his cheeks go red. Even after his admission to hospital, and with Paul and his gang safely in the bag, he had been unable to summon up the courage to tell Morgan about the diary. Morgan had learned of it from Winstone; on his next visit to the hospital he had told David in no uncertain terms what he thought of him. But you had to hand it to the old boy, David reflected; he might blow his top, but the fury didn't last. He had referred to the diary just now as calmly as though it had never been a bone of contention between them.

Would he have been as genial had the case been less successfully concluded?

Morgan took a deep draught of tea. 'That doesn't sound like a mass of information, does it? But when you're not squeamish about method you can get a lot from quite a little.'

David made no comment. At that moment even the thought of Wilhelmina could not cheer him. It was galling to contrast his own stubborn stupidity with Morgan's magnanimity, and as he munched his bread and jam he carefully avoided his godfather's eyes. This is where we came in, he reflected sourly — with me as the prize idiot. They search my flat for the diary — I'd told Paul I'd be in Rotherhithe that evening — and when that fails Winstone is detailed to do the suffering husband act and slip me a clue. 'Robert' means nothing to them, but they reckon I'm just about bright enough to check with the diary. Then they follow me; and when I give their chap the slip, thinking he's a copper, they resort to more direct methods. They knock me out and pinch the diary and get to Lumsden that way.

'Who knocked me out?' he asked. 'Dunn?'

Morgan was not happy on the wooden chair. It was hard and small, and his posterior spread and sagged over the edges, which bit into his flesh. Still holding the cup, he stood up and went over to the window.

'Baker,' he said. 'Dunn is a little too impetuous, and at that stage you still had possibilities.'

'But only until the Sunday, apparently,'

David said bitterly. 'Was that Dunn? He wasn't very clever with the knife.'

'No. That was a little chap named Boretti, one of Dunn's apprentices.' It was warm by the window, and Morgan undid his jacket and moved away. He perspired easily, and he did not want his collar to go limp. 'By then, you see, they knew all about Lumsden. They picked him up on the Friday night, having got his address from the diary.' He gave his godson another of his sly smiles. 'You had gone home, tired of waiting and satisfied with leaving a note. They were a little more persistent.'

David scowled. That damned diary again! Why must he keep referring to it? He pushed the bed trolley away and lit a cigarette.

'If they were so blasted thorough, why did they wait until Tuesday before disposing of him? During those four days he might have changed his mind and gone to the police.'

'A good question, David.' The superintendent put his cup back on the trolley. 'You couldn't spare one of those pillows,

383

could you? That chair's damned hard.'

'Help yourself.'

At David's request he wound up the back rest. Then he returned to his chair and settled himself on the pillow, a bland look of contentment on his round face.

'Robert Lumsden seems to have been quite a lad. As you suspected, he was interested not in the girl but in her money. He told Brenn-Taylor so. When they picked him up he was quick to realize that he was reasonably safe until and unless he gave them the name of the girl. So he refused. But he also made them an offer. Although they had been married only a few days, he was all in favour of his wife's death provided he was not involved. He suggested he should take her down to Cornwall on the Sunday, and they could dispose of her there. Make it look like an accident, with an alibi for himself, and on the day he got her money he would hand over a thousand quid for their services. Plus, of course, the promise to keep his mouth shut about the Rotherhithe affair.'

'The swine!' At their first meeting

David had rather liked Lumsden. 'I'm surprised the gang trusted him.'

'They didn't. They made him put the offer in writing and sign it; with that in their possession he dared not go to the police. They told him he could have it back when he paid up.'

'And he was fool enough to believe them?'

Morgan shrugged. 'Hadn't much choice, had he? Even without his help it wouldn't have taken them long to find the girl, and then it would be curtains for both. At least his offer seemed to give him a chance — plus the exciting prospect of enjoying the money without being encumbered by the girl.' Thoughtfully he stroked his heavy jowls, taking pleasure in their smoothness. 'He couldn't know he was already earmarked for death. A thousand smackers was peanuts to that mob, and they weren't risking their necks for peanuts.' The superintendent leaned back and flexed the muscles of his arms, the chair tilting dangerously under his weight. 'That night they killed Nora Winstone and tried to kill you. They reckoned it was in the bag.'

And so it would have been, thought David, had he not interfered. He got some comfort from that. But he did not make this point to Morgan; Morgan would undoubtedly belittle it. He said, 'I suppose Dunn and Baker went down to Pendwara on the Saturday to establish some sort of an alibi. But how about Paul? What would he have done had I not asked him to join me?'

'He'd have been in the vicinity, directing operations without actually putting in an appearance. You provided the opportunity for him to be right on the spot, with yourself as his guarantor of respectability. Not in person, of course; you were not expected to arrive at Pendwara. Come to that, you were not expected to arrive anywhere. But your telephone call to your uncle gave him the necessary credentials.'

David nodded glumly. It was galling to learn how completely Paul had used him, but even more bitter to reflect on how readily he had offered himself for use.

The negress was back. She tottered

into the room with her cheerful smile and said to David, 'You've got another visitor. A young lady.' And then, with a sidelong glance at the superintendent, 'I said you was busy with the police.'

'That'll be Susan,' David said. 'It's all right, nurse, thank you. She can come in.' As an afterthought he asked, 'You've no objection, sir, have you?'

'Yes, I have. I'm sorry, David, but this is confidential.' David was puzzled by the broad smile that lit his godfather's face. Under the circumstances it was unexpected. 'Ask her to wait, nurse, will you? Tell her I shan't keep her long.'

'You'd better not,' David warned when the nurse had left with the tray. 'Not if you value her good opinion. Susan doesn't like being kept waiting.'

'What woman does? However, we're nearly through.'

In a voice carefully modulated to avoid monotony, Morgan summarized the rest of the story. On the Sunday evening Winstone had been detailed to discover how David was progressing. When David, on his way to see Susan, had dropped him off at Notting Hill, Winstone had telephoned Paul the information that David not only knew where the Lumsdens were in hiding, but meant to visit them on the morrow. Paul could not risk that. David must be liquidated immediately; and since Dunn was already in Cornwall the task was given to Boretti.

'And he bungled it,' David said, with some satisfaction.

Morgan nodded. 'He lacked Dunn's skill with the knife. So now they cooked up a new plan; to steal a car and run you off the road on the way down. That was Boretti again. Boretti and Fenner, the sixth member of the gang. He's a waiter at the Seventy-Seven. Or was. Right now he's in Brixton.'

'They couldn't care less, I suppose, that Winstone happened to be in the car with me?'

The superintendent smiled. 'A slight lack of co-ordination. They didn't know about Winstone. You had refused him a lift the night before, and they thought that still went. Nor did they bother to tell Winstone the new plan, or you certainly wouldn't have found him outside your flat the next morning.'

David echoed the smile. The knowledge that his enemies had also made mistakes made him feel better. 'Why was he so keen on a lift? What was he planning to do?'

'Nothing violent. Fix the car on the way down, perhaps; I'm told he's a bit of a mechanic. Delay you somehow, anyway.'

Paul's plan had been simple enough. Lumsden would take his wife down to lonely Tremmaes Cove for a picnic, and Dunn and Baker would follow. As Lumsden saw it, the two thugs would dispose of the girl, and be ready to testify later at the inquest that it was an accident, that her husband (the obvious suspect) had been nowhere near her at the time. Paul and his men saw it differently. They had no intention of attending any inquest. The 'accident' would involve both husband and wife, and Dunn and Baker would then make themselves scarce; and unless they had actually been spotted in the cove (and they would take precautions against that) it would occur to no one that two complete strangers might have found their way down there unaided, let alone commit murder. Why should they?

'They had fixed the job for Monday,' Morgan continued, 'but because of the rain Wilhelmina could not be lured from the caravan. Not that it mattered. There was no apparent need for haste. Boretti and Fenner would have taken care of you, and the police were nowhere. It rocked them when you and Winstone turned up on the Tuesday.'

David stubbed out his cigarette. 'I'm glad I managed to cause them some discomfort.'

'Not a lot, I'm afraid. Paul isn't easily disconcerted. He sent Dunn and Baker to the camp site to warn Lumsden that you would be around, instructing him to play it tough at first and then appear to yield. But he was to insist that he and the girl had the afternoon to themselves. And that seemed to wrap it up. True, you were around; you might even do a little snooping. But Paul was there to keep tabs on you.' Morgan grimaced. 'Had you not insisted on going down to Tremmaes you would never have known he was involved. You and he might have continued as friends until the law finally caught up with him. As it was you forced him to show his hand. Not that it worried him. What, after all, was one more murder?'

'What, indeed?' David agreed. 'Although he might have had some difficulty in explaining my disappearance. He had gone out with me. My uncle knew that.'

'No difficulty at all. He would claim to have stayed on the cliff-top. Who would expect a one-armed man to attempt such a tricky descent? Did you?'

David admitted he did not. 'I gather those two johnnies on the motor cycle were genuine campers. They had no connexion with the gang; it was just a coincidence that one of them had lost the top of a finger. Yet Winstone couldn't have known they would be there to confuse me. Why did he mention the finger at all?'

'Because you were so insistent that he must have noticed something that he invented the first deformity that came into his mind. Or so he says.' Morgan stood up, adjusted the hang of his jacket and the set of his tie, and ran a careful hand over the thinning grey hair. It still had a wave which he was anxious to preserve. 'It's time I collected your other visitor, David. We've kept her waiting long enough.' He eyed his godson with disfavour. If David had shaved that morning it had been hastily done, for already his chin and cheeks were grey with patches of stubble. Certainly he had not used comb or brush on that unruly mop of his. 'Is it possible to get one's hair cut in hospital?' he asked pointedly.

'I don't know,' David snapped. 'What's more, I don't care.'

Why does the old buzzard always manage to get my goat? he reflected when Morgan had gone. Does he do it deliberately, out of a mistaken sense of duty, a sort of I-must-keep-the-young-devil-up-to-the-mark notion? He's not a bad old stick really, and he's been pretty decent over this business. More than decent. If it hadn't been for him I wouldn't be alive.

It was Inspector Nightingale who had

told David of the events leading up to his rescue. David's anger at Susan's betrayal of a confidence had been short lived; and, in fact, because of the accident to the Alvis, her betrayal had given the police little help. When Morgan realized that David had somehow managed to slip unnoticed past the police cars waiting at Redruth and Truro, he had immediately instigated a search in the Helston area. But it had been from Rotherhithe that the real lead had come. On the Tuesday morning Nightingale had visited Einsdorp in hospital, and had learned of Wilhelmina's marriage and disappearance and of David's interest in the young couple. That had been enough for the inspector; anything that had interested David interested him. A visit to Lumsden's lodgings, where David's letter lay unopened in the hall, had clinched the matter. The letter mentioned Pendwara, and it was to Pendwara that Nightingale and the superintendent had gone, after alerting the local police. Pendwara boasted only the one inn. David's uncle had put them more fully in the picture, and it was he who had suggested Tremmaes as a likely spot for a murder.

He was still brooding on the drama at Tremmaes, from the gloom of which only the one bright consolation emerged — that in saving Wilhelmina he had ensured Paul's conviction for the murder of Constable Dyerson, and thus earned his godfather's gratitude — when Morgan returned. But the girl who followed him into the room was not Susan. She was a curvaceous brunette in a tight fitting two-piece of soft pink, and on her head a little white cap with a dangling pom-pom. The dark eyes under the spiky brows surveyed him cautiously, as though uncertain of her welcome.

David sat up with a jerk that made him wince.

'Judy Garland! What on earth brings you here?'

'Me,' Morgan said. He was standing very erect, contracting his stomach muscles. 'I thought you might like to see her.'

'Of course I do.' David realized that his pyjama jacket was undone, and hastily fastened the buttons. 'Who wouldn't? But why should she want to see me?'

'I heard you was hurt,' the girl said. 'I'm sorry.'

Her voice was subdued, and David had the impression that this was not an answer to his question but a timid — even an apologetic — approach. He gave her a friendly and appreciative grin. 'I'm fine,' he told her, and patted the bed. 'Come and sit here. Leave the chair for the aged and infirm.'

The look the superintendent gave him was searing in its contempt. The girl declined his offer, but the cockney voice was more confident as she said, 'Thanks, I'll stand.'

She moved to the foot of the bed and rested her arms on the high trolley, her enormous eyes contemplating him. Embarrassed, David turned to his godfather. 'What's all this in aid of?' he demanded. 'How did you come to meet Judy?'

'She came to meet me.' Morgan surveyed the girl with pleasure. 'She is Robert Lumsden's girl-friend. Or was until he married Wilhelmina Einsdorp. When she discovered how he had deceived her she decided, very sensibly, to pay me a visit.'

'Why you?'

'Well, perhaps not me personally. But I happened to be at the station when she called.' Airily he waved a well-manicured hand to dismiss the argument, and smiled at the girl. 'Shall I tell him, Miss Garland, or will you?'

She shook her head, blinking her long lashes at him. 'You tell him, please.'

Morgan moved to the chair, then paused. He could not sit while the girl stood.

'You failed to get the full story, David,' he said. 'Lumsden married Wilhelmina, but he was in love with Miss Garland. And she was in love with him.' He looked at the girl. 'That's so, isn't it?' She lowered her eyes and nodded. 'From Lumsden's point of view the marriage was one of convenience; he was reluctant to renounce Miss Garland, but still more reluctant to relinquish Wilhelmina's nest-egg. After his meeting with Brenn-Taylor he realized he need do neither; he was about to become a widower with prospects. So before departing on his so-called honeymoon he told Miss Garland that he would be away for a few days, but hinted that on his return his circumstances might be considerably improved.' Morgan turned again to the girl. 'I know he had kept the marriage a secret, but had you no inkling of his interest in Miss Einsdorp?'

'I knew he took her to the cinema sometimes,' she said. 'I thought he was just being kind. I wasn't — well, jealous.'

David could believe that. A girl with Judy's looks would have no cause to be jealous of Wilhelmina.

'I'm sorry,' he said. 'His death must have come as a great shock to you.'

She nodded, the pom-pom dancing. 'I was that upset I didn't know what to do. It wasn't only him being killed, you see, but finding out he was married. I got to thinking about how he'd deceived me. And then I thought — well, maybe he lied about the shooting too. Maybe he hadn't been to the police like he said he would.

So I went myself, just to make sure.'

There were no tears, her voice was firm. She might have been upset, David concluded, but her heart wasn't broken. Yet there was something here that puzzled him.

'What's all this about shooting?' he asked. 'What shooting?'

There was a pause. Judy was looking at Morgan, obviously expecting him to answer. David looked too. Hands clasped behind his back, feet well apart, the superintendent regarded his godson with an enigmatic smile.

'Well?' David demanded.

'I'm afraid you had it all wrong, David,' Morgan told him, with obvious relish. 'It was Miss Garland, not Wilhelmina, who was with Lumsden on the night Dyerson was shot.'

David shook his head in bewilderment. 'But Lumsden told me himself . . . ' No, that wasn't true. Lumsden had not told him, he had merely omitted to deny David's assumption. 'You mean — it was you who saw the shooting, Judy? Not Wilhelmina?'

'That's right,' she said, her voice a whisper. 'And I wish I hadn't. There was his face, you see — real evil it was — and the empty sleeve and . . . ' She shuddered. 'Oh, it was horrible!' Her chin came up, and she looked defiantly at Morgan. 'I know you think it was wicked of me not to tell the police, but Robert said not to. He said it would be all right, that he'd see to it. And I believed him.'

'I don't think you're wicked,' he assured her, smiling. Judy Garland's lush beauty and gay, uninhibited nature had appealed to him greatly, but he had reluctantly decided she was not for him. He could not see her as the wife of a senior police officer. 'Lumsden knew what he was about. He was due to be married in two days time; to admit to having been out with another girl that night might have wrecked all his plans. So he kept his mouth shut. Yours too.'

David sank back on the pillows. Now he was really confused. 'Where was Wilhelmina, then?' he asked weakly. 'And how about Nora? Why should she spy on

Judy and Lumsden? It doesn't make sense.'

'Doesn't it?' Morgan fished for an acid-drop, then changed his mind. 'Nora Winstone mistrusted Lumsden, she had no wish for him to marry her daughter. If she could prove to Wilhelmina that he was interested in someone else it might disillusion the girl.' He shrugged. 'Or maybe she recognized Lumsden's red hair, and automatically assumed his companion to be her daughter. Miss Garland and Wilhelmina are about the same height and build.' He favoured Judy with an intimate smile. 'I grant you that otherwise there's no resemblance, but in the dark it was a mistake easily made. As for Wilhelmina — as she said, she went to the cinema and then for a walk. Lumsden had told her he would be busy, and she did not fancy spending the evening at home. She was excited at the prospect of her marriage. It might not be easy to conceal her excitement from her parents.'

David reached for a cigarette and lit it. In his confusion he did not think to offer one to the girl. As Morgan had said, it made sense. It explained why Wilhelmina had said nothing of the shooting to her parents, as she surely would have done had she witnessed it; after all, her father had been seriously injured in the raid. It explained too why she had made no mention of it in the note she had left for her mother before departing on her honeymoon; to the girl it had been only a honeymoon, with nothing sinister behind it.

Presumably the switch in names had first suggested itself to Lumsden when the gang had picked him up on the Friday night; it protected Judy, and at the same time promised to dispose of an unwanted wife. From then on, however, he had to ensure that the deception was maintained. Perhaps that accounted for the elaborate arrangement he had devised for his wife's death. Had he merely told the gang her name and left them to choose the time and place and manner of it, they might have questioned her first. It explained too why he had been so anxious at Pendwara to keep David and his wife apart. A few words from Wilhelmina then, and everything could go wrong for him.

Well, it had gone wrong — although not as Lumsden had feared. Lumsden had died, and Wilhelmina, thanks to him, was alive. The glow of complacency began once more to creep over David, only to fade as he realized that now even that consolation was denied him. He had saved a life — but not *the* life. Wilhelmina was of no interest to the police. He had not given Morgan his vital witness. Morgan had found her for himself.

He was silent for so long, lying back on the pillows with his eyes closed and the cigarette smouldering unheeded in the ashtray, that Morgan, who had been talking quietly to Judy, said suddenly, 'By Themis, I believe the lad's asleep! We've worn him out. Or I have.'

David kept his eyes firmly shut. He had had enough of his godfather for one afternoon, and he was too dispirited to be able to enjoy the girl's company.

Judy said softly, 'Poor boy! He looks very pale. Do you think he's all right?'

'Of course he's all right.' The ashtray rattled on the cabinet as Morgan stubbed out the cigarette. 'However, we'd better go before he wakes.'

'Would he like me to come and see him again, do you think?'

Morgan contemplated her gravely. Attractive as he found her, he was thinking of Susan. Susan was in love with David, she would not thank him were he to encourage a friendship with a girl as seductive as Judy. And he was fond of Susan. He could not understand what she found in his irresponsible young godson to appeal to her; but if David was what she wanted . . .

'Better not, my dear.' His tone was confidential. 'Susan — his fiancée, you know — she might misunderstand.' David heard the sound of the superintendent's bowler being tapped into position on his head. 'Come along. We'll have a cup of tea somewhere, and then I'll run you home. It must be a deadly journey by bus.'

You old lecher, thought David, as he heard the door close — wishing Susan on to me just to obviate competition! There ought to be a law prohibiting policemen from fraternizing with beautiful witnesses. Or perhaps there's one already. I must look into that. It might provide material for a little refined blackmail.

He drifted gently into sleep.

THE END

We do hope that you have enjoyed reading this large print book.

Did you know that all of our titles are available for purchase?

We publish a wide range of high quality large print books including:
**Romances, Mysteries, Classics
General Fiction
Non Fiction and Westerns**

Special interest titles available in large print are:
**The Little Oxford Dictionary
Music Book, Song Book
Hymn Book, Service Book**

Also available from us courtesy of Oxford University Press:
**Young Readers' Dictionary
(large print edition)
Young Readers' Thesaurus
(large print edition)**

For further information or a free brochure, please contact us at:
**Ulverscroft Large Print Books Ltd.,
The Green, Bradgate Road, Anstey,
Leicester, LE7 7FU, England.
Tel:** (00 44) **0116 236 4325**
Fax: (00 44) **0116 234 0205**

Other titles in the
Linford Mystery Library:

THAT INFERNAL TRIANGLE

Mark Ashton

An aeroplane goes down in the notorious Bermuda Triangle and on board is an Englishman recently heavily insured. The suspicious insurance company calls in Dan Felsen, former RAF pilot turned private investigator. Dan soon runs into trouble, which makes him suspect the infernal triangle is being used as a front for a much more sinister reason for the disappearance. His search for clues leads him to the Bahamas, the Caribbean and into a hurricane before he resolves the mystery.

THE GUILTY WITNESSES

John Newton Chance

Jonathan Blake had become involved in finding out just who had stolen a precious statuette. A gang of amateurs had so clever a plot that they had attracted the attention of a group of international spies, who habitually used amateurs as guide dogs to secret places of treasure and other things. Then, of course, the amateurs were disposed of. Jonathan Blake found himself being shot at because the guide dogs had lost their way . . .

THIS SIDE OF HELL

Robert Charles

Corporal David Canning buried his best friend below the burning African sand. Then he was alone, with a bullet-sprayed ambulance containing five seriously injured men and one hysterical nurse in his care. He faced heat, dust, thirst and hunger; and somewhere in the area roamed almost two hundred blood-crazed tribesmen led by a white mercenary with his own desperate reasons for catching up with the sole survivors of the massacre. But Canning vowed that he would win through to safety.

HEAVY IRON

Basil Copper

In this action-packed adventure, Mike Faraday, the laconic L.A. private investigator, stumbles by accident into one of his most bizarre and lethal cases when he is asked to collect a fifty thousand dollar debt by wealthy club owner, Manny Richter. Instead, Mike becomes involved in a murderous web of death, crime and corruption until the solution is revealed in the most unexpected manner.

HIRE ME A HEARSE

Piers Marlowe

Whenever Wilma Haven decided to be wayward, she insisted that she was seen to be wayward. So perhaps she was merely being consistent when she hired a hearse before committing suicide, then proceeded to take her time over the act in a very public place. However, Wilma died not from her own act, but by the murderous intent of an unsuspected killer, and Superintendent Frank Drury of Scotland Yard becomes embroiled in his most challenging case ever.